Instead, speaking the truth in love, we will grow to become in every respect the mature body of him who is the head, that is, Christ.

—Ephesians 4:15 (NIV)

MYSTERIES *of* BLACKBERRY VALLEY

Where There's Smoke
The Key Question
Seeds of Suspicion

MYSTERIES *of* BLACKBERRY VALLEY

Seeds of Suspicion

ELIZABETH PENNEY

Guideposts

A Gift from Guideposts

Thank you for your purchase! We want to express our gratitude for your support with a special gift just for you.

Dive into *Spirit Lifters*, a complimentary e-book that will fortify your faith, offering solace during challenging moments. Its 31 carefully selected scripture verses will soothe and uplift your soul.

Please use the QR code or go to **guideposts.org/spiritlifters** to download.

Mysteries of Blackberry Valley is a trademark of Guideposts.

Published by Guideposts
100 Reserve Road, Suite E200
Danbury, CT 06810
Guideposts.org

Copyright © 2025 by Guideposts. All rights reserved. This book, or parts thereof, may not be reproduced, stored in a retrieval system, or transmitted in any form or by any means, electronic, mechanical, photocopying, recording, or otherwise, without the written permission of the publisher.

This is a work of fiction. Apart from actual historical people and events that may figure into the fiction narrative, all other names, characters, businesses, and events are the creation of the author's imagination and any resemblance to actual persons, living or dead, or events is coincidental. Every attempt has been made to credit the sources of copyrighted material used in this book. If any such acknowledgment has been inadvertently omitted or miscredited, receipt of such information would be appreciated.

Scripture references are from the following sources: *The Holy Bible, King James Version* (KJV). *The Holy Bible, New International Version* (NIV). Copyright © 1973, 1978, 1984, 2011 by Biblica, Inc. Used by permission of Zondervan. All rights reserved worldwide. www.zondervan.com.

Cover and interior design by Müllerhaus
Cover illustration by Bob Kayganich at Illustration Online LLC.
Typeset by Aptara, Inc.

ISBN 978-1-961442-57-3 (hardcover)
ISBN 978-1-961442-58-0 (softcover)
ISBN 978-1-961442-59-7 (epub)

Printed and bound in the United States of America

Seeds of
Suspicion

Chapter One

Growing up, Hannah Prentiss enjoyed taking leisurely bike rides through the countryside around her hometown of Blackberry Valley, Kentucky. Nothing was better than the sun on her face, the wind in her hair, and views of fields and woods unspooling as she pedaled along a winding rural road.

On this fine August Monday, as the owner of a farm-to-table restaurant called the Hot Spot, Hannah drove with purpose. She was on her way to the King Farm, owned by Elaine Wilby, who also worked as the hostess at Hannah's restaurant. Elaine grew berries and vegetables, and as part of Hannah's commitment to local farms, she was personally picking up a small order. While the produce, meat, and dairy were usually delivered, she enjoyed visiting her suppliers now and then, walking through the fields or barns, patting cows and tasting samples.

Especially tasting samples.

As she signaled and turned in to a long driveway marked by an open gate and a faded painted sign, her mouth watered. Blackberries were in, and they were her primary interest today. She needed them for the Blackberry Festival Chef Cook-Off that was happening at the end of the week.

As she approached the simple, two-story gray farmhouse with its navy blue shutters, the front door opened and Elaine stepped out onto the porch. Grinning widely, she waved and then waited while Hannah parked on the edge of the main drive.

Elaine wore a faded red bandanna over brown hair threaded with gray, jeans, a sleeveless blouse, and red garden clogs. Quite a difference from the sleek, sophisticated Elaine who served as the Hot Spot hostess every evening. About ten years older than Hannah's thirty-five, Elaine was a widow with a college-age son named Blake. He was headed to the University of Kentucky for his freshman year in a couple of weeks.

"Can I get you some sweet tea?" Elaine called as Hannah got out of the car.

"After," Hannah said. "Business before pleasure." She knew that Elaine would also have something delectable and home-baked to offer.

Elaine hopped off the porch to join Hannah. "That's fine. I already picked and packed what you ordered. Want to drive to the barn?"

"Sure."

Hannah heard scratching and whining behind the front door below the half-screen. "Hold on." With a shake of her head, Elaine returned to the house and opened the door again. Banjo, a medium-size mutt with floppy ears and a black spot around one eye, bounded out, his tail going a mile a minute. Elaine had recently adopted Banjo from a local animal shelter. So far, it was a match made in heaven.

Elaine and Banjo climbed into the front seat, and they set off toward the main barn.

"How is everything?" Hannah asked.

To her surprise, the normally cheerful Elaine scowled. "You know that article Marshall wrote about my farm?"

Marshall Fredericks was a food critic for the local newspaper. His historical feature article entitled BLACKBERRY VALLEY'S FAMOUS LOST ONION—AND QUEEN had been a departure for him. To Marshall's delight, papers across the country had picked it up.

"I loved it," Hannah said. "Who knew onions used to be so big around here? Not to mention the Onion Queens. What a hoot." Years ago, Blackberry Valley held an annual Onion Festival to celebrate a once important crop. The last festival had been in 1932.

Elaine leaned her elbow on the window ledge and propped her chin on her fist. "That part was fine. I wish I hadn't mentioned that I had Blackberry Red onion seeds around here somewhere. I've had dozens of calls since the article went national. People want to buy them from me, including some hotshot professor from Virginia. He wants to add the onion to his vegetable heritage project."

Hannah pulled up in front of the barn. Banjo immediately started barking, launching himself toward the open window on Elaine's side. "Easy there," she said, grabbing his collar with one hand and unlatching the door with the other.

Once they were out, she let go of his collar, and he bolted through the open barn door.

Elaine called him, but when he didn't return, she rolled her eyes. "I'd better go grab him. There's a bunch of stuff in there he could get into."

Hannah followed her into the barn. Elaine didn't keep any farm animals, so the space was dedicated to her produce business. In one corner, she'd set up a washing station and packing area. Several glass-front refrigerators, a couple of chest freezers, and tables stored produce for distribution. Shelves held preserves, pickles, and jams Elaine made for sale from excess fruit and vegetables.

Banjo was in another area of the barn, where old horse and cow stalls still stood. He nosed at something on the worn wooden boards.

"Give me that," Elaine said, bending to pick the item up. It was a blue baseball cap with a University of Kentucky emblem. She dusted it off against her leg. "I wonder where this came from." She snorted. "Probably Blake. I tell him he sheds like a molting chicken."

Hannah laughed. Her own mother had said something similar when she and her brother were teenagers.

Elaine hung the cap on a nail. "Let's go out to the garden." She picked up two baskets. "We'll try some blackberries right out of the patch."

They walked out of the barn and headed toward the fields. The growing area included an extensive stand of blackberry bushes to the far left, rows of crops, and a hoop house Elaine used to start vegetables. A small cabin, the original home on the farm, stood under an ancient red maple. A young man with curly blond hair sat on the cabin steps, strumming a guitar.

"Excuse me," Elaine said. "I need to go talk to Phoenix."

Hannah stayed where she was, enjoying the day and the views across the rolling fields. From where she stood she could see the next farm, which featured a stately three-story house with a sweeping veranda. She recalled that the Combs family lived there.

Although she couldn't make out individual words, Hannah could tell that Elaine was displeased with the young man. Hands on hips, she leaned over him as she talked, scowling.

After laying aside his guitar, Phoenix put up his hands. Him, she could hear clearly. "I'm just waiting for Blake. He ran to town for something. I promise we'll get it all done."

Elaine gave a reply, chin bobbing in emphasis, and started back toward Hannah. Behind her, Phoenix ducked into the cabin, guitar in hand.

"Sorry," Elaine said when she reached Hannah. "He's a good kid, but I have to stay on him every minute."

Hannah clucked in sympathy. Having worked in restaurants with a wide variety of employees, she understood the frustration. "Where did he come from?"

"I put an ad on a farming group page, and he was the only one to respond. I think all the other potential farmhands had already been snapped up. That was my mistake. Next year, I'll advertise earlier."

"It's nice that you've given him a place to stay." Hannah glanced over her shoulder at the cabin. Phoenix marched toward the barn, head ducked, wearing a ball cap and sunglasses against the hot sun.

"Wow," Hannah said when they arrived at the blackberry patch. Elaine grew a popular variety called Triple Crown. The thornless canes required trellises to support the large, juicy berries. Thornless berries ripened later than thorny varieties, so they were the focus of the Blackberry Festival.

Elaine grinned. "Aren't they gorgeous? Go ahead, try one."

Hannah popped a blackberry into her mouth. A sweet, sun-ripened, slightly tart flavor washed over her taste buds. "Yum." Visions of how she could use this stellar fruit in recipes flooded her mind. Blackberries had always been a favorite of hers, and she'd invented one of her most popular dishes back in LA: blackberry burrata pizza with basil.

A lanky figure came running across the field toward them. Elaine's son, Blake. Hannah always thought the handsome young man resembled his mother with his dark hair and deep brown eyes. Banjo greeted him with leaps of joy.

"Good boy, Banjo," Blake said, rubbing the dog's ears. He looked up. "Hey, Hannah."

"How are you?" Hannah asked. "Enjoying the summer?"

Blake's eyes lit with eagerness. "For the most part, yeah. I've been horseback riding a lot with my girlfriend, Kylie Jacobs. We also go swimming, kayaking, four-wheeling, and bike-riding with our friends. So, yeah, I'm busy."

"Plus working," Elaine put in, her voice teasing.

"In between our fun," Blake teased back. "I wanted to check in with you and see what the priorities should be."

Elaine had a ready answer. "Please review the board for orders that have to go out today and load the truck. You two can make deliveries after lunch. Except Hannah's order. She's taking that with her."

"You got it." Blake grinned at Hannah. "By the way, Kylie is running for Blackberry Queen. Be sure to vote for her."

"I will," Hannah said, smiling. The Blackberry Queen contest was relatively new, and Hannah wasn't familiar with it.

As her son started off, Elaine said, "Hold on a sec. Did you drop a blue UK hat in the barn?"

Blake halted, his brow furrowed. "No."

"What about Phoenix? Does it belong to him?"

Blake shook his head. "I don't think so. I've never seen him wearing a UK hat."

Mother and son were both starting to look agitated. "What's going on?" Hannah asked. It had to be about more than a ball cap.

Elaine tugged at the bottom of her blouse. "We're not sure. It's just that ever since Marshall wrote that article, strange things have been happening around here. Small, so you think you're imagining them, but definitely happening. Right, Blake?"

He nodded. "Yeah. Like a door is open that I was pretty sure I shut. Things are moved around. Mostly in the barn, but also the tool shed, tractor garage, and even Phoenix's cabin, according to him. Though he's a slob," he added. "So it's hard to tell if that's part of the weird stuff going on around here, or if it's just him."

Hannah was concerned. "Have you reported it to the police?"

"Reported what?" Elaine's shoulders rose. "Nothing's missing or even damaged."

"But someone was in your barn." The thought of an intruder was distressing. Whether they'd disturbed anything or not. Hannah couldn't think of a single good reason someone would want to sneak around another person's property.

"It was probably a customer. Or someone looking for one of the boys." Elaine plucked a couple of blackberries off a bush.

Hannah sensed Elaine was ready to close the subject. "Well, if things escalate…"

Elaine dropped the berries into a basket. "I know where you're going with that, and don't worry. My guard is certainly up."

Leaving it there, Hannah began to pick berries as well. Their baskets were almost full when Banjo let out a bark before tearing off across the field.

Elaine put a hand over her eyes to watch the dog. "You've got to be kidding me."

A bareheaded man wearing sunglasses, a blue shirt with rolled-up sleeves, and loose canvas pants made his way toward them. When Banjo reached him, he stopped to greet the dog.

"Who is that?" Hannah asked.

"My neighbor. Cooper Combs. Another thorn in my side. He recently moved back here from Louisville." Elaine continued plucking berries, her movements a little fiercer than strictly necessary.

"Should we run away?" Hannah joked.

That made Elaine smile and shake her head. "I wish. But it's better to get it over with. Otherwise, he'll hound me."

A motor sounded, and Hannah saw a small refrigerator truck back up to the barn door. The boys were loading produce as requested.

Cooper continued toward the patch. Once he reached them, he called out in a pleasant drawl, "Hey, Elaine. How y'all doing?"

Elaine raised her head. "Hi, Cooper. What's up? Oh, this is Hannah Prentiss. She owns the restaurant where I work. Hannah, this is my neighbor, Cooper Combs."

Hannah and Cooper nodded to each other.

Cooper watched as Elaine returned to picking, hands in his pockets and rocking on his heels. Elaine wasn't making it easy for him, Hannah realized.

The longer he stood there, the redder Cooper's face grew. Finally, he burst out, "Elaine Wilby, you know as well as I do that your family stole those seeds from mine, and I want them back!"

Chapter Two

Hannah winced at the hostility in Cooper's voice. *Those seeds again.* Marshall's article really had stirred up a hornet's nest.

Elaine took her time answering. Hannah knew her friend well enough by now to guess that she was making sure her words and tone were under control before she spoke. "That's ridiculous, Cooper. The Blackberry Red was developed by my great-great-great-grandfather. We have notes on it somewhere." She continued to pick as she spoke.

"Stop with those berries," Cooper demanded. "We need to talk about this, and I deserve your full attention."

Elaine lifted her head, eyes flashing. "There's nothing to discuss. I don't know where the seeds are, and even if I did, I wouldn't give them to you. King Farm owns the rights to that variety."

Cooper crossed his arms, his gaze shrewd. "Oh, did you patent them? I had no idea."

"Patent? Why, no, we didn't." Elaine seemed alarmed at the idea.

Hannah had heard about patenting seeds during many restaurant-industry debates. Companies did it to protect the research that went into developing a certain variety.

Cooper nodded. "Didn't think so. Who's to say the onion didn't originate with us? Maybe we let your family grow them. We were generous that way, I'm sure."

Elaine stared at him, apparently nonplussed. She finally rallied. "And who's to say it wasn't the other way around? If your family created them, why don't you have them?" She lifted her chin. "I've seen the seeds. Have you?"

A sly grin slid across Cooper's face. "Not yet." His gaze roamed over the berry bushes. "I'll let you keep picking." With a nod of farewell, he started back across the field.

Banjo watched, leaning against Elaine's legs as though to comfort her. "Aren't you a good boy?" she cooed to him. "Even if you are a traitor. Greeting Cooper like that."

"That was interesting," Hannah said. "He really is hot on the trail of those seeds, isn't he?"

"He certainly seems to be," Elaine agreed. "And I guess I really blew it, telling him I'd seen them. Now he knows for sure they're around here somewhere."

Elaine was right. She'd confirmed what she'd told Marshall in the article, that the seeds were on her farm. Remembering Cooper's sly expression, Hannah wondered if her admission was what he'd been after.

"You'd better make sure everything's locked up," Hannah said. "Maybe Cooper is the one behind the odd things going on."

"Cooper?" Elaine's brow furrowed. She glanced toward his retreating figure. "You think he'd stoop that low?"

"Maybe, if those seeds are valuable enough. What is it about Blackberry Red that gets people so worked up?"

Elaine glanced into Hannah's full basket. "Why don't we talk about that over a nice glass of sweet tea?"

Back at the house, they sat at the island in Elaine's comfortable kitchen with its natural wood cabinets, terra-cotta floor, and granite countertops. After filling two glasses and setting out a plate of butter pecan cookies—no doubt made with pecans from the farm—Elaine said, "Make yourself comfortable. I'm going to grab a scrapbook my gran put together."

Banjo at her heels, Elaine left the kitchen.

Hannah took a sip of tea and then chose a cookie. If only Blackberry Reds were still grown. Red onions were excellent raw, so she used them in salads and slaws or on sandwiches and burgers. They were also good pickled, caramelized, or grilled.

Elaine returned, carrying a large album in one arm. She perched on the stool next to Hannah and placed the book between them. "I'm so grateful that my great-grandmother sorted out all the old family photos and added names and dates."

"What was her name?" Hannah asked.

"Olive. She married Lemuel King, the younger brother of the missing Onion Queen, Clara." Elaine stopped at a page and pointed. "This is Clara and the 1932 court."

The photo showed a line of young women, hands on hips and wearing knee-length dresses. A label below gave their names.

"There's Clara." Hannah pointed to a blond. "Oh, and look, there's Mabel Prentiss. She was my great-great-aunt. I didn't know a relative of mine was in the contest."

"She's really pretty." Elaine peered more closely. "I can see the resemblance."

Hannah laughed. "Thanks."

"There's Cooper's great-grandmother," Elaine said, pointing to a dark-haired woman. "Ada Young. The Youngs owned the farm next door until Ada married Rodney Combs, the local stationmaster." Ada was labeled the first runner-up.

Elaine pointed to a picture of Clara and Mabel standing arm-in-arm under a big maple tree outside what was now Elaine's house. "Looks like our ancestors were besties."

Hannah grinned. "That's awesome."

Elaine continued to leaf through. "No more pictures of Clara. A lot of Olive and Lemuel though." These included a wedding photograph and then a growing family on the farm. She flipped back. "You had a question about Blackberry Red."

A clipping from a newspaper had been pasted into the scrapbook. LOCAL ONION A STATE FAIR FAVORITE.

Hannah read the article, which detailed Blackberry Red's success at the 1929 fair and the ribbons the onion had won at the county and local levels as well.

"That's impressive," Hannah said.

"My ancestors used to grow onion sets from seeds." Elaine tapped a printed ad. "Home gardeners and other farms would buy the sets and plant a crop. Everyone loved Blackberry Red. It was sweet and quite a good keeper for a red onion."

The ad copy read, *Nothing sweeter than a Blackberry Red onion. Our own variety, sold only at the King Farm since 1880. A customer favorite.*

"I want to try them," Hannah said with a laugh. "Oh, the recipes I could create."

Elaine took a sip of tea. "Well, if I find the seeds and they're still viable, I'll grow some for you. We'll introduce them at the Hot Spot."

Hannah loved that idea. "Any clue where they could be?"

Her friend waved her hand. "Could be anywhere. I vaguely remember coming across them as a kid. I didn't like onions back then, so I didn't pay attention."

"It's neat that our ancestors were friends." Hannah paged back to the photo of Clara and Mabel. "What happened to Clara?"

Elaine shrugged. "Nobody knows. Apparently, there was a huge scandal of some kind, and Clara ended up leaving town. After that, we didn't grow the onions anymore. Whether that was directly related to the scandal, I can't say."

Marshall's article had heavily implied that Clara's departure and the demise of the Onion Festival were tied together. Journalistic license, perhaps. Hannah made a mental note to ask him if he knew any details he hadn't printed.

"Why didn't they keep having the festival anyway?" Hannah asked. "Blackberry Reds weren't the only onions grown around here."

"Our family started the festival," Elaine explained. "Without the Kings' leadership, it fizzled, I suppose. Plus, it was the Depression. People had a lot of other things to think about."

All of that made sense to Hannah. "I had no idea one of my relatives was an Onion Queen contestant. But I should ask my dad. He might know something. Or my uncle might." Hannah's father, Gabriel Prentiss, lived with his older brother, Gordon.

"Give him a call if you want." Elaine rose from her seat. "I need to check on the boys anyway. Be right back."

Hannah picked up her phone and made the call. Her father answered immediately. "Hello, favorite daughter."

Hannah laughed. "I'm your only daughter." Hannah had one brother, Andrew. Their mother had passed away about eight years ago, and both were close to their father.

"Then it sure would be embarrassing if you weren't my favorite. What's up?" Dad asked.

"Not much. I'm planning my entry for the cook-off on Friday night." Hannah paused to gather her thoughts. "But I'm calling to ask you about your great-aunt Mabel."

"I don't know how much I'll be able to tell you. She died when I was a teenager."

"Did you know she was on the Onion Queen court in 1932?"

"You mean the contest mentioned in Marshall's article?"

"Exactly. And she was Clara King's friend. I'm at Elaine's, and we're looking at old photos. Elaine said there was some kind of scandal in 1932."

Dad laughed. "A ninety-year-old scandal. How riveting."

Hannah had to laugh too. "True. Anyway, Mabel's name rang a bell, and I wondered if there was anything about her in the historical materials we gave the library." The library maintained a local collection of books, private papers, photographs, and other memorabilia.

"Her diaries," Dad said promptly, surprising Hannah. "Your grandmother said nothing in there was too personal about our family, so she donated them. Slice-of-life stuff from the good old days, I suppose."

Seeds of Suspicion

A scandal and a runaway Onion Queen. Were the old days actually good, or did they only seem so in the glow of nostalgia?

Blackberry Valley
August 7, 1932

"He's looking at you." Mabel Prentiss gently elbowed her best friend's side.

"Hush," Clara King said. "We're in church." She rounded her pretty blue eyes at Mabel, an expression that made her look like a Kewpie doll.

The organist was playing "In the Garden." All around them the residents of Blackberry Valley were settling in the pews, dressed in their Sunday best and redolent with perfume and hair pomade.

The young man in question glanced around as he made his way down the aisle, ushered along by the mayor of Blackberry Valley, no less. He was very handsome with his dark hair and a pencil mustache, and his gray suit was expensive, fitting like a glove.

"That's the new stationmaster," Mabel whispered. "Rodney Combs."

Mabel's parents had discussed Mr. Combs at the dinner table the previous night. "I understand he's well-connected," her father had said. "Friends in high places at the L&N."

The Louisville and Nashville Railroad shipped freight and passengers all over the Southeast. Stationmaster was an important position, with authority for railroad operations, staff, safety, and maintenance. As for social standing, they were counted among their location's elite.

"I'm sure this assignment is a stepping-stone for him," her mother replied as she passed the potatoes to Mark, Mabel's older brother. She gave Mabel a significant look. "Maybe you and your friends should make a point of showing him around, since he's not married yet. It would be the neighborly thing to do." Mama often bemoaned what she considered a shortage of suitable suitors for her daughter and other young women in town.

At the time, Mabel had been certain the new stationmaster would be older and portly, maybe with a habit of chewing tobacco. Now she revised that assumption and reconsidered her mother's suggestion.

Another young woman seemed equally impressed with Mr. Combs, Mabel noticed as the mayor and his companion settled in a pew. Ada Young actually twisted

Seeds of Suspicion

around in her seat to greet the newcomer, a startling breach of protocol during a church service.

Mabel did her best to be charitable, the way her mother and Sunday school had taught. When it came to Ada, though, she had difficulty at times. The girl could be downright mean.

Just the other day, she'd come up to Clara on the street. "Don't be thinking you have the Onion Queen contest in the bag," Ada had said with a toss of her brown curls. "I'm going to give you a run for your money."

Clara had laughed. "That's wonderful, Ada. A little friendly competition never hurt anyone."

Ada and her best friend gaped as Clara and Mabel sauntered off arm in arm to the drugstore for an egg cream.

Mabel saw that Ada wore the exact same expression right now. Rodney Combs was looking over his shoulder at Clara, who studied her hymnal. Then the pastor stepped behind the pulpit, and Rodney's head snapped forward, as did Ada's.

Interesting times were ahead. Better than the usual boring old Blackberry Valley summer.

The Hot Spot's kitchen was dim and cool when Hannah stepped inside carrying a box full of King Farm produce. No one was there, as she'd expected, although her head chef, Jacob Forrest, sometimes came in to try new recipes on Mondays.

That was what she would be doing later this afternoon. Elaine and the other staff were going to taste-test her pizza creation. When she'd floated the idea of entering the cook-off, the decision for the Hot Spot to enter had been unanimous.

After placing the produce in the walk-in cooler, Hannah realized she had time for another outing before lunch. She decided to run over to the library and take a look at Mabel's diary and anything else in the collection pertaining to 1932. *A scandal,* Elaine had said. Hannah was curious to find out exactly what that meant.

She hopped back into her Subaru Outback to drive to the library. Maybe while she was there, she'd browse the newly added books and find one to check out. Not that she had much time to read, especially in the summer when business ramped up. Still, she enjoyed relaxing with a good book and a cup of coffee or glass of sweet tea. She'd gotten her love of reading from her mother, who had brought Hannah to the library almost every week growing up.

Head librarian Evangeline Cooke looked up from her computer when Hannah walked in. "Good morning, Hannah. How are you?"

Hannah stopped beside the desk. "I'm great. How about you?"

"Can't complain." A big smile creased Evangeline's cheeks. "I'm really looking forward to the festival. My husband and I have a ritual—visiting the arts-and-crafts booths and then getting a bowl of blackberry crisp with vanilla ice cream."

"That sounds fun. The Hot Spot will be in the cook-off Friday night. From what I understand, the competition is fierce." When Hannah had found out that chefs from high-end restaurants and inns in the surrounding area were competing, she'd been surprised. She'd pictured competing against home cooks rather than professionals. Not that that necessarily meant a change in quality, as numerous reality TV series could attest. However, it did mean that her competitors would likely know sophisticated techniques, as she did, which meant those wouldn't give her a leg up.

"How exciting," Evangeline said. "That's one of my favorite events. What are you making?"

Hannah almost told her then thought better of it. She wanted to surprise and amaze her audience. The last time she'd made the pizza had been in LA, and it had gone over very well there. Evangeline was a good friend, but she'd tell everyone in town about Hannah's dish.

"It's a secret," she said. "Be sure to come to the contest and cheer me on."

"I will," the librarian promised. "Anything I can help you with today?"

Hannah glanced toward the local history room. "I'm doing some research, but I think I can find my way around. I'll let you know if I have any questions."

"You need anything, just holler." Evangeline settled herself at the computer. "Well, not *holler*. This is a library, after all." She let out one of her silvery laughs.

Hannah laughed as well as she headed for the local history room. The small space was filled with shelves of various sizes plus a few file cabinets. Besides the diary, Hannah was also interested in local newspapers, which were bound in volumes.

The shelves were organized by subject and type, so Hannah readily found Mabel Prentiss's diary from the 1930s. She pulled it from the shelf and put it on a table. Maybe Evangeline would let her check it out, since it had belonged to Hannah's family. The library didn't normally lend materials from the local history room. They were too rare and of general interest.

Then she went around the corner to the newspapers—and almost bumped into a young man who'd gotten there first. He held a bound edition. "Oops. Sorry." Then Hannah took a good look at him. "Phoenix?"

Shifting from foot to foot, he stared at her, puzzled. "Yes?" He obviously didn't know who she was.

"I'm Hannah Prentiss, Elaine's friend. I saw you—" Hannah's words faltered when she remembered what she'd witnessed. Elaine had been annoyed with her young farmhand and quite vocal about it. "Anyway, hi."

"Hi," he replied, sidling over a step or two. "I'll get out of your way."

"No, don't go on my account," Hannah protested. "I can look at something else until you're done."

"That's okay." He slotted the book into its spot. "I'm just here during my lunch. I'd better head out to the truck." He hesitated then added, "I got all the deliveries done before taking a break."

"I'm sure you did." Hannah wondered if he thought she would report back to Elaine. Well, she wouldn't. It wasn't any of her business when Phoenix took a break. "See you later," she called as he strode away.

Then Hannah ran her finger over the newspapers on the shelves, searching for 1932. To her surprise, that year was in the very volume Phoenix had chosen.

Was he looking into the Onion Queen scandal as well?

Hannah shook her head. Probably dozens of people in town were. Something about that article—and the mystery of the seeds—was really intriguing.

She carried the book to the table, where there was plenty of room to leaf through it. Like many old newspapers, this one was both wider and taller than current publications.

She began to flip pages, not looking for anything in particular except mention of onions and the Onion Queen contest. Right away she was captured by the glimpses of long-ago days. The local headlines, a spelling bee as noteworthy as a car accident. Recipes from a food column called Grandma's Kitchen. Hannah sat up. *Awesome.* She loved food columns, especially unassuming ones featuring regional and traditional dishes. The column on the page she was looking at featured a recipe for blackberry jam cake.

Good idea for a Hot Spot dessert. Hannah took a picture of the recipe and sent it to Jacob.

Looking more closely at the Grandma's Kitchen column, Hannah saw it was submitted by a women's group from the same church Hannah attended. That meant the group, which Hannah now belonged to, had been around for decades. Maybe they had put together a cookbook at some point. She'd have to check. If they hadn't, maybe she could suggest it.

Nothing like authentic local flavor.

Ah. Here we go. NEW STATIONMASTER TAKES POST. Elaine had mentioned Rodney Combs, the stationmaster who married Ada, Clara's main rival for Onion Queen. Cooper Combs's great-grandfather.

The article was glowing, with quotes from the mayor and others saying how happy they were to welcome Rodney to Blackberry Valley. Apparently, the previous stationmaster had been elderly and, after his passing, there had been some anxiety about getting a good replacement. Rodney's previous posting had been in Ellisville, in neighboring Warren County.

A grainy black-and-white photograph taken outside the station showed men in suits identified as Rodney, the mayor, Mr. David King, and Mr. Clarence Prentiss.

Hannah's ancestor. She studied the photograph closely, thrilled to find it, then snapped a picture of both the article and photo.

She found mentions of the upcoming Onion Festival in the next few newspapers. One included the same photo of the contestants Elaine had shown her. The text described each young woman in complimentary terms, including descriptions of their "shining locks" and "sparkling eyes." Also noted in the article was that these contestants often tended Blackberry Valley's onions with their "delicate hands" using the "utmost care."

Hannah grinned. Talk about a marketing ploy. Indeed, she soon came across an advertisement for Blackberry Red that featured an illustration of a young woman holding up a very large onion. QUEEN OF ONIONS, the headline read. DON'T SETTLE FOR LESS THAN THE AUTHENTIC BLACKBERRY RED, A PROPRIETARY VARIETY FROM THE KING FARM. Below that it read, *Sweet, yellow, white, and other reds available too.* The ad had been placed by King Farm, and in Hannah's eyes, the text furthered Elaine's claim that the onions had been developed by her family.

She photographed the article about the contestants, and the ad as well. If Elaine ever did find the seeds, she could use some of this vintage flavor in her marketing. People loved learning about a connection to the past, about heirloom fruits and vegetables.

Hannah kept going.

TRAIN STATION ROBBED. DAYLIGHT THIEF STEALS CASHBOX.

That headline certainly caught her attention. Reading the article, she learned that while the stationmaster and other railroad employees had been outside dealing with a switching problem that had "almost caused a collision between two trains," someone had stolen the cashbox used for ticket sales and freight shipments. A hand from King Farm, Wilson Barnes, who had been working on Onion Festival floats nearby, didn't see anyone enter or leave the station. Anyone with information was asked by the police to come forward.

The connection to the King Farm intrigued Hannah, so she took pictures of that article as well. Then she checked the time. After noon. She really ought to grab some lunch and get set up for the pizza tasting.

A text message chimed on her phone. It was from Micki, a former restaurant coworker in California. HEY, HANNAH. YOU NEED TO SEE THIS. SERIOUSLY, WE'RE ALL FLIPPING OUT.

There was a link at the bottom of the message. Hannah clicked on it.

A video on a social media site started to play. Hannah recognized the young woman as Corrie Rice, a chef she used to work with.

"Hi, gang. It's Corrie. I'm so, so glad to have you join me for this edition of *Corrie Rice Cooks, Home Edition*. For those of you new to me, I adapt my most popular restaurant recipes for the home cook."

Corrie picked up a pint of fresh, juicy blackberries and showed it to the camera. "It's berry season, so I've been daydreaming about wonderful ways to use these beauties. Today I'm going to show you how to make one of my signature dishes: Blackberry Burrata Pizza."

Chapter Three

Hannah stared at the video in disbelief. Then she forced herself to calm down and not jump to conclusions. Maybe Corrie's recipe was totally different.

Keeping the volume low so as not to disturb anyone, Hannah watched the entire thing, more sickened with every moment.

Her initial reaction was correct. Corrie had stolen her recipe and now claimed it as a signature dish of her own.

That was exactly what Hannah had said in her application for the cook-off—that she would be preparing a signature dish that was a well-tested fan favorite. She hadn't said what she was making, wanting it to be a surprise.

How should she respond to Corrie? Just ignoring the encroachment didn't seem fair. Hannah was tempted to write a comment blasting the other chef. Or maybe a subtly snide approach, such as, *I see you learned from the best.*

The thing was that Corrie was three thousand miles away. She could make Hannah's recipes all day long, and Hannah would never be the wiser. But with social media, here it was, right in her face. Open to everyone, including friends, family, and customers in Blackberry Valley.

Horror flashed over Hannah. What if people thought *she'd* stolen *Corrie's* recipe? What was she going to do?

She took a deep breath. First things first. It was time to have lunch. After putting the newspapers back, she carried the diary out to the main room. Evangeline raised her head with a smile as Hannah approached the desk.

"I have a favor to ask," Hannah said. "This diary belonged to my great-great-aunt, Mabel Prentiss. We donated it to the library."

"I remember," the librarian said. "Along with other fascinating documents. It was generous of you."

"Well, if it's all right with you," Hannah said tentatively, "I'd like to borrow it back. Marshall's article about the Onion Queens in 1932 fascinates me, and Mabel was one of the contestants. I'd love to read her thoughts about the event."

Evangeline shrugged. "I don't have a problem with it. Usually, those materials don't circulate, but this is a different situation, isn't it? The diary belongs to your family."

"Thank you so much. I'll take good care of it, I promise." Hannah tucked the book carefully into her shoulder bag.

"That article sure did stir up a lot of interest in that era," Evangeline commented. "I've had a bunch of people in here asking where to find more information. Something about the story really captures their imagination."

People including Phoenix, the farmhand? Hannah didn't ask, since that would be too nosy. There were other incidents from 1932 he could have been looking up, after all.

Or maybe he wanted the seeds.

Hannah immediately squelched that uncharitable thought. What would Phoenix do with them? Would he really be so bold as to search his employer's property?

She sure hoped not.

"Is there anything else I can help you with?" Evangeline asked.

Hannah walked over to the display of new titles. "I'm going to look for a book while I'm here." Something relaxing, a beach-read sort of story. She had enough excitement in her life right now.

Later that afternoon, Hannah had pizza dough rising and the topping ingredients waiting in bowls for assembly. Her plan was for each person to make their own small pizza, so that meant five, including one for her. Then she'd take their feedback and maybe tweak the recipe.

Doing well at the cook-off would help bring exposure to the restaurant. A lot of people in the area didn't know it existed, even though the old firehouse she'd renovated was a pretty visible building.

While she waited on the pizza dough, Hannah puttered around in the kitchen, checking inventory and mulling over the week's menus. Jacob had written them up for her review and approval. With their focus on local produce, this week's dishes included a sweet-corn-and-potato chowder, caprese salad with local tomatoes and basil, and a delightful Asian slaw made with cabbage and carrots.

Delicious, she wrote across the page before putting it into his inbox.

The back door opened, and Elaine slipped in. "Hello again. How's your day been?" She wandered over to the food prep island to study the toppings. "My berries are lovely, aren't they?"

"They're awesome," Hannah said. "I can't wait to see how they do on the pizza."

Elaine pursed her lips then said, "Pizza? That's your entry? I never thought of putting blackberries on pizza."

"A lot of people haven't. That's why I've been keeping my recipe for the cook-off under wraps. I want the element of surprise."

Her friend laughed. "And you'll have it. I don't think anyone has ever entered a blackberry pizza."

Elaine's mention of the past reminded Hannah of her research. "Guess what? I borrowed Mabel's diary back from the library. I can't wait to read it. Oh, and I found some interesting articles." She pulled out her phone and brought up the images.

They were scrolling through, discussing the news articles, when Raquel Holden and Dylan Bowman, the waitstaff, walked in.

"Blackberry pizza. Great concept." Dylan was twenty, only a little older than Blake, Hannah realized. Although he could be clumsy while waiting tables, he always earned an A for effort. Plus, customers adored him with his curly red hair and amiable personality.

Raquel, who was a few years older but equally enthusiastic and open, squealed. "I just saw a chef making that online. I was thinking, wow, the Hot Spot should do that. And here you are, Hannah. You're amazing."

Hannah had a sinking feeling. "Who was the chef in the video?"

Raquel whipped out her phone and tapped the screen. "Corrie something."

"You don't have to show me." Hannah sank down on a stool. "Guys, I need your advice."

Before she could share her tale of woe, the door opened one more time to admit Jacob. "Hey, what's up?" he greeted them. Jacob was lean and lanky, with a scruffy beard and green eyes. His laid-back demeanor belied his intensity as a chef. He was highly creative and a wonder to watch.

"Hannah was asking our advice," Dylan said eagerly.

Jacob's gaze scanned the island. "Burrata with berries? I'm in."

"Not about that. Well, not *only* about that," Hannah said, although she was glad to have Jacob's seal of approval. She trusted his culinary instincts, even if his recipes were a little elaborate at times.

Hannah took a deep breath. She hadn't planned to bring Corrie up, but with Raquel mentioning her, she had no choice.

"I used to work with Corrie," Hannah said.

"Who's Corrie?" Jacob inquired.

"Show everyone, Raquel," Hannah said with a wave of her hand. It would save time if they knew what she was talking about. "The first few minutes will be enough."

Raquel slid over next to Jacob and played the video so everyone could see it. When she pushed the pause button, there was an uneasy silence.

"The blackberry burrata pizza is my invention, one hundred percent," Hannah said. "Corrie was working with me when I invented it. In fact, she made fun of it at first. Until it sold out."

She couldn't decide what annoyed her more—that Corrie had tried to discourage Hannah's creativity or that she'd then claimed the result as her own.

"Now, as you see, she's calling it one of her signature dishes." Hannah frowned. "I guess she didn't think I'd ever see the video."

"That is so not cool." Dylan took out his phone. "I'm going to post a comment. She can't get away with this."

Alarm shot through Hannah, and she regretted that the subject had even come up. "No, Dylan, don't. The last thing I want is to start an online war with Corrie. Those never end well."

Dylan put his phone down with a grunt of disgust. "If you say so. I just think she shouldn't get away with it."

"I agree," Hannah admitted. Now that she'd become aware of Corrie's recipe theft, she couldn't ignore it. The question was, how should she deal with it? It would require some thought—and prayer.

Jacob gave her a sympathetic look. "It's a tough one for sure." He moved closer to the island. "I'm excited to try blackberry burrata pizza though. The original."

Hannah put the topic of Corrie aside for later. "Okay, I thought I'd have us each make our own pizza." She passed out the individual serving pans. "Let's get started."

After she divided the dough, everyone got to work lining the pans. Raquel started a playlist on her phone, and Hannah smiled at her happy crew, enjoying their camaraderie and lively banter even when the restaurant was closed. This was what she had hoped for when dreaming of her own restaurant. She'd worked many places, and each one, regardless of the food or reputation, was influenced by the attitude of the owner and chef.

Cooking could be a dream job or a nightmare. She tried to create a welcoming, supportive atmosphere for her staff, to help them flourish.

"What do you think?" Dylan held up his pan for the others to see. He'd placed the basil leaves, blackberries, and the ball of burrata cheese in an artistic pattern.

The others murmured approval. "Nice work," Jacob said. "I couldn't have done better."

A flush crept up Dylan's neck, and he beamed.

Hannah grabbed a pizza peel. "Into the ovens they go. Let's set a table while they cook."

Raquel and Dylan raced through the kitchen doors, and soon they were laughing as they set up a table in the back.

Elaine switched on a single light just overhead, and Hannah took drink orders. Jacob helped her ferry them to the table.

The timer went off, and Hannah retrieved bubbling-hot pizzas from the oven. She lined them up, and each person took slices from their own creation.

"Let's say grace," Hannah said when they were all seated. Everyone bowed their heads, and she led the prayer. "All right, let's dig in," she said after the amen.

For a few minutes, the only sounds were mutters of appreciation and the tinkle of ice cubes as they ate and drank.

"This is my new favorite." Raquel laughed. "Along with my other favorites anyway." She enjoyed just about everything made at the Hot Spot, announcing a new top choice every week.

"Very good," Jacob said. "We should add this to the menu while the local berries are in season."

"I think so too," Hannah said. "After the cook-off. Hopefully, we can promote it as a prizewinning recipe."

"I'll make sure to post that on our social media," Elaine said. "Blackberry burrata pizza, the *original*."

"Let me handle Corrie first, okay?" Hannah smiled at her friend, appreciating the support but not wanting to start something with her former colleague, even in a more subtle way.

Someone rapped at the front door, despite the sign that read Closed. "I'll go," Hannah said, not wanting to interrupt her staff's meal.

As she approached the door, she saw the visitor was a tall man wearing a straw hat, white linen slacks, and a white shirt. *A brave outfit to eat a meal in*, she thought, amused. If they were serving, which they were not.

Hannah unlocked the door. "Good evening. I'm sorry, but we're closed tonight."

The man peered beyond her into the dim recesses of the room. "I'm actually looking for Elaine Wilby. Her son said she was here."

"I'll see if she's available," Hannah offered. "May I tell her who is asking?"

He lifted his chin proudly. "I'm Professor Timothy J. Buttonwood, from the University of Virginia at Charlottesville. She'll know why I'm here. We've corresponded."

Elaine had mentioned a professor while they picked blackberries. He was also interested in the onions. *Get in line*, Hannah wanted to tell Timothy J. Buttonwood. Instead, she said, "Hold on. I'll be right back."

At Elaine's invitation, Hannah joined her and the professor in a booth. Raquel brought fresh glasses of iced tea before returning to cleanup duty.

"I'm sorry I interrupted your staff meal," Professor Buttonwood said. He pulled out his wallet and extracted two business cards.

Seeds of Suspicion

A peal of laughter echoed in the kitchen. "It's fine," Hannah said. "We were trying out a recipe for the town's cook-off later this week."

He slid the cards across the table. "Ah, yes. The Blackberry Festival. I'm looking forward to attending. These rural festivals have a long history, as I'm sure you know. They were a way for our ancestors to celebrate a successful harvest after toiling all summer."

"They had the right idea," Elaine said. "My farm is pretty small now, but it's still tons of work. Which I love." She chuckled. "I guess it's in my genes."

By the way Elaine fiddled with her straw paper, Hannah guessed she was nervous about this conversation. The onions had brought her and her farm a lot of unexpected attention.

"Very interesting you should say that," the professor went on. "As part of my work, I trace family lines from settlement to the present when investigating a particular heirloom vegetable they grew. The stories of farmers and food are fascinating."

Heirloom vegetables, open-pollinated varieties passed down from generation to generation, differed from hybrids, which were deliberately cross-pollinated to create a plant with the best qualities of its parents.

"Some heirlooms are hundreds of years old," he continued. "The oldest known is the Judean date seed, which, when found, was over two thousand years old. It actually germinated."

"So my onion seeds might still grow," Elaine said.

The professor's eyes lit up. "Did you locate them? I'd love to add them to my inventory. While heirlooms can be found worldwide, I'm focusing on vegetables grown in Appalachia for a database and potential book called *Appalachian Heirloom*. So many wonderful plants in this region. Such rich history."

Elaine shook her head. "Sorry to mislead you. I haven't found them. Yet." She shrugged. "I've been wondering whether they would even sprout, that's all."

Professor Buttonwood leaned forward. "Is there anything I can do to help you find them? Part of the fun is tracking heirlooms down. It sounds like your onions might pose the greatest challenge yet."

Hannah glanced at Elaine to gauge her reaction. In her view, the professor was being rather forward. Although it would be wonderful to have Blackberry Red included in a recognized heirloom plant directory. Provided Elaine found the seeds.

Elaine, who was now dunking her straw up and down in her tea, did seem uneasy. "Well, I don't need help looking. I can handle that just fine. Thanks for the offer though."

The professor's enthusiasm dimmed slightly, but then he rallied. "When you do find the seeds, you'll need a good test garden to grow samples. How about I help you find the best spot on your property? I've got connections at a lab for soil testing. There's a lot more to it than the basic tests most people get. Trace minerals and whatnot."

Elaine didn't answer for a moment. Then she said, "How can I refuse such a generous offer? Expertise like yours doesn't come along every day."

Only when lured by the promise of a rare and beautiful onion, Hannah thought. Hopefully Elaine wasn't making a mistake by allowing this pushy professor onto her property.

Blackberry Valley
August 8, 1932

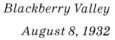

Mabel halted her bicycle near the farmhouse porch. "Hello, Mrs. King," she called with a wave. Clara's mother was visiting with Mrs. Young, Ada's mother. Both women rocked in chairs while drinking iced tea. "Mrs. Young. My mother sends greetings."

"Hello to her too," Mrs. King said. "Clara is down at the barn. Can you remind her that the meeting is in half an hour?" To Mrs. Young, she said, "Can't drag that girl away from the farm lately. She loves it so much."

Was it the farm or something—someone—else? Mabel kept that thought to herself.

"Can't blame her," Mrs. Young said. "You have the finest farm in Blackberry Valley."

Mrs. King inclined her head. "Appreciate you saying that. Though I do envy your spread. Your corn is looking mighty fine."

Mrs. Young shrugged. "We're doing all right with both sweet and field corn. Something about our land makes it grow and grow."

"Same here, with our red onions. They're going to restaurants and hotels as far away as Florida and Maine. All up and down the East Coast."

While the ladies continued to trade gentle boasts, Mabel started pedaling again. She guessed it was up to her to drag Clara to the meeting. Sometimes she wondered if Clara really wanted to be Onion Queen. She truly did deserve it. Not only was she beautiful and talented and active in the community, her family was the premier grower of the famous Blackberry Red onion. Without that, they wouldn't even have an Onion Queen.

Maybe they'd have a Corn Queen instead. Mabel smiled at the idea of wearing a crown of woven cornstalks. Ada would definitely claim that prize.

Farther along the lane, Mabel spotted Clara by the barn. She stood next to a tractor talking to Wilson Barnes, the hired hand who did most everything around the King farm. This year's shortage of hired help meant that Wilson shouldered a much larger share of the work, according to Clara.

Clara herself wasn't above weeding the onions. She'd also helped with planting, as had Mabel on her own farm. *Nothing wrong with honest work*, Mabel's mother always said. *But wear gloves to save your manicure.*

Sometimes Mabel studied photographs of her great-grandmother. She hadn't seemed to worry about manicures, being too busy raising a bunch of children and working with her husband to maintain the farm. Later generations had benefited from that hard work, rising a station or two in Blackberry Valley's social hierarchy.

The Great Depression seemed to have put a crimp in those ambitious plans. Mabel had left the normal school in Louisville for now, but she hoped to return when the economy improved. Her dream was to be an elementary school teacher.

Mabel halted her bike with a flourish. "Hello," she called as the wheels skidded on the dirt.

Wilson lay on his back under the tractor, banging on something, but Clara glanced over, her eyes bright, as if she'd been laughing. "Hello. How are you?"

"I'm fine, thanks." Mabel hopped off and engaged the kickstand. "Your mother said to remind you about the meeting."

"Pass the wrench, please," Wilson said, his voice muffled. Clara bent and placed it in his hand. "Thanks."

"You might want to get ready," Mabel said, noticing that Clara had a smudge of something on her cheek and wore an old dress.

Clara curled her lip as she smoothed her skirt. "Not exactly queen attire, is it?" She giggled. "I have half a mind not to change, just to see the ladies' expressions."

"You're awful." Mabel tried to scold, but the laugh she tried to hold back came out in her tone anyway.

From where she stood she could see several automobiles rolling up the drive, bringing the rest of the committee and contestants. Today they were going to run through the contest rules, order of events, and the judging.

"Everyone else is arriving," she said with some urgency. "Come on, Clara. Your mama is going to be so annoyed."

Clara studied the new arrivals as they spilled out of the vehicles with much chatter and laughter. "Oh, look," she said, touching Mabel's arm. "Ada caught a ride with our new stationmaster."

Mabel saw Ada leaning on the open driver's window of a shiny new roadster. She'd seen the vehicle around town and parked near the train station. "I guess she's setting her cap at the biggest fish around."

Wilson pushed out from under the tractor, grinning. "I guess the new big fish is leaving the rest of us bachelors in the dust, huh, Clara?"

Clara still watched Ada and Rodney, but her easy smile was nowhere in sight. "Hush, Wilson. He can't hold a candle to any of the men in Blackberry Valley." She folded her arms over her chest. "There's something about Mr. Combs I just don't like."

Chapter Four

After staying up late to read Mabel's diary, Hannah inadvertently slept late the next morning. Not that she had to be up terribly early. The Hot Spot didn't open until four. She was usually in the kitchen around noon, taking deliveries, doing paperwork, and whatever else was needed.

Jacob came in around then for food prep, and the servers showed up an hour before opening to set up tables and stock condiments and the like.

I need a jump start today, she thought as she stumbled toward the shower. And she knew the perfect place to get one: Jump Start Coffee, owned by Jacob's brother, Zane.

The coffeehouse was hopping when Hannah pushed through the door half an hour later. Customers lined up waiting to be served, and most of the tables were full.

Someone called her name. Marshall Fredericks, food critic and author of the viral Onion Queen article, pointed to the empty seat at his table. Hannah nodded, indicating she would join him.

Hannah liked Marshall and looked forward to catching up with him. Although his first review of the Hot Spot had been critical, he'd given the restaurant another chance and was now one of its biggest fans. Hannah thought he was also a fan of Raquel, and she was interested to see what might develop there.

Zane was behind the cash register. "Hey, Zane," Hannah said when she reached the head of the line. "Can I get an egg-and-bacon sandwich on an English muffin and a large coffee, please?" She pulled her card out of her wallet.

"Coming right up." Zane punched the order into the register. "Jacob said you have a stellar entry for the cook-off." He pushed his glasses up with his thumb and grinned. "He said he'd have to kill me if he told me what it was. So I didn't ask."

"Good." Hannah slid her card into the reader. "I want the element of surprise."

Zane relayed her order to the kitchen. "We're slammed already, and the festival doesn't start for two days. Did I tell you we're doing a coffee cart?"

"No, but that's a great idea. I heard there'll be a lot of tourist business downtown too."

"Oh, yeah. Some visitors come just for the festival, but plenty decide to explore. Especially since our chamber is so good about promoting us all." Zane handed Hannah the receipt.

She scooted along the counter to wait for her order so Zane could take his next customer. "Talk to you later."

"Oh, Hannah," Zane called. Hannah moved back. "You wouldn't believe how fascinated visitors are with the Onion Queen story and those Blackberry Red onions. Some of them have mentioned Elaine and the Hot Spot, so you might get some curiosity seekers."

"Thanks for the heads-up," Hannah said, wondering if they would get a flood of diners due to the story, which had mentioned Elaine's place of employment along with her farm. Elaine was becoming famous, whether or not she wanted to be.

Such flares of notoriety were usually brief, lasting until the next human-interest story hit the headlines. While it was her restaurant's turn in the spotlight, Hannah resolved to impress every single customer. And to support Elaine however she could.

Hannah placed her coffee, sandwich, and a glass of water on a tray and made her way to Marshall's table.

The reporter smiled a greeting then closed his laptop and put it into his messenger bag. "How's it going?"

Hannah set her tray on the table. "Great, thanks. Getting ready for the festival and the cook-off." Her phone pinged with a text.

"I'm looking forward to the cook-off." Marshall picked up his mug. "I'm doing a big feature on it for the *Chronicle*."

"Not judging?" If anyone could evaluate food, it was Marshall.

"No way. I need to stay on good terms with all the chefs." He laughed. "Or else they'll bar the door when I show up."

"Makes sense." Hannah took a bite of her sandwich, enjoying the salty goodness of crisp bacon and tender egg. She dabbed her mouth with a napkin. "I didn't realize how hungry I was."

Marshall stood. "I'm going up for a refill. Be right back."

While he was gone, Hannah checked her phone, seeing a text from Lacy Minyard, her best friend and supplier for the restaurant. Lacy and her husband, Neil, ran Bluegrass Hollow Farm, which produced the best eggs in Blackberry Valley.

HEY. HAVE A HUGE FAVOR TO ASK.

Hannah smiled. Her friend had a tendency to be dramatic. GO AHEAD.

WE JUST LOST A JUDGE FOR THE BLACKBERRY QUEEN COMPETITION. SHE'S HAVING EMERGENCY SURGERY. CAN YOU FILL IN?

Hannah sighed. She was already so busy this week. Still, she almost never said no to Lacy, who was always there for her. WHAT DO I HAVE TO DO?

WE'RE INTERVIEWING THE CONTESTANTS AT MY HOUSE TOMORROW AT TEN. THE CONTEST IS SATURDAY EVENING AT SEVEN. IT'S JUST THOSE TWO COMMITMENTS. I'LL SEND A LINK TO THE PAGEANT WEBPAGE. THERE'S A SCHOLARSHIP, AND THEY'RE GREAT YOUNG WOMEN.

That didn't sound too onerous. It would probably be fun. Hannah also liked the idea of encouraging young people.

I'LL DO IT.

THANK YOU! YOU'RE A LIFESAVER.

Marshall returned with his refill and sat.

"I just agreed to be a judge in the Blackberry Queen competition," Hannah told him. "Can't say no to Lacy."

"Not many of us can. She's a force around these parts," Marshall said. "Now that you know I'm not judging the cook-off, I might as well tell you what I'll be up to. One of the Louisville television stations is sending their lifestyle reporter to the festival. They've tapped me to help coordinate what they cover, which will include the cook-off."

"That's amazing." But Hannah had a suspicion about their sudden interest in a local festival, even if it was fun. "Is this because of your article?" She picked up her cup and took a sip.

Marshall's expression was slightly smug. "Yeah, it is. You know, I was proud of that article when I submitted it, but I never dreamed it would take off the way it has. If only you could predict what will hit, huh?"

"Something about the missing Onion Queen has really touched hearts," Hannah said. "My great-great-aunt was a contestant that year."

"Mabel Prentiss, right? I saw her name."

"She left a diary," Hannah said. "I'm reading it now."

Marshall sat straight up. "Get out. Does she talk about the competition?"

Hannah nodded. "She was Clara King's best friend."

"Can I read it?" Marshall asked. "I wouldn't write about anything in it without running it by you first."

"Of course," Hannah said. "I'll let you look at it when I'm finished. It's usually kept in the history room at the library."

Marshall grimaced. "I guess I didn't dig deep enough. I spent a lot of time in the library while working on the Onion Queen story."

Hannah thought about the question she wanted to ask him then said, "Your article seemed to suggest that Clara's disappearance and the demise of the Onion Festival were related. Did you have any particular reason to think that?"

He shook his head. "The timing, that's all. The year she competed, 1932, was the final year of the festival. The King family were leaders in local onion production, so it seems possible to me. Maybe they bowed out and no one else took it on."

"That's sounds likely," Hannah said. "Now we need to know where she went."

"Agreed." Marshall tapped his fingers on the table. "Figuring out what happened to Clara King would make a great follow-up story. Everyone wants to know. And so do I."

Hannah was intrigued by the idea of discovering the rest of the story as well. "I'm not a writer, so go for it, Marshall. Meanwhile, Elaine is fending off people who want the seeds."

"I bet. Heirloom vegetables are big now because people are discovering how good they taste. Plus, the history angle is interesting, the fact that our ancestors grew those crops."

"That's what Professor Timothy J. Buttonwood said," Hannah said. "Have you met him? He's from the University of Virginia and wants to add Elaine's onions to the database of heirloom vegetables he's building. Appalachian heirlooms."

Marshall frowned. "That kind of rings a bell. I'll check him out." He picked up his phone and began searching.

The traffic in and out of the coffee shop had been constant, and Hannah had barely paid attention to the customers. She turned and looked when the door opened yet again.

Blackberry Valley's fire chief, Liam Berthold, waved at Hannah as he stepped in line. Hannah returned the greeting. He was two years older than she, so although they'd attended school together, they hadn't run in the same circles. Since she'd come back to town, they'd struck up a friendship. Today he was with Colin Steele, the local sheriff.

Marshall also waved then gestured to the empty chairs at the table. "I've been meaning to catch up with the sheriff," Marshall said. "If you don't mind."

"Of course not." She checked her coffee level. Leave or get a refill? Another cup, she decided. She wouldn't turn down a chance to visit with Liam.

Picking up her cup, Hannah pushed back in her chair and stood.

By the time she returned, Liam and the sheriff had settled into their places. "Hey, Hannah," Liam said, setting her phone on the table. Hannah knew he'd taken it to change his contact in her phone to another of his ridiculous nicknames, which was why she'd left it there. It was an ongoing joke between the two.

"Hi, Liam," she replied. She checked his contact and chuckled. "Or should I say, 'Chief Sparky'? That's terrible."

"In my defense, I haven't had my coffee yet," Liam replied.

"Colin, how's Geraldine?" Hannah asked.

The sheriff's eyes lit up, as they so often did at the mention of his wife. "She's great. Super excited about the festival. Thanks for asking."

Hannah smiled at his enthusiasm. "You're welcome."

"And speaking of the festival, a TV station in Louisville called us today," Colin added. "They let us know they'd be filming the events."

"I'm glad to hear they contacted you," Marshall said. "I wanted to make sure you knew about it. They've asked me to show them around while they're in town."

"It's pretty exciting that they're filming the cook-off," Hannah said.

"Thinking it might be your big break?" Liam teased. "Maybe you'll be offered your own cooking show."

He was being funny, but his remark reminded her of Corrie.

She must have made a face, because he quickly added, "Sorry. I was only joking. I mean, you're a fabulous chef, so you certainly deserve your own show, but—"

"Stop before you dig yourself too deep," Colin advised. "When Geraldine gets that expression, it means tread with care."

"It's not what you said," Hannah reassured Liam. "It's just that I know someone who's making a name for herself that way. Unfortunately, she's currently featuring one of my recipes."

"What?" Liam's brows drew together. "Who is it?"

Hannah pondered what to say. "It's really not important. I'm going to handle it." Though she had no idea how yet. She was tempted to tell them all about it, but she knew that wouldn't be wise. Even though she trusted the three men at the table, she didn't want any mention of the issue, however inadvertent, to taint her entry.

The men seemed to accept her explanation and continued their conversation. Colin told them about how the deputies would rotate duty so there would be ample police presence at the festival.

"The event is pretty family-friendly," he said. "There shouldn't be too many troublemakers. I think having our people visible helps keep things calm though."

"We'll have a truck on-site as well," Liam said. He winked at Hannah. "In case one of you chefs sets something on fire."

She laughed. "I appreciate your forethought." She glanced at the clock. "On that note, I'd better get going." She began to gather her things.

Liam and Colin got up as well, said their goodbyes, and made their way out of the coffee shop.

"Hannah," Marshall said, "before you go."

Hannah paused to hear what he had to say.

Marshall's expression was troubled. "The professor you mentioned? I knew I'd heard that name before." He held up his phone. "I'll send you the link. He's not at the university anymore."

Chapter Five

Hannah got the link, but before she could open it, a call came in from a supplier. And with that, she was off and running with Hot Spot business.

She walked into the kitchen to find Jacob pacing around while studying his phone. "You got the message too," she guessed, since he was in earlier than usual. Their shipment of grass-fed beef would be delayed until the next day.

Jacob nodded. "I'll move the carne asada tacos to tomorrow night." The spicy and tender tacos, with the beef finished to a slight char under the broiler, were a customer favorite.

"What do we have in the walk-in?" Hannah started in that direction.

"Already checked. We have plenty of chicken, so I'm using that." He tapped his phone. "How about baked chicken breasts with a crunchy honey topping? Perfect with potato wedges and green salad. I'll call it Candlelight Chicken."

"Sounds delicious." Kind of like fried chicken, only healthier and with no vats of hot oil. "You should probably think about another backup recipe for tomorrow in case the beef is delayed again." Hannah headed toward the office. "I'm going to catch up on paperwork. If you need me, holler."

In the small office, Hannah powered on the computer and began opening a stack of mail. Once the computer booted up, she checked her email. A lot of vendors sent bills electronically.

Hannah didn't love paperwork, but it did give her a good sense of what was going on in the business. Even without sales numbers, she could see loss or growth from the amount of stock they had to order. Trends in what had to be replenished. Mastering grocery supplies was one of the trickiest parts of running a restaurant. Running out was far from ideal, but so were overages, which then had to be repurposed into other dishes. Food waste was a huge no-no, both ethically and as a hit to the bottom line.

Jacob spoke to her from the doorway. "Any ideas about dessert? I'm feeling uninspired at the moment."

Hannah thought for a moment. "Actually, yes. Blackberry jam cake. I found a recipe in an old newspaper."

"Sounds good." His brows drew together. "Make our own jam, or what?"

"You don't have time," Hannah said. She recalled the display of jars she'd seen at the King Farm. "Fortunately for us, Elaine sells it." Elaine was coming in later, but Hannah could go pick up some jam so Jacob could get to work. She'd take a sandwich and eat lunch on the way.

She searched through her phone. "I'll get the recipe to you. Let's figure out how much jam you'll need." After sending the recipe to Jacob, she texted Elaine to put dibs on the jam. Elaine reported that she had plenty.

"It's a go," Hannah told Jacob.

"Awesome. I'll get busy scaling up the ingredients." Not only would the cakes themselves be larger, but he would also be making more than one.

"I'll head out and get what you need," Hannah said.

Jacob was still ciphering and checking his notes against what they had in stock. "Sounds good. Thanks. It'll just take me a few more minutes to figure out how much."

By the time Hannah paid some invoices then logged off, Jacob had the answer for her. In the kitchen, she gathered ingredients for a sandwich: ham and cheese, sweet pickle, mustard, and hearty rye bread from Sweet Caroline's Bakery. "Want one, Jacob?"

He glanced up from slicing chicken breasts into serving sizes for the supper service. "Sure. Thanks."

Hannah put together the sandwiches, wrapped hers in wax paper, and added a small bag of chips. A travel mug of ice water, and she was ready to roll. "See you soon. Call if you think of anything else you need."

The sun was high overhead, and downtown Blackberry Valley was hot and drowsy. Pedestrians sauntered along the sidewalk, and the ice cream shop was packed.

Hannah ate her lunch as she cruised along in the Subaru, thinking that life couldn't get much better. When she'd worked as a chef, she'd had much less freedom. Now she not only set the restaurant's—and her own—hours, but she could also take a break for a ride or a walk when she wanted to.

On the flip side, the full responsibility of the Hot Spot's success was on her shoulders. That meant late-night and early-morning hours, juggling money, and taking up the slack whenever and wherever needed.

She wouldn't trade it for anything.

As she turned in to King Farm, her relaxed mood was rudely interrupted. A battered blue pickup truck barreled toward her, right down the middle of the long driveway. She had to swerve abruptly, her right-side tires crushing the grass on the shoulder.

A hand lifted in apology, and then the truck was gone, wheeling onto the main road and roaring away.

Shaken, Hannah continued up the drive. Who was that? She hadn't recognized the vehicle. Elaine had texted to meet her at the barn, so Hannah went directly there.

Her friend stood near the open doors, talking to Blake and a young woman with blond hair in a high ponytail. Elaine waved as Hannah parked.

"Who was that in the blue pickup?" Hannah asked as she climbed out. "They almost hit me."

Elaine huffed. "Sorry about that. I had to fire Phoenix." She rubbed both arms as if chilled despite the blazing heat. "I feel awful."

Blake laid a hand on his mother's arm. "I feel bad too. But he wasn't doing his work." He glanced at the young woman. "Thankfully, Kylie is able to fill in for today."

Kylie ran her fingers through her ponytail. "I'm all done with my summer job, so I don't mind at all. I'll be busy starting tomorrow though, what with the competition and all."

Elaine gestured toward the barn. "I've got the jam ready, Hannah." To her son, she said, "Can you pick tomatoes? We have to make a delivery this afternoon."

The young pair walked off in the direction of the field, Blake pulling a cart of five-gallon buckets.

"I'll take some tomatoes if you have extra," Hannah said. "Five pounds?"

"Sure." Elaine put her hands to her mouth. "Pick Hannah five pounds, please."

Blake gave his mom a thumbs-up.

The women walked into the barn. Banjo, who had been lounging in the shade, came to greet them. "So sorry about Phoenix," Elaine said again.

"Don't worry about it," Hannah said. "I'm fine." She hoped the young man would be too. It was a blow to be fired, even if it was a reasonable consequence.

As if picking up on Hannah's thoughts, Elaine said, "I hope he'll be okay. I have no idea where he's going or what he's going to do." She showed Hannah a box of jars sitting on a table. "Here's your jam."

Hannah pulled out a jar to admire the deep purple contents. "It looks fantastic."

"Got to use the leftover berries somehow. I freeze a lot for pie and other desserts." Elaine patted the box. "Jacob is making cake?"

"Yes. I found an old recipe when I was looking through newspapers at the library." She thought of an update to share. "I've been reading Mabel's diary. You'd probably enjoy it too. She talks about Clara a lot."

Elaine peered at a tray of blackberries in a glass-fronted fridge. "I would love to read it when you're done." She glanced over her shoulder. "Any clues to the mystery of why she left yet? Or where she went?"

"Not yet. So far, Rodney Combs, the stationmaster, is new to town. Clara seems to like a farmhand named Wilson. He was nearby when a money box was stolen from the station. I think that might be the big scandal. I didn't see any other exciting headlines."

"Could be." Elaine turned away from the refrigerator. "Need any more whole berries? They would make a nice decoration on the cake."

Hannah wondered why she hadn't thought of that. "You're absolutely right."

A man entered the barn, and Hannah recognized Professor Buttonwood. He wore the same straw hat, but today he had on khaki shorts, a T-shirt with a UV logo, and a pair of laced boots. His boots and lower legs were dusty, and he carried a water bottle.

The professor stopped short when he noticed Hannah. "Good afternoon. The Hot Spot, right?"

"That's right. How are you, Professor Buttonwood?" Hannah thought of the link from Marshall she still hadn't opened. Was it any of her business? Maybe, as Elaine's friend. She made a mental note to check it later.

With a laugh, the professor took off his hat and wiped his face with a handkerchief. "Please, call me Timothy. I'm roasting. That's why I came in, to get more water." He replaced the hat, tucked away the handkerchief, and went over to a water dispenser.

"Timothy is taking soil samples," Elaine explained. "He's starting with the existing gardens before moving out to other areas of the farm."

"That does sound like hot, dusty work," Hannah said.

Timothy drank deeply then wiped his mouth with the back of his hand. "You need to dig down six to eight inches for each sample. I've created a numbering system keyed to a farm map, Elaine. That way we'll be able to match results to specific areas."

Elaine nodded. "Great idea. Thank you."

The professor topped off his water bottle and capped it. "By the way, what's that old house in the woods at the edge of the hayfield? Does it belong to this farm?"

"It does," Elaine said. "Field hands used to live there when we had more help. There's an old well out there somewhere. I don't think that area is safe anymore."

Timothy nodded. "I'll be sure to avoid it. I'm going back out for another hour or so."

"Stop by the house for sweet tea," Elaine said. "And a snack."

"What a nice offer. I sure will." He touched the brim of his hat in a salute and strode out of the barn.

Elaine shook her head. "He's doing all that work, and I still haven't found the seeds. Not that I've had time to search."

"Any other mysterious events?" Hannah was worried that someone else would find the seeds first.

"Not over the last day or so." Elaine pointed to the UK ball cap hanging on a post. "Still don't know who that belongs to. And I doubt the sheriff would bother with a DNA sample," she joked.

The mention of the sheriff reminded Hannah of other news. "Guess what? A television station in Louisville is sending a lifestyle reporter to the festival. Marshall will be acting as their guide around town."

Elaine clapped her hands. "That's exciting. Maybe the Hot Spot can get some good exposure out of it."

"Your farm as well," Hannah said, thinking of the blackberries she'd be using for her cook-off entry. "Unless you don't want any more press."

"Probably don't need it." Elaine rolled her eyes.

Hannah winced. "Zane at Jump Start said a lot of people are talking about the Onion Queen story. Marshall expects it to die down soon though."

"We can only hope," Elaine said fervently.

Getting the sense that Elaine needed to get back to work, Hannah moved toward the box of jam jars. "Can you write up a receipt while I load these? You can bring the tomatoes later if you want."

She was hauling the box out to her car when Kylie approached. "We have the tomatoes in the barn," she said to Hannah.

"I'll be right back to get some," Hannah told her. She put the box of jam jars in the back of the car then returned to the barn to pick out tomatoes and put them on the scale.

"I gave Phoenix the name and number of my contact at the rec department," Kylie said to Elaine. "They need help. Maybe they'll give him a job."

Elaine looked relieved. "That makes me feel better."

Once Kylie left the barn, Elaine told Hannah, "I honestly don't have anything against Phoenix. He just didn't work out as a farmhand." She paused. "I told him he could stay here until he found another place. He refused and took off."

Hannah wasn't surprised that Elaine had shown compassion even after firing someone. "Don't beat yourself up too much. I've had to let people go as well. In the past, I mean. Not here in Blackberry Valley. I've been very fortunate."

As Hannah carried her tomatoes out to the car, she said a quick prayer for Phoenix, that he would land on his feet and figure out where he was meant to be.

Something Hannah hoped everyone would find in life.

Blackberry Valley
August 8, 1932

Clara and Mabel raced to the house. Mabel left her bike on the grass and followed Clara inside and up the staircase to her bedroom.

Her mother waited there, arms folded and foot tapping. "Where have you been? Everyone is downstairs and waiting on you."

"I'm sorry, Mama." Clara grabbed the fresh dress that Mrs. King had laid out on the bed. "I'll be ready in no time." She dashed out of the bedroom toward the bathroom, to wash up and change.

Mrs. King perched on the bed instead of going back downstairs. "What am I going to do with her, Mabel?"

Mabel was startled. Partly because it wasn't like Mrs. King to confide in her, but mostly because she could see nothing wrong with Clara's behavior.

"I'm not sure," she said, hoping to end the conversation before Clara came back.

Clara's mother sighed deeply, clasping her hands together. "What does she see in that Wilson Barnes? I have half a mind to ask my husband to fire him. He's getting too big for his britches."

Mabel was alarmed. "Don't do that, Mrs. King. You know how hard it is for people to find work nowadays. Plus, who could replace him? Wilson can do everything around here." Wilson worked in the fields, took care of the livestock, and maintained all the machines and vehicles on the farm. Without his help, Mr. King and Clara's younger brother, Lemuel, would be overwhelmed.

Mrs. King raised her brows. "You make good points, Mabel. Are you sure there's nothing untoward between that man and my daughter?"

Mabel had never seen anything more than friendship between the pair. Clara seemed happy around Wilson, lighter and more joyful, but she wasn't going to mention that to her mother in case Mrs. King misinterpreted it.

"I haven't noticed anything like that," she finally said. "Besides, Clara wouldn't allow it. She's the finest girl I know. That's why she'll be the Onion Queen. She deserves it."

Mrs. King's features relaxed into a smile. "She is something special, isn't she? Her father and I want her to have a husband who is worthy of her." She rose to her feet and moved toward the door, pausing to pat Mabel's shoulder. "You're a good friend, Mabel. See you downstairs."

Clara trotted into the room, her face rosy and shining. She sat at her dressing table and began combing her hair. "What was Mama going on about?" Her eyes were troubled in the mirror's reflection.

Mabel made sure to close the bedroom door. Then she moved close to Clara. "She's worried about you and Wilson." She saw her own face twist in the mirror. "She thinks something's going on."

Clara dropped her comb with a gasp. "She said that?" Her eyes snapped with anger. "How dare she? Wilson has been nothing but a gentleman."

"Hold on," Mabel said. "I told her that. I also said you're the finest girl I know and that you deserve to be Onion Queen."

Clara hopped up to give Mabel a hug. "Thank you. You're the best." After letting go, she leaned close and whispered, "Can I tell you a secret?"

Mabel nodded, even though something told her she might not like Clara's revelation. But Clara had been her best friend since they were toddlers making mud pies. What else were best friends for?

"Wilson and I are falling in love," Clara whispered. "Isn't that wonderful?"

Clara's confession made it hard for Mabel to concentrate as the contestants and the committee members milled around the Kings' dining room, filling plates with finger sandwiches and cookies. While Mabel could understand the attraction between the pair, she was worried.

Mrs. King had made it very plain that she considered Wilson beneath her daughter. And now Clara's mother had sidled close to Mrs. Thompson, who cooked and cleaned for the new stationmaster at the cottage the railroad had provided for him.

"What sort of man is he?" Mabel heard Mrs. King ask in a low voice.

"Tidier than most," Mrs. Thompson practically bellowed. "Barely have to do a thing. Not a fussy eater either. Likes everything I make."

"Are you talking about Mr. Combs?" Ada Young asked with a flutter of her lashes. "He's just the nicest thing. A real gentleman."

Mrs. King's expression was sour when she studied Ada's flushed face. Not only was Ada the main rival for the Onion Queen title, she was now a contender for Rodney Combs. And Mrs. King clearly wanted Rodney for Clara, at least as an option. Mabel had years of experience reading such situations.

"We're having him over for dinner this week, along with a few other local dignitaries," Mrs. King said loftily. "He said he's greatly looking forward to it."

This remark only confirmed Mabel's theory. "What do you think about that dinner party?" she whispered in Clara's ear.

Clara made a face, quickly smoothing her features when Ada glanced their way. "The food will be delicious. I know that because I'm cooking it."

Mabel hid a giggle behind her hand as Mrs. Young announced, "Let's get started, ladies. We have a lot to do before the competition."

Everyone settled in the living room, on sofas and chairs and even the piano bench. Mrs. Young detailed the sequence of events, the interviews and parade and stage competition. "We'll have a dress rehearsal on Friday night," she said. "People will be attending from all over the county, so we want to give them a quality performance. Right, girls?"

The contestants echoed agreement. Mabel's belly clenched with nerves. She was going to play "Amazing Grace" on her flute. How she hoped she didn't make a mistake. She'd been practicing every spare moment.

"In a few minutes, a reporter from the *Blackberry Valley Chronicle* will be here to take a group photograph." Mrs. Young turned to Mrs. King. "The porch will be the best spot, don't you think?"

"I do," Mrs. King agreed. "I'll have our hired hand move the furniture aside so the girls can line up against the wall." Glancing at her daughter, she looked ready to say more but then rose to her feet. "I'll go tell him."

Apparently, Mabel hadn't reassured her about the nature of Clara's relationship with Wilson as much as she'd hoped.

A car engine rumbled outside, announcing the arrival of the reporter. As they trooped out the front door onto the porch, Mabel saw that Rodney Combs had given the man a lift. Ada gave Rodney a wave and a big smile.

Mrs. Young ushered them into place, and the reporter aimed his box camera in their direction. "Smile, ladies," he said. "On three. One...two..." The shutter clicked. "Now please stay where you are. I'm going to need your names in the order you appear in the photograph."

"This is so exciting," Marjorie Evans, another contestant, gushed while the reporter worked his way along the line, jotting down details. "I've never been in the paper before."

"Count your lucky stars," Rodney quipped. "It's not always a good thing."

Some of the girls giggled.

"I don't know what you mean," Marjorie said. "You looked terribly handsome in the paper last week."

"Aw, doll," Rodney said. "You're too good to be true."

Clara discreetly rolled her eyes at Mabel, who hid a smile. Rodney Combs appeared set on charming his way through the unattached women in town. When it came to Mabel and her best friend, he wouldn't get far. They were decidedly unimpressed.

Chapter Six

The Blackberry Queen interviews were held the following morning at one of Hannah's favorite places in Blackberry Valley, Bluegrass Hollow Farm. Cars filled the farmyard. Not only were the committee members here, but so were the contestants. Hannah also recognized a couple of the contestants' mothers in the crowd. As she approached the farmhouse, the sound of laughter and chatter drifted through the windows.

She started walking faster, eager to join the fellowship and fun.

The back door was open, so Hannah knocked on the frame of the screen door and entered the kitchen, which was filled with the aroma of fresh-brewed coffee.

Lacy dashed into the kitchen with a carafe. "There you are." She gave Hannah a one-armed hug and then hurried to the coffeemaker. "Go make yourself at home."

Hannah followed the direction she pointed, stepping into a scene of pandemonium. The dining room and adjacent living room were full of guests. Harriet stopped by the dining room table to grab a chocolate chip cookie.

"Hey." Elaine came up to Hannah. "I see you also got roped in?" She laughed. "I'm not a judge. I'm the stage coordinator."

"Wonderful." Lacy returned with the carafe, and Hannah moved over to pour herself a cup. "Good turnout, Lacy."

Lacy rested her hands on her hips, surveying the room with satisfaction. "Six young women competing, five judges, and a few helpers. This year's competition is going to be the best ever." She clapped her hands and announced, "I think it's time to get started."

With much milling about and chatter, everyone found a seat. Hannah sat on a folding chair along the dining room wall next to Elaine.

Lacy remained standing, and Hannah noticed a pile of printed handouts on the sideboard beside her. "Welcome, everyone," Lacy said as she picked up the stack and passed it to Kylie, who was seated closest to her. Kylie took a packet and passed the rest along.

"Before we get into the agenda for the week, I'd like everyone to introduce themselves," Lacy went on. "I'm Lacy Minyard, competition coordinator. Also chicken mama and egg salesperson."

Hannah laughed along with the others and looked around the room. She recognized the members of the committee and most of the young women, but some only by sight from seeing them in the Hot Spot.

Lacy gave an overview of the competition history, and Hannah thought about her own great-great-aunt and the Onion Queen pageant. The Blackberry Queen contest offered scholarships to the winner and two runners-up. All competitors were given a court title and a certification recognizing their efforts. From what Lacy said, both competitions were a way to support young women in their endeavors.

"Community service is a big part of our judging," Lacy said. "We want to hear about what you've been doing in town or in your college community. During the festival, you'll be volunteering with children's activities, the kickoff celebration, the cook-off, and other events. You'll wear these." She reached into a box and pulled out a dark purple T-shirt printed with BLACKBERRY QUEEN COURT and the date. "And these." She reached in again and took out a tiara.

Everyone exclaimed over the costumes as Lacy doled them out. Most of the young women put their tiaras on right away, laughing and chattering.

The contestants would also be in a parade on Friday morning. The main competition would be on stage in the park early Saturday evening, followed by a dance.

"We're doing short personal interviews this morning," Lacy said. "Those will be in my office, one at a time. The rest of you can socialize and enjoy the refreshments while you wait your turn. Coordinators, you'll be talking about logistics and setting up volunteer assignments with the girls as they wait. We'll have lunch when the interviews are over. Sandwiches and salads are in the fridge, along with lemonade and sweet tea."

Elaine leaned toward Hannah. "She's really good at this."

"She sure is." Hannah was proud of her friend's organizational abilities, not to mention her talent at building relationships. She was great at matching people with tasks suited to their gifts and skills. That must mean she thought Hannah had what it took to be a pageant judge.

Hannah followed the other judges into Lacy's office, where they were given paper to jot notes and rank a contestant's answers to several questions.

What makes you unique? What accomplishments are you most proud of? Tell us about your personal goals. Tell us how you've overcome a challenge.

They were great questions, and Hannah found herself eager to hear the answers. One by one, the young women entered the room, seated themselves somewhat nervously in the "hot seat," as Lacy called it, and did their best.

They were all charming, intelligent, and interesting. "I'm rooting for them all," Hannah confessed to Miriam Spencer, a senior member of the committee. "How can we narrow it down to a winner and two runners-up?"

"It's always difficult, dear," Miriam told her. "Just remember, they're all winners, among Blackberry Valley's brightest and best. Like you and Lacy. I'm proud of what you two have done with your lives."

"Why, thank you." Hannah was touched to hear this praise from a woman she admired and respected. "We have lots of wonderful role models."

When Hannah returned to the dining room, she spotted Elaine carrying a platter of sandwiches to the table. "Those look good."

"They sure do." Elaine peeled away the plastic wrap and examined the fillings. "Chicken salad, egg salad, and deviled ham."

The others lined up at the table, filling plates with food and pouring glasses of tea or lemonade. "You know how to do things right," Hannah said when Lacy came up beside her.

"Thanks." Lacy grinned. "Guess where the egg salad came from?"

"The upside of raising chickens," Hannah joked. "All the eggs you can eat."

"And then some." Lacy moved on to make sure other guests had what they needed.

Hannah sat with Elaine again, and this time Kylie was beside them. "Mom had to go to work," she said to Elaine. "I'm still riding with you, right? To your place, to help Blake?" She glanced at her phone. "Have you heard from him? He hasn't answered my text."

Elaine checked her own phone. "No, I haven't. That's odd." She put her sandwich down and began poking at the screen. "He usually checks in to see what he should do next." She put her phone to her ear and listened as it rang. "No answer."

"Is that like him?" Hannah asked. Most people kept their phones close, but maybe Blake wasn't one of them.

Elaine shook her head. "Not at all. He knows to keep his phone on him in case something happens and he needs help. Especially when he's way out in the fields, where nobody can hear him shout."

Kylie devoured the rest of her sandwich in two bites. "We need to go. Maybe something happened to him."

Elaine immediately stood. "Hannah, I'll talk to you later."

"No way. I'm coming with you." If Blake was in trouble, Hannah wanted to be there to provide support and whatever else was needed.

After a quick goodbye to Lacy, the trio were on their way. As Hannah followed Elaine's car down the road, she prayed that Blake was okay. She'd heard of far too many farm accidents such as overturned tractors, life-threatening cuts from tools, and sprained or broken limbs due to a fall. Even the most sensible and cautious person could get hurt in a split second.

At the King Farm, Elaine drove straight to the barn, and Hannah did the same. They both parked and jumped out.

"Where should we check first?" Kylie asked, glancing around frantically. "There are acres of fields. I wish I had my horse. We'd cover the ground in no time."

Hannah tried to bring a sense of order and calm. "Where was he working today, Elaine?"

"In the blackberry patch." Elaine took out her phone and dialed. "I'll try him again."

A phone rang nearby, and they all looked around to find it.

"There it is," Kylie said. She trotted over to where the device lay on the grass. "He must have dropped it."

"Maybe Banjo is with him." Elaine whistled for the dog. "Let's see what direction he comes from."

Hannah immediately heard barking, and Banjo wiggled out between the barely open barn doors. Once free, he ran over and leaped at Elaine, still barking frantically.

"What's up, boy?" Elaine asked. "Do you know where Blake is?" Her mouth twisted. "I know, I know. It's foolish to ask a dog."

"Maybe not." Kylie pointed at Banjo, who was running back to the barn. "He wants us to go in there."

Elaine went to the door and tugged it along the rails, making the opening wide enough for them to enter. Hannah's heart was in her throat. If the dog had heard Elaine, why hadn't Blake? Why hadn't he called out?

Inside, the barn was dim and quiet. "Blake?" Elaine called. "Blake, are you in here?"

"I'll look in the loft." Kylie was already halfway up the ladder. "He's not up here," she called down a moment later.

A knocking sound came from the rear of the barn. Elaine raced in that direction. Hannah hadn't been in this part of the structure before. They passed old stalls, tools hung on the walls, and aging equipment. At the very end was a door with an old-fashioned thumb-latch handle.

The rapping came from the door. Then Hannah heard a faint voice. "Mom? Mom, help!"

Banjo pawed at the door, whining.

"Blake," Elaine shouted. "I'm coming." She tugged at the door latch before noticing there was a padlock hanging on a hasp right above it. "Phew," she said. "It's not locked."

Elaine pulled out the padlock and yanked the door open. "Blake?"

Kylie turned her phone's flashlight on and swept the dark space. "There he is. Blake, what happened?"

She and Elaine went in to check on the young man while Hannah hovered outside. "Do I need to call an ambulance?"

"Maybe," Elaine said. "Let me check him out."

Blake sat on the floor, holding the back of his head. "Someone tackled me, Mom. Next thing I knew, I was shoved inside this old storage room."

Chapter Seven

Blake insisted he was fine, that his head injury wasn't serious. Elaine and Kylie helped him out of the storage room and into the main part of the barn, where his mother could take a better look for herself.

Elaine gently pushed his hair aside to reveal a definite egg on his scalp. "I'm going to run you to the emergency room so they can check it out. I'm worried you might have a concussion."

Blake said, "Seriously, I'm okay."

"I didn't raise you to argue with your mother and her instincts," Elaine said sternly.

"Yes, ma'am." The corners of Blake's mouth twitched with amusement.

"What happened?" Kylie asked. She was standing nearby, watching anxiously, her arms crossed. "Who tackled you?"

Hannah wondered the same thing. Elaine had said that they'd been plagued by mysterious occurrences. With Blake being attacked, whoever was behind those odd happenings seemed to be escalating their efforts. Did this incident have anything to do with the seeds? Or was there another reason someone would go after Blake?

"I didn't see the person," Blake said. "I came into the barn, and someone jumped me. They put a sack over my head and pushed me inside the storage room. I tripped and banged my head on something."

Elaine gasped. "They put a sack over your head?"

Blake gestured. "It's in there. I managed to get it off." He sneezed and then groaned, holding his head.

Kylie and Hannah hurried to the storage room door and peered inside, Kylie's phone light bobbing around the dark enclosure.

Hannah saw a heap of burlap on the ground. "Don't touch it," she warned as Kylie started toward it. "We need to call the sheriff, Elaine. Someone assaulted your son. We can't ignore this any longer." The burlap sack indicated to her that the trespasser didn't want Blake to identify them.

"Was it Phoenix?" Elaine asked Blake.

"No way," Blake said firmly. "He wouldn't do something like that. We're friends."

Hannah was impressed by Blake's defense of the young man. Although Phoenix had seemed harmless enough to her. Certainly not a criminal type.

Elaine didn't look convinced. "I'm going to call the sheriff and ask him to check this out. We'll leave everything exactly the way it is. Blake, I'm taking you to the hospital."

His injury didn't seem urgent enough to require an ambulance, so Elaine's plan made sense. "If you can't work tonight, that's fine," Hannah told her. "I'll fill in."

"Thanks, Hannah. I'll try to make it, but I'll call you either way."

Kylie stepped forward. "We found your phone out on the grass." She held it out to him.

"Thanks." Blake put the phone in his pocket. "I must've dropped it when I was loading a cart."

Elaine shook her head. "The car is right outside the door. Let's go. Kylie, I'll drop you off at your house."

With Hannah and Kylie following, Elaine helped Blake out to the car. After he was settled in the passenger seat, Elaine said, "I'm going to lock the main gate, so you should leave ahead of me, Hannah." Her gaze fell on Banjo. "And I'd better put you in the house before we go."

"Of course." Hannah started toward her vehicle as Kylie climbed into Elaine's back seat. "Keep me posted, okay?"

Elaine promised to give her an update after Blake saw the doctor.

All the way to town, Hannah pondered the question. Who would attack Blake? And why? It was possible that the person hadn't targeted him specifically, but rather anyone who came into the barn and interrupted whatever the intruder had been up to.

Looking for the seeds? That seemed likely. Maybe it was Phoenix. He probably knew about the onion seeds. Everyone else did, apparently.

Hannah recalled the hat Elaine had found. Did it belong to the intruder? If only there was a way to tie the hat to a particular person. Sure, they could get DNA from it if the sheriff's department agreed to test it, but who would they match it to?

She doubted the department would go for it. Anyone could have left the hat, like another friend of Blake's or even someone stopping by to pick up an order. The hat might not have anything to do with what happened.

If only Elaine could find the seeds. That would put an end to all this. Maybe Hannah should volunteer to help. Although she had a full plate, as did Elaine. However, with the incidents escalating, maybe finding the seeds needed to be a priority.

Hannah would suggest this approach to Elaine. Perhaps they could fit it in between the Hot Spot, the Blackberry Queen contest, and the cook-off.

Feeling overwhelmed by her to-do list over the next few days, Hannah exhaled.

How had so much come up so quickly?

Hannah was in the middle of food prep with Jacob when Elaine called. She put her phone on speaker so the chef could listen in. He was concerned about Blake as well.

"Good news," Elaine said. "No concussion. He just has to take it easy for a day or two." Hannah could hear the relief in her friend's voice. "Take it easy and Blake don't go together, believe me. Still, I have him on the couch watching his favorite movies with Banjo. Which means I'll be in."

"Great news," Hannah said. "If you want the night off, though, please feel free."

"He'll kill me if I keep hovering," Elaine said. "He has me on speed dial, and I'll check in periodically as well."

"Did you have the sheriff come out?" Hannah asked. She'd told Jacob about the mysterious events, so he was up to date.

"They sent Deputy Holt. Alex." Elaine gave the first name because Alex had a twin sister, Jacky, who was also a deputy. "He took Blake's statement and poked around the barn. I also showed him the UK baseball cap I found. He said he couldn't do much with it unless they had a sample to compare it to."

So Hannah'd been right about that. "Well, with Blake being attacked, that might change things. Though we don't know for sure that it was Hat Man who jumped him."

Elaine chuckled. "Thanks for the nickname. Yeah, Hat Man is a mystery. Especially now."

"Why's that?" Hannah asked.

"Because the hat is gone. I wanted to show it to the deputy, and I couldn't find it. Blake said he didn't touch it. You didn't move it, did you?"

"Wasn't me." Had the intruder grabbed the hat? Maybe it had belonged to him, a connection that he didn't want to risk being made.

Noise at the back door announced the arrival of the waitstaff. "We'll talk more later," Hannah said. "Thanks for the update." She would ask Elaine about getting together and searching for the seeds later.

"I'll be there shortly." Elaine hung up.

"Wow," Jacob said. "This whole thing is nuts." He stirred the pot of beans that would be served with the carne asada, which was currently marinating.

The beef order had come through that morning, and Hannah was excited to sample the spicy dish.

"What's on the menu tonight?" Dylan asked as he and Raquel put on aprons.

While Jacob took them through the printed list, which Raquel would use to make a chalkboard menu, Hannah ducked into her office to catch up on calls and emails.

Wednesday night was usually quite busy, although Friday and Saturday were the busiest. Driving into town on the way back from King Farm, Hannah had definitely seen a lot of traffic. The summer tourist season was in full swing, and the festival drew even more visitors.

An email from the chamber of commerce reminded Hannah that the Hot Spot was to provide appetizers for the festival's kickoff tomorrow evening. The Sample and Schmooze event was designed to highlight the businesses in downtown Blackberry Valley. Attendees would buy tickets they could redeem for various items.

Sudden anxiety gripped Hannah. She'd barely given the event a passing thought with everything else that had been going on. Pushing back her chair, she jumped up and hurried out to the kitchen. "Jacob, how are we doing for Sample and Schmooze?"

He didn't pause in his work. "All set. You and I talked about how much we'd need based on what the chamber said. You've had enough on your plate lately, so I just took care of it. I hope that's all right."

"So we have everything?"

"More than enough. In fact, I'm going to put the same appetizers on our menu tomorrow night to make prep easier."

"Thank you, Jacob. I'm so glad you're on top of it."

"That's my job," the chef said lightly. "Helping you keep all the balls in the air." He mimed juggling.

Hannah laughed. "By the way, we got great feedback on the blackberry jam cake. I'd say we should offer it at the festival, but the church is selling their famous blackberry crumble there."

"Glad people liked it. And no problem. We don't want to compete with the church. Tonight's dessert is vanilla cake topped with a fruit compote and whipped cream."

Elaine entered through the rear. "Hello, hello. Got here as quick as I could."

Hannah glanced at the clock. "You're fine. Raquel did the menu board already, so that's off your plate."

Elaine glanced into a mirror and smoothed her hair. "Wonderful. By the amount of traffic I ran into, I think we'll be busy tonight."

"Glad to hear it." Hannah started back toward her office. "I'll be out to help in ten." She would float as she usually did, helping Jacob or in the dining room as needed.

The doors opened at four, which was early, so traffic was modest at first. But it picked up as dinnertime approached, and Elaine had to make a waiting list. Some wandered away while others stuck it out, determined to eat at the Hot Spot.

As Hannah surveyed the full dining room, she allowed herself to feel a moment of satisfaction. This was exactly what she had dreamed of: a full house of happy patrons laughing and talking and enjoying excellent food.

Circling the floor, she murmured encouraging words to Raquel and Dylan then swooped in to refresh water, bring a condiment, answer a question. As she made her way through, her attention was caught by two men dining together. Cooper Combs, Elaine's neighbor, and Professor Timothy J. Buttonwood, who was taking soil samples at Elaine's farm.

The hair on the back of Hannah's neck rose. What business did they have together? Cooper had bluntly stated that he thought his family should get credit for the seeds. Timothy wanted them for his collection.

Their water glasses were low, so she picked up a pitcher and went over. "How is everything?" she asked. They had ordered the carne asada, and both had made significant dents in their meal.

Cooper finished chewing and patted his mouth with a napkin. "Fantastic. I can't believe I haven't been in here before. But I usually wait six months to a year to make sure the restaurant is going to stick around."

Seriously? This insensitive remark tempted Hannah to pour water on his head. Instead, she injected sweetness into her voice as she filled his glass. "Well, I'm glad you decided to join us. We've passed the six-month mark here, so I'm optimistic."

"I'm enjoying every single bite," Timothy told her. "I make a point of choosing farm-to-table restaurants everywhere I go. It's important to support them."

Timothy was now her favorite out of the two men, although Hannah wasn't sure about either. She still hadn't checked the link Marshall had sent her about the professor. She was really off her game lately.

She could also be completely off base suspecting a conspiracy between the pair. Why would they come to Elaine's place of work if they were up to no good?

"Thank you for dining with us," Hannah said, knowing she needed to move on. People were leaving, which meant their tables should be cleared so new customers could be seated. "Let us know if you need anything else."

The men nodded, and Hannah left the table. As she walked away, she heard Cooper say, "So you've helped farmers through the seed-patent process. What's needed to prove a claim?"

Chapter Eight

It was nearing ten o'clock, closing time. Cooper's words had lingered in the back of Hannah's mind the rest of the night, an undercurrent to the hubbub of a busy restaurant. Her impression was that he still hoped to find the onion seeds and stake a claim. Timothy, as a vegetable crop expert, probably knew the ins and outs of the fine print involved.

Hannah was annoyed on Elaine's behalf. If those seeds were located, they belonged to the King family, not Cooper Combs. The advertisement she had found claimed that the variety had been proprietary to the Kings.

"You two can go home," Hannah told the servers. "I'll finish up and put your tips aside." The last two parties were having dessert, and she had to stay and close out the register anyway.

"That sounds great," Raquel said. "I've already got the silverware ready for tomorrow."

"And the service station is clean and stocked," Dylan added. They'd carried out these tasks in between waiting on the last two tables.

"Great. I'll vacuum." Hannah preferred to do it at night rather than in the morning.

Elaine was already gone, released early to tend to Blake. He was fine, but Hannah could tell that Elaine was worried. Hannah had taken over her duties and hadn't had a moment to bring up searching for the seeds. She'd do it tomorrow.

She also hadn't had a chance to mention the conversation between Cooper and Timothy to Elaine. There hadn't been a spare moment all evening.

Hannah perched on a stool behind the register, taking a short break while the patrons finished their meal. *Phew.* She'd been run off her feet all night.

A quick glance through the slips revealed that sales had been very good. She couldn't do anything else yet, so she took out her phone.

She would check out the link Marshall had sent. Hannah found his text and opened the web page.

Professor Resigns after Controversy. Hannah hurriedly skimmed the article, which detailed a disagreement between Professor Timothy Buttonwood and his department head. At issue was an accusation of double-dipping and lack of permission from the dean for a side project Timothy had taken on—his research of Appalachian heirloom vegetables. He had resigned weeks ago but still passed himself off as a professor at the university. Hannah didn't like that.

One of the parties stood, gathering purses and jackets. Hannah set her phone aside to ring them up. The other group left soon after, and Hannah was alone in the restaurant. She locked the door and began to put chairs up on the tables so she could vacuum.

About halfway through the room, Hannah strode toward the back. Although she knew she had Timothy's card, she wanted to double-check it.

In the office, she unlocked the desk drawer and pulled out her handbag. She searched through it and found the card. It was as she remembered. Timothy's card said he was a professor at the University of Virginia in Charlottesville.

Why was he misrepresenting himself? He had even worn a T-shirt with the school logo while collecting soil samples at Elaine's farm. Did he think a professor position gave him more authority?

Hannah had to admit it did. He came across as an expert in the field. And he claimed the backing of an institution of higher learning.

The problem was, it wasn't honest. In Hannah's experience, people who shaded the truth about one thing were likely to do it with another.

She had to share this with Elaine. Tomorrow, at a reasonable hour.

Hannah put the card in the top drawer of the desk where she could easily lay hands on it. She still had to finish vacuuming and close out the cash register.

Thank goodness her commute was short. She could crawl upstairs to bed when she was done.

Blackberry Valley
August 11, 1932

"Look at this dress." Standing in front of the mirror, Clara made a face at herself. "Mama insists I wear it tonight at the dinner party."

Mabel didn't like the ruffly pink dress either. "At least she's not making you wear it in the pageant."

Clara rolled her eyes. "I would quit, and she knows that." She picked up a brush from her dressing table and began to tug it through her hair. "She's trying so hard to push me toward Rodney Combs. I can't stand it."

"I'll protect you." Mabel sat on the edge of Clara's bed, waiting until it was time to go down. Her parents were also attending the party, as was her brother. "Maybe you should pay Mark a lot of attention tonight to discourage Rodney. Mark's nice. Quite handsome too." She put one hand under her chin and fluttered her lashes. "Runs in the family."

As she'd hoped, Clara laughed. "You're both knockouts. I don't think I'd better though. That would be dishonest. Besides, Mark's already sweet on someone else."

Mabel knew that was true. Mark was only attending the dinner party because their mother had twisted his arm. "So...," she began, making sure her gaze was on the bedspread instead of her friend's face. "Anything new with Wilson?" Frankly, she was curious to know if Clara and Wilson had made declarations of love to each other yet.

Clara blushed bright red. "Not really." She slapped her brush down on the dressing table.

"I'm sorry," Mabel said. "I didn't mean to pry. You're my best friend, and I want you to be happy."

Clara's head was bowed now, and Mabel thought she saw the glimmer of tears. "Have you ever wanted something that's impossible?" Clara asked. "Something that everyone is against?"

"Not yet," Mabel said cautiously. She'd never had a desire put to the test. She'd gone to teaching college with her parents' blessing. She didn't have a sweetheart, and she hoped when she finally did, he would be like her father—kind and loving.

Her friend twisted a handkerchief in her hands. "I was raised to listen to my mother and father, to honor them. And I do. I just know that—"

The bedroom door opened to reveal Mrs. King. "Clara, are you coming?" Her gaze shifted to Mabel. "Don't you look lovely, dear." Mabel had come in the back, unlike her parents and brother, who'd gone to the front door.

Mabel slid off the bed and stood. "Thank you, Mrs. King. Clara and I are about ready to come down. Clara just needs to pick out a necklace. Right, Clara?"

Clara, who hadn't met her mother's gaze, nodded and took a seat at the dressing table. She flipped open the jewelry box that held a jumble of necklaces, bracelets, and rings. Far more than Mabel had at home.

"Don't be much longer." Mrs. King swished out of the room, leaving the aroma of perfume behind.

The warm sound of masculine laughter met Mabel and Clara when they came downstairs a few minutes later. Their fathers, along with Mark and Rodney, chatted near the parlor fireplace. Mrs. King and Mama bustled about in the dining room, setting out platters and bowls. Lemuel, Clara's younger brother, was eating in the kitchen. He had plans to go to a movie with friends.

"Should we help?" Mabel asked, ready to start in the direction of the dining room.

Clara shook her head. "Mama said for me to mingle. I'm sure she means you as well."

The two young women entered the living room.

"There you are," Mr. King said. "Rodney, you remember my daughter and her friend, don't you?"

Rodney performed a half-bow. "How could I forget? How nice to see you, Miss King, Miss Prentiss."

Clara smiled. "Welcome to our home. When you see the best tablecloth out, you know Mama is whipping up a feast." Everyone laughed.

"You're in the Onion Queen pageant." Rodney addressed Mabel. "What's your talent?"

Mabel felt her cheeks heat under his scrutiny, amiable as it was. So far, she'd only observed the stationmaster from a distance, watching him interact with others. He had a lot of charm, she had to admit. A way of looking at a person that felt admiring yet respectful. No wonder Ada Young was so taken with him.

"I play the flute," Mabel said. "I've had lessons for years, plus I've been in the band at school." It was much less glamorous than Ada's ballet dancing or Clara's singing.

"She's really good," Mark said. He grinned. "Once we got past the first year of practice. Thought we had a scared bird in the house."

"Oh, Mark." Mabel cuffed her brother's arm gently then blushed again. Rodney would think she was a hoyden.

He didn't seem to notice. He turned to Clara and asked about her performance at the competition, making sounds of approval when she told him about the song she had chosen.

Mrs. King appeared in the doorway. "Dinner is served."

Mr. King sat at the head of the table, Rodney on his right, Clara on his left. Mabel was next to Rodney. Once everyone was settled, Mr. King said grace. Then he opened his napkin and placed it on his lap. "Let's eat."

They passed around the serving dishes of fried chicken, potato salad, pea salad, coleslaw, and cucumbers, tomatoes, and onions in vinegar.

Mark, who was on Mabel's other side, whispered, "Salads as far as the eye can see."

Mama sent him a reproving glance, and he subsided with a covert smile.

Mabel returned the smile, glad her brother was there. He certainly took some of the starch out of the gathering.

Mr. King led the conversation, which was focused on Rodney's position, the railroad in general, and what the new stationmaster thought of Blackberry Valley. His previous position had been in Ellisville, about thirty miles away in the adjacent county. Mabel had visited there a few times over the years. She had cousins who lived there, on her mother's side.

"One of the finest towns I've ever had the pleasure of living in," Rodney said. "Not too big, but not too small either." He threw a twinkling smile around the room. "Upstanding, friendly folks. Even with the challenges our country is facing, I can see signs of great prosperity to come. I've never seen such rich, productive farmland, for one thing."

"Do you think so?" Mr. King sounded anxious. "The coal mines closing was a great blow to our state. At least here we grow a lot of our own food, with surplus to sell. Onion sales have been holding steady, thankfully."

Mrs. King made a clucking sound. "I'm sure Rodney doesn't want to talk about such topics during dinner, dear." She held a plate out to the guest of honor. "Another biscuit?"

Rodney took one. "Thank you. And I don't mind at all, Mrs. King. It's important for me, as a representative of the railroad, to have a finger on the pulse of the local economy, so to speak. We want to make sure there is capacity to carry all of Blackberry Valley's goods to market. And ensure that supplies can make their way here as well."

Clara shifted in her seat. "Plus, we like our train trips to Louisville, don't we, Mama?" To Rodney, she explained, "We go shopping there twice a year. We stay at a hotel and take in a movie or go to a play."

Mabel had been invited along on a few of those trips, and she'd loved every minute. She'd been glad to get back to Blackberry Valley though. She was a country girl at heart.

"I've got prospects of promotion to Louisville—or Nashville," Rodney said, his chest puffing out. "I plan to make the most of every opportunity that comes my way."

Mr. King beamed his approval. "Young men with ambition and good sense built this country. I can tell you're one of them."

Rodney sat up straighter, accepting the compliment like a cape draped around his shoulders. Then, perhaps sensing he'd been the topic of conversation too long, he leaned forward and addressed Mark. "Pretty snappy roadster I saw you driving tonight."

Mark laughed. "I could say the same to you. I rebuilt mine after I got it for a song. It's already ten years old."

The men started talking about automobiles, which didn't interest Mabel in the least. She did notice how animated her brother became. Rodney had won him over.

Another thing Mabel noticed was Mrs. King's smile as she watched the banter. Clara's mother glanced at her daughter frequently, as if checking her reaction. Clara appeared to be barely paying attention, although her expression remained perfectly polite. When Mrs. King briefly allowed her annoyance to show, Mabel felt a flash of concern for her friend.

Mrs. King hoped for a match between the station agent and Clara, regardless of Clara's feelings about the man. Mabel's friend was a good and obedient daughter. Would she be pressured into a marriage she didn't want?

And why was Mrs. King acting this pushy? She never had in the past. Mabel wondered what was behind the change in the woman who had practically been her second mother. What was it about Rodney Combs that made her willing to doom her daughter to a life of unhappiness with him?

Chapter Nine

Hannah slept like a log, awakening around eight. She rolled out of bed and padded to the kitchen to make coffee. She had time to sit and relax over breakfast before diving into the day, which would be even busier than usual. Tonight was the kickoff event for the Blackberry Festival.

In honor of the day, Hannah sprinkled a few blackberries on her cereal and sat at the counter to eat. Between bites and sips of coffee, she read a daily devotional, researching the Bible verses for additional insights. Next, she said a prayer for the day, her loved ones, and other requests shared by friends. Then she checked her phone for messages.

An uneasy feeling reminded her that she needed to tell Elaine what she had discovered about Timothy Buttonwood. Not only was he friendly with Cooper Combs, but he wasn't teaching at the university any longer. So what was he doing in Blackberry Valley? Was he really working on an Appalachian directory of heirlooms, or had that ended along with his job?

Marshall sent her a text that included an image of a lanyard badge that read, Tour Guide. The name of the TV station's lifestyle show was below, and his text read: It's official! We're doing local color shots today and then filming the kickoff.

She typed, THRILLED FOR YOU! SEE YOU THERE. Perhaps Marshall would have an opportunity to be the lifestyle show's restaurant critic. He would be great at that.

The thought of being on camera reminded Hannah of Corrie Rice. There was another issue she'd set on the back burner. She could ignore the recipe theft, she supposed. It would be easier.

Despite that thought, Hannah navigated to Corrie's social media page. A sick feeling dropped into her stomach when she brought up the post featuring the blackberry burrata pizza.

There were thousands of reactions and comments. Knowing she shouldn't, that it wasn't good for her peace of mind, Hannah scrolled through and read some of them.

What a creative combo... never would have thought... going to try it... family loved it, even my picky eater...

Hannah practically slammed the phone down. That had been a mistake. While she was careful not to indulge in pride, she couldn't help but feel that those compliments belonged to her.

Maybe she tweaked the recipe. In that case, it was Corrie's version getting the accolades. Although she claimed to have invented the dish, which was still a problem.

Hannah picked up the phone again and brought up the post under the reel, which provided the recipe. No, that was her original recipe. Scaled down for the home cook, of course.

Feeling paranoid, she checked out the recipes posted after the pizza. Nothing of hers, thankfully.

She drummed her fingers on the table. What should she do? Blasting Corrie on social media was not an option. Send her a private message? Maybe. What if Corrie didn't see it? Or just ignored it?

Hannah knew the right thing to do was call her former colleague. After a lot of prayer. Right now, she had to get control of her anger and hurt. It wasn't fair that Corrie benefited from Hannah's hard work. She wasn't giving her credit, although that wouldn't be enough. Even if she'd credited the recipe to Hannah, proper etiquette required that she ask Hannah's permission to post it.

A honk in the parking lot caught her attention.

Hannah ran to look out a front window. A red pickup truck sat on the street below, Dylan and another young man standing beside it. There was something in the truck bed she couldn't quite make out.

She rapped on the window until they noticed then gestured that she'd be right there.

After hastily donning jeans and a T-shirt and sliding her feet into her shoes, Hannah went down the stairs and outside. "Hey, Dylan. What brings you here so early?"

"I'll show you," Dylan said. "Hannah, this is Seth Bagsby. Seth, this is Hannah Prentiss, owner of the Hot Spot."

Seth, a lean, muscled young man, shuffled his feet and touched the brim of his ball cap. "Nice to meet you."

Hannah nodded and smiled, following Dylan to the rear of the truck. The bed held a small barn-shaped shack with HOT SPOT painted on a sign over the door. Stacks of fruit and vegetable crates, sheaves of cornstalks, and a mini chicken coop complete with fake chickens rounded out the display.

Dylan climbed aboard the bed. "I decided to make this as a surprise, for the parade. Seth helped." He clapped on a straw hat and

Seeds of Suspicion

leaned on a hoe. "We'll add a couple of banners with stuff like, 'Hot Spot: Fine farm-to-table dining.' I know you're super busy with other festival stuff, so I'll ride on the float. Maybe Raquel too."

Hannah was touched. With all her other responsibilities for the festival, she hadn't given an entry in the Friday morning parade a single thought. "It's fantastic, Dylan. Thank you." She turned to Seth. "And thank you too. Are you going to be on the float?"

Seth ducked his head. "I just helped build the barn."

Hannah admired the float some more. "Great job. Do you live in town?"

"I do. I'm a hand at the Combs farm. I also work at the animal shelter part-time."

"Busy," Hannah murmured. Elaine's dog, Banjo, had come from the shelter. "Thanks again, Seth. Do either of you want coffee?"

They both shook their heads. "I need to get back," Seth said. "Thanks though."

"See you later, boss," Dylan said, walking to the driver's door. He hopped in, and soon the truck ambled out of the lot.

Dylan must have borrowed the truck, which was sweet of him. Interesting that Seth worked for Cooper Combs. It was nice of him to work on the float.

Back upstairs, Hannah poured another cup of coffee. Realizing she hadn't talked to her father for a couple of days, she picked up her phone and called him. "Good morning, Dad," she said when he answered. "Want to come over for coffee?"

"Only if you let me bring the muffins," was his response.

A short while later, Hannah and her dad sat at her counter, drinking coffee and nibbling on blackberry streusel muffins from Jump Start.

"Yum," Hannah said. "I wonder if we'll be sick of blackberries by the end of the week."

"Never," Dad declared. "We only get them a short time, and I make sure to eat all I can while they're here."

Hannah's dad had a hearty voice and laugh, and just being near him made Hannah smile. He'd had that effect on his customers during his years as an electrician. "My skill is electrifying," he often said, one of his trademark jokes.

"So what's new, sweetie?" Dad asked. "Ready for the festival?"

"I think so," Hannah said. "We've got the opening ceremony tonight, and I'm in the cook-off tomorrow night. Dylan made a Hot Spot float for the parade, and I'm now a judge for the Blackberry Queen competition."

Dad whistled. "That's quite an honor."

"I know." Hannah grinned. "I've met the girls, and they're all fantastic. It's going to be hard to pick a queen. And speaking of that, I've been reading Mabel's diary. She was an Onion Queen contestant in 1932."

"Now that you mention it, I remember seeing a picture of her in the lineup."

"From what I'm gathering in Mabel's diary, Clara King's parents wanted her to marry the stationmaster, a man named Rodney Combs. He ended up marrying Ada Young after Clara disappeared."

"Hmm. I don't recall hearing any of that," Dad said. "When I was a kid, I didn't pay much attention to old people's stories." He grinned. "As I thought of them back then. Now I'm the one telling old people's stories."

"There was a robbery at the train station under Rodney's watch," Hannah said. "Not sure yet if that has anything to do with Clara or not."

"The Kings have always been prominent here," Dad said. "If you look through past town government or church organizations, you'll see their names. It's only in the last couple of generations that their role has dwindled. Elaine's trying to keep the farm going alone, which is a huge task. My grandparents sold our farm, so I never got to live there. Only had a garden patch."

Hannah took another bite of muffin. "That's where I got my love of farm-to-table. Well, garden-to-table. It must be in our blood."

"Definitely," Dad said. "Although I'm down to a potted cherry tomato plant." He polished off his muffin. "I always got the impression that there wasn't much love lost between the Combs family and the Kings. The Kings' farm used to be larger, but they sold off some of the land to the Combses. After that, there seemed to be bad blood."

"When was that?" Hannah asked, wondering whether she could verify the land transfer. The county office should have that information.

"The midthirties, I think."

Hannah glanced in the coffee cups. "Let me get you a refill." She got up to fetch the carafe. "I think bad blood still exists, on Cooper Combs's part anyway. He came over to Elaine's while I was there picking blackberries earlier this week. He said the Blackberry Red onion belonged to his family."

Dad snorted. "After it got a big write-up. I've seen that before—people coming out of the woodwork when they think there's a dollar to be made."

Hannah appreciated her father's pragmatism. "You're probably right, although the land transfer might muddy the water. What if the Blackberry Red did originate on land that now belongs to the Combses? Although, in an old newspaper ad, the Kings claimed the variety as proprietary. They grew sets and sold them." She swirled her coffee in her mug. "I wonder if Elaine has any old farm ledgers. Those might give us more evidence." Farms kept crop records. The issue would be whether they still existed.

"I don't suppose you have a photo of the ad you were talking about," her dad said.

"Actually, I do. It's here on my phone." She showed her father the picture. "Looks like they grew a bunch of varieties. The Blackberry Red was the most popular, I'm guessing. And now it's gone."

"Keep digging, sweetheart," Dad said. "You'll get there."

Sensing he was preparing to leave, Hannah asked, "Can I get your advice about something else?" She brought up the pizza video Corrie had made and handed it to him.

A furrow appeared between his brows. "That's interesting." He sounded slightly skeptical. Dad wasn't a particularly adventurous eater.

"The thing is, I used to work with her. That's my recipe. I created it."

His eyes flew up to meet hers. "She stole it? Wow, talk about nerve." He glanced down again. "Looks like it's popular with her viewers."

"Exactly," Hannah said. "I could ignore it, pretend I never saw the post. But another chef sent it to me, which means people in my network know about it."

"So you feel like you should say something. To set the record straight." Dad nodded. "Give her a call. Tell her she needs to stop claiming it's her recipe."

Hannah gnawed at her bottom lip then said, "You make it sound so easy. I guess I'm chicken. I don't like confronting people."

"Who does?" Dad chuckled. "Sometimes, though, you have to. She might be stealing recipes from other people too. Or more of yours. That's not an honest or ethical way to build a reputation." He slid off the stool. "You never know, she might thank you."

"Maybe. Thanks for your input, Dad." She slid off her stool to walk him to the apartment door. She gave him a kiss on the cheek. "See you at the kickoff?"

"Gordon and I will be there." He headed down the staircase.

Hannah finished her coffee, planning to jump into the shower next. Then her phone rang with a call from Marshall.

"Hey, Hannah." He sounded a little nervous. "I have something to run by you. Don't feel like you have to say yes, okay?"

Hannah was getting nervous. "Go ahead, Marshall. What is it?"

"Jada from the lifestyle show wants to feature you and the Hot Spot in the segment about Blackberry Valley."

Hannah was both startled and flattered. "What does that mean, exactly?"

"I told her about the restaurant, how you incorporate so many local foods in your menu. And that you're going to be in the cook-off Friday night. Plus, you buy produce from Elaine, so they want to go there too. The home of the Blackberry Red onion."

"Wow. Okay. They can film me, but they'll have to ask Elaine, of course." Hannah doubted her friend wanted any more publicity about those onions. "When are they thinking?"

"Um, later this morning. A quick interview at the restaurant, in the kitchen. If you're good with it, I'll have them call you."

Later this morning? "Give me half an hour before they call, okay? I, er, have a couple of things to take care of." Like showering and fixing her hair and makeup.

"Definitely. See you soon."

As Hannah headed to the bathroom, she realized something. If she was going to be on the air at the cook-off, so would her blackberry burrata pizza.

She had to talk to Corrie before Friday night. Otherwise, people would think Hannah had stolen Corrie's recipe, not the other way around.

Chapter Ten

At exactly eleven, Hannah and Jacob were in the Hot Spot kitchen with fresh aprons on, the place spotless, and a tasting menu of local foods on the counter.

Someone rapped on the front door. Hannah hurried through the restaurant to answer. Outside the glass, she saw Marshall, a dark-skinned woman with cornrows, and a blond woman lugging equipment.

Marshall ushered the small crew inside first. "Folks, this is Hannah Prentiss, owner of the Hot Spot." He introduced Jada, the TV station's lifestyle reporter, and Tiffany, her camera operator.

Jada turned a blinding smile Hannah's way as she extended a hand. "So lovely to meet you. We're going to be filming around Blackberry Valley for the next few days."

After the introductions, they began making their way through the restaurant. "This is the old fire station," Hannah explained. "Hence the name."

"Hot Spot," Jada murmured. "Perfect." She took in the high ceilings and other features that spoke to the building's history. "What a beautiful use of the space. Tiffany, let's take a couple of shots. Okay, Hannah, we're going to give you a collar mic. Don't worry too much about what you say. We're going to edit it down, okay?"

Tiffany attached the device, and then Hannah repeated what she'd told Jada about the Hot Spot. Jada then asked about Hannah's background.

"I grew up in Blackberry Valley." Hannah went on to explain how she had gone away to culinary school and then worked in California, naming the restaurants.

"This is a homecoming for you then," Jada said. "Blackberry Valley is the kind of place you want to come home to, isn't it?"

Eventually, at their direction, Hannah led them into the kitchen. She introduced Jacob, and after they clipped a microphone on his collar, Tiffany began filming Jada and Marshall sampling food described by Hannah and Jacob. After a while, Hannah forgot about the camera and fell into the swing of enjoying food and people's feedback on hers.

They were wrapping up when the back door opened and Elaine entered, a flat of vegetables in her arms. "I'm sorry. I didn't mean to interrupt." Her gaze went right to the camera.

"We're finished." Jada advanced on Elaine, smiling, her hand out. "I'm Jada Jackson."

"Elaine Wilby," Elaine said. "I work here, and I also have a small farm. The Hot Spot buys my produce."

"Elaine Wilby," Jada mused. "Blackberry Red onions, right?"

Hannah was sure her friend did not want to talk about onions. But Elaine answered, "Yes. We used to grow them many decades ago."

"So I understand." Standing with arms folded, Jada tilted her head. "I saw some posts online from another farmer." She addressed Tiffany. "What was his name?"

"Cooper Combs." Tiffany was winding cords and putting them inside a case.

Seeds of Suspicion

Jada turned back to Elaine. "He claims his family developed those onions. Any truth to that?"

The blunt question seemed to fluster Elaine at first. Then she rallied. "I don't believe so. Besides, it's a moot point. They haven't been grown for decades, and no one has the seeds. Which might not even germinate at this point anyway."

Jada seemed to accept that. "Okay. How do you feel about having us come out to the farm to film?" When Elaine looked doubtful, she put up a hand. "We'll focus on the blackberries. Promise. Hannah told us you're providing them for the Hot Spot's cook-off entry."

Elaine nodded. "That would be okay. What time did you have in mind?"

"Tomorrow, after the parade?" Jada pivoted toward Hannah. "Can you join us? I'd love shots of you and Elaine in the berry patch."

"I can do that," Hannah said. As long as she had the afternoon to focus on preparing for the cook-off. Hopefully, they wouldn't be interrupted by Cooper this time. The last thing they needed was his antics caught on camera.

Once the crew left, Hannah and Jacob got to work prepping the appetizers. They were making finger-friendly antipasto skewers and mini-quiches with bacon, spinach, and cheese.

"That was fun," Jacob said as he rolled out pastry for the quiches. "Thanks for including me."

Hannah smiled at him. "Of course I included you. The Hot Spot wouldn't be what it is without you." Jacob was talented and experienced, and they worked well together. Many chefs wanted to be in charge, but Hannah was firmly top dog in her own place. It was her vision, and Jacob was helping bring it to life.

"Aw, thanks." Jacob stopped rolling. "Did I tell you the new idea I had?" He went on to describe a recipe that was a little elaborate for the Hot Spot.

Hannah waited until he finished describing it then made a couple of tactful suggestions to bring the new dish in line with her style. His creativity was essential. Without it, her well of ideas might eventually run dry. The last thing she wanted was her clientele complaining that they were bored with the menu.

Once the appetizers were ready and in the walk-in, they moved on to prepping the night's menu. In peak summer weather, salads were hugely popular. Hannah washed lettuce, sliced cucumbers and tomatoes, cut beets into matchsticks, and shredded carrots. Jacob marinated the chicken and beef that would be grilled and sliced to top the salads.

"Everyone loves our poppyseed and honey mustard dressings," Hannah said. "We probably should make more."

Jacob began to gather the ingredients for the dressings. It was true that they could buy them readymade, but their patrons had shown a clear preference for the Hot Spot's versions.

They worked in tandem, pausing only briefly for lunch. The rest of the team arrived around three. Hannah was going to the kickoff at four thirty.

"Want to help me set up at the park?" Hannah asked Elaine. They would use a cart to transport the food the short distance. Since they didn't need to take a vehicle, they could leave parking room for those coming from farther away.

"I can do that," Elaine said. "Raquel can seat people until I get back."

They usually didn't get many customers until after five anyway. With the event at the park, they might be slow until it ended around seven.

Hannah ran upstairs to shower again and change. The film crew would be there, and she wanted to look her best.

When she returned downstairs, she put on a clean apron and made sure she had gloves on the cart for food handling. Besides the trays of food, they were transporting small paper plates and napkins.

People milled around and inside the large canopy tents set up for the event. Vendors were already setting up booths for the next day, and over at the playground, children ran and shrieked with laughter. Music played over loudspeakers, adding to the festive scene.

Hannah found her steps quickening as they approached the tents. She was in the mood for a fun evening.

Elaine touched her arm, and when Hannah followed her friend's gaze, she saw Phoenix sitting on a picnic table strumming his guitar and singing for a group of people who'd clustered around him.

"Do you think he attacked Blake?" Elaine glared at the young man. "Maybe he came back to the farm and didn't want Blake to see him."

Hannah was alarmed by Elaine's intensity, although she could sympathize. What had happened to Blake could have been so much worse.

"I'm going over there," Elaine said.

Before Hannah could object, Elaine marched toward the picnic table. Hannah glanced from Elaine to the cart. She couldn't push it over the grass, so she finally left it and darted after her friend. They weren't going that far away.

Phoenix had his head bent over his guitar as he strummed and sang, so he didn't notice his former employer approaching. Elaine circled around until she stood right in front of him.

He sang the last few bars, ending the song with a flourish of notes. When he noticed Elaine, he jerked backward, startled.

"Were you at the farm yesterday?" Elaine demanded. The onlookers began to drift away, some muttering and glancing back over their shoulders. "What were you doing there?"

Without responding, Phoenix tucked his pick into his pocket and carefully laid the guitar inside its case.

Elaine moved even closer, practically looming over the young man. He snapped the latches on the case closed.

"Elaine," Hannah said, "don't do this here." The park was far too public for such a conversation.

"Did you attack my son?" Elaine asked, her hands on her hips. "Answer me."

Remaining mute, the young man shook his head, picked up the guitar case, and loped away across the grass.

The kickoff was a great success. People thronged the tents, making their way through and handing over tickets to sample appetizers, sweet treats, and beverages. The Blackberry Queen contestants were volunteering, so Hannah didn't need Elaine to stay. Kylie ended up helping at the Hot Spot table.

"Now there's trouble," Kylie called.

Hannah looked up to see Blake coming through the line, tickets in hand. He grinned when he reached the table.

"Hey, Kylie. Hannah." Blake leaned over the table, peering at the skewers and quiches. "Those look tasty."

"They're super good." Kylie's gloved hand hovered, waiting for him to choose. "Are you feeling better?"

"One hundred percent." Blake pointed to his selections. "I'll be back in the fields tomorrow."

Kylie put the food on a paper plate. "You're coming to the parade, though, right?"

"Wouldn't miss it." Blake gave Hannah his ticket.

"The Hot Spot has a float," Hannah said. "Dylan surprised me with it. He worked on it with a guy named Seth."

Jada Jackson approached, Tiffany right behind her with the camera. Hannah had been anticipating this, and she smoothed her apron, hoping she wasn't too disheveled.

"They're filming the festival for a lifestyle show," she explained to Kylie and Blake. "Stand up straight and smile."

"How are we all doing here?" Jada asked as she approached. She gestured to the plate in Blake's hand. "That looks delicious."

Kylie jumped in. "We have antipasto skewers and spinach-bacon quiches from the Hot Spot."

Jada made an approving sound. "Local ingredients, am I right?"

"You bet." Hannah listed the various farms that had supplied the ingredients.

Jada asked Blake and Kylie a couple of questions before moving on.

"Phew," Blake said. "I was nervous." He lifted his plate with a rueful smile. "Almost dropped this on the ground. Would have been a waste of great food."

Kylie made a face. "You get used to it after a while. I sure have, being in horse shows and now a pageant." She turned to Hannah. "You said something about Seth?"

"Seth Bagsby. He built the float with Dylan."

Blake shrugged. "Oh, yeah. Seth. He works at the animal shelter. He helped Mom adopt Banjo."

He also worked at Cooper Combs's farm, but Hannah supposed she shouldn't hold that against him. She checked the platters. "We're almost out of food. Good thing the event is winding down."

Only a few people were in line now, including Liam Berthold, who was next.

Hannah waved, smiling. "Hey, stranger," she said. "Made it just in time."

Liam scanned the almost empty dishes. "I see that." His eyes met Hannah's. "Which do you recommend?"

Hannah's gloved hand hovered. "Both, of course." At his nod, she placed the appetizers on a plate. "Enjoy."

He didn't move. "What are you doing after this?" He nodded toward the stage, where fiddlers played a lively tune. "Hanging around to listen to music?"

Hannah sighed. "I wish. I have to go back to the Hot Spot to help with dinner service."

Liam glanced at his plate. "Maybe I'll swing by and have something to eat. This won't hold me, delicious as I know it is."

"Maybe I'm biased, but I think that's a great idea." Hannah was pleased. "We've got a delicious menu this evening." At the moment, with Liam's brown eyes gazing into hers, she couldn't remember what was on it. As he moved away with his plate, Hannah hoped he would dine at the Hot Spot tonight.

Despite her family and friends trying to set up blind dates and Hannah's insistence she didn't want to date right now, the town's fire chief was someone she wouldn't mind getting to know better.

Chapter Eleven

Around seven thirty, Hannah was on her way back to the restaurant with a much lighter cart. She left a scene of merriment behind—music, dancing, children playing, festivalgoers enjoying all of it.

She was rarely outside the Hot Spot when it was open. As she approached, she could see inside the restaurant through the windows. Raquel smiled as she placed plates in front of a couple. Dylan listened attentively as he took an order.

Hannah paused for a moment, her heart filled with gratitude and warmth. The Hot Spot looked friendly and inviting, the kind of place that drew in passersby. They'd find good food and good company, enjoy a few laughs, and leave with lifted spirits.

"Need some help with that?" Liam was coming along the sidewalk.

"Oh. No. Just checking out my place." Hannah grinned. "I never see it from this angle."

Arms folded, Liam studied the restaurant. "I like what you've done with it. We weren't sure what would happen to the building once we built the new station. Which is far larger and more efficient. Not as charming and historic though."

"I'll take efficient when it comes to fighting fires," Hannah told him. "Are you going in?" She didn't want to presume.

"I am." He moved toward the entrance. "I'll get the door for you."

"Actually, I'm going to take this in through the rear." Hannah didn't want to run dirty wheels through the dining room, not to mention the rattling noise of the cart. She'd park the cart in the back area.

In response, Liam led the way around the building, apparently determined to help her.

Hannah followed with the cart, certainly not planning to refuse. Some people might leave Hannah to her chore and go inside without further thought. Liam was thoughtful and considerate.

He proved it further when he opened the back door for her and waited until she had rolled the cart inside.

"Thank you," she said.

"My pleasure. I'll see you in there." He went around the building again, to the front.

"How'd it go?" Jacob asked.

"Fantastic." Hannah began unloading the cart. "As you can see, no leftovers."

"That's what we like." Jacob added sliced chicken to a big bowl of salad. "We're just starting to get busy here."

"That's what I figured." Hannah quickly finished unloading the cart. "Where do you need me?"

"Help with these orders?" Jacob moved at a controlled yet brisk pace. "I had six tables come in at once."

"Let's do it." Hannah washed up and got to work helping put together orders. She'd been doing it so long that her movements were almost automatic. There was a rhythm, a sense of satisfaction in preparing and plating a meal to her own high standards. Each dish was a work of art, perfectly composed and delicious. It was both meditative and refreshing.

Raquel burst through the doors to pick up. "Liam is asking for you, Hannah."

She had all but forgotten him. "Tell him I'll be out soon. We're almost over the hump. Right, Jacob?"

"Almost," the chef replied.

Raquel carried her order out, returning a few minutes later to say, "Guess who just walked in? Marshall and the TV crew."

"They're stalking us," Hannah said with a chuckle. "Who's got the table?"

Raquel tapped her chest. "Me. You know I'm Marshall's favorite." She dimpled. Raquel and Marshall had been circling each other for weeks now. Hannah was confident that dating was the inevitable next step. "Anything I should steer them toward tonight?"

Jacob shook his head. "Everything is good. We haven't run out of anything yet."

"Thanks." Raquel headed back to the door then halted. "Oh, Sheriff Steele just joined Liam. I'll have his order in a minute."

Liam was already on dessert, so Hannah was glad that the sheriff would delay him for a while longer. Maybe she could nip out soon to say hello.

As if reading her mind, Jacob said, "If you want a break, now is good. I know you have elbows to rub." He chuckled.

"Okay. Fifteen minutes, then you can take a break." This way, Hannah could say hello to the television reporter and her camera operator.

Hannah changed her apron before pushing through the doors. Liam was seated near the back. She caught his eye and held up a finger to indicate she'd be with him soon. He nodded.

"Good evening," Hannah said when she reached Marshall's table. "Welcome to the Hot Spot." No sign of the camera, she was glad to note. They must be finished filming for the night.

Jada glanced up from the menu with a big smile. "Hello again. What do you recommend tonight?"

Hannah knew from experience that saying, "All of it," wasn't a helpful answer. So she said a few words about each entrée, pointing out their most appetizing attributes so that Jada could make a decision based on her own individual preferences.

Raquel arrived at the perfect moment to take the orders.

"Enjoy," Hannah said. "Raquel will take good care of you." She crossed the room to Liam's table.

He pulled out a chair for her. "Join us?"

Hannah sank into the chair with a sigh. "I can stay for a few minutes. It's a busy night. I would have been out sooner, but Jacob was swamped. Hello, Colin."

The sheriff returned the greeting. "Great turnout at the opening event, I thought."

"It was," Hannah agreed.

Dylan came by. "Sweet tea, Hannah?"

"Love one, thanks." Hannah turned back to the men. "I see you chose the blackberry jam cake, Liam." She'd considered not repeating the dessert that week, but it had felt appropriate for the first night of the festival.

He cut off a forkful. "It's fantastic. My grandmother used to make it."

"The recipe is from an old newspaper article," Hannah said. "I found it when researching the Onion Queen story and Clara King. Turns out my great-great-aunt, Mabel Prentiss, was best friends with Clara. I'm reading Mabel's diary now."

"That's cool," Colin said. "You have deep roots in Blackberry Valley."

"Very much so." Hannah thanked Dylan, who had brought over the tall glass of tea. She took a long, refreshing drink. "No one out west drinks sweet tea. At least, not properly made sweet tea. I missed it."

"Another way there's no place like home," Liam said with a smile.

She recalled another discovery she'd made in the old newspaper. "While I was researching, I found out there was a robbery at the train station around the time Clara disappeared. A cashbox was taken."

Colin perked up. "Interesting. Did they find the thief?"

"Not sure." Hannah smiled at Raquel as the server dropped off the sheriff's meal. "There might have been a follow-up article later. I didn't have time to look."

Colin poured dressing on his salad. "We might have the file in the archives."

Hannah sat up straighter. "Really? I have no idea if it's related to Clara's disappearance, but Elaine told me there were rumors of a scandal. That was the only thing I found that might have qualified." She gave him the details she remembered, that the theft had been during daylight while the stationmaster was occupied with a problem on the track outside.

The sheriff picked up his fork. "I'll ask the evidence-room deputy to take a look." After a couple of bites, he said, "Take this with a grain of salt, since I don't know all the particulars. The chances of someone grabbing the cash when the stationmaster happened to be otherwise occupied are pretty slim. It might have been an inside job."

After closing, Hannah was too wired to go to bed right away. Instead, she puttered around her apartment, tidying up and picking out clothing for the events ahead. She'd wear her professional chef's jacket for the cook-off, but the pageant judging was another matter.

Her closet held several pretty sundresses that didn't see nearly enough use. She took them out of the closet one by one, holding them up to herself in the full-length mirror. The pink floral print would be perfect with white, low-heeled sandals.

As she put a load of laundry in the wash, she thought about the contestants. Kylie continued to impress Hannah as one of the top choices for Blackberry Queen. Tonight, she'd jumped right in to help with the tasting event, and she'd done an excellent job. If she approached everything else in her life with that same cheerful work ethic, she was sure to be successful.

Once her chores were finished, Hannah curled up with a glass of ice water, a cookie, and her phone. The situation with Corrie nagged at her, and with the cook-off tomorrow night, she couldn't put off the conversation any longer.

She checked her contacts and found the number. Corrie was on the West Coast, which meant it wasn't too late to call.

Hannah swallowed, her throat suddenly dry. She took a sip of water.

Then she took a deep breath, trying to compose her thoughts. *Start off friendly. Don't accuse.* Maybe it was all an innocent mistake.

She might believe that if it had been another recipe, one that hadn't been bantered about when Hannah first made it.

She recalled the scene perfectly. She'd pulled the pizza out of the oven and placed it on the counter to cool before cutting.

"What's that?" Corrie had demanded, wrinkling her nose. When Hannah told her the toppings, Corrie had said, "I'm not a fan of fruit on pizza." She shuddered. "Like pineapple."

"Try it," Hannah had urged, slicing the pie into triangles. Other coworkers, including the one who had told her about Corrie's claim to the pizza, gathered around.

When the others were effusive in their praise, Corrie had tried a bite—then eaten the whole piece. "Not bad," she finally admitted.

Fast forward a year or so, and now Corrie was presenting the recipe as it if were an amazing feat of her own culinary creativity. Hannah's midsection clenched with anger.

She bowed her head and prayed, knowing that if she carried these difficult emotions into the call, she would lose control.

When she was ready, Hannah pressed the phone icon, holding her breath while waiting for the call to connect.

"This number is no longer in service," an automated voice intoned.

Hannah laid her head back against the sofa cushion. A reprieve. She'd tried.

And she'd have to try again. She couldn't let this go. Hannah found the original text her old coworker, Micki, had sent. Perhaps she had an updated number for Corrie.

After texting to ask, Hannah got up and retrieved Mabel's diary. Maybe a return to 1932 would help her sleep. She paused after an entry where Mabel mentioned Clara's dislike of Rodney—at the same time Mrs. King seemed to be trying to push the pair together.

Hannah thought about the blind dates she'd gone on, where a friend or relative had thought someone was perfect for her and had been so wrong. This situation sounded similar. Since Rodney had gone on to marry Ada Young, he might have felt the same way.

According to Mabel, Clara had an actual aversion to Rodney Combs. Hannah knew the feeling. Some untrustworthy people hid their true nature behind social niceties. From what she'd read, Rodney appeared to be charming and adept at making friends and fitting into new situations.

Hannah recalled the comment the sheriff had made about an inside job. Had Rodney been involved? All she had right now was a suspicion, though it carried more weight since it was from a seasoned lawman. As stationmaster, Rodney had certainly been well-placed to know what he could and couldn't get away with. Passengers and freight shippers paid for transport. Valuable cargos were sent by rail.

If Rodney was crooked—and that was a big *if*—maybe there was something in his history to show it. Although he hadn't lost his job with the railroad—which meant that, if he was the thief, he'd gotten away with it.

Hannah knew she was reaching, spinning theories out of whole cloth as the old saying went. She needed to go back to the library and confirm or deny this line of inquiry. That wouldn't happen until after the festival, unfortunately. Unless... In the past, Hannah had come across sites that posted old newspapers in a digital format.

She quickly found one she'd used before then navigated to the article about Rodney's arrival in town from Ellisville. A little digging, and she found newspaper archives from the Ellisville area and narrowed the search to Rodney's name.

The first result was from January 1931.

> *The engagement of Miss Ann Ellis and Mr. Rodney Combs was announced Saturday during a luncheon hosted by Mr. and Mrs. Hiram Ellis at the Ellisville Country Club. The wedding will take place in June. Mr. Combs is the stationmaster in Ellisville for the Louisville and Nashville Railroad.*

Rodney Combs had been engaged the year before he arrived in Blackberry Valley. From the bride-to-be's last name, Hannah guessed her family was prominent in Ellisville. Exactly like the King family in Blackberry Valley.

Why hadn't the wedding gone forward? Maybe the answer to that would reveal Rodney's true nature.

Blackberry Valley
August 12, 1932

"They're here," Mabel called as Rodney's sleek new roadster pulled up in front of the house. She snagged her coat off the hallway tree in case it was chilly later.

Mama bustled into the hallway. "Do you have a fresh hankie? And don't forget your change purse."

Mabel showed her mother the small handbag. "I'll be fine, Mama." She extended a cheek for the kiss she knew was coming. "It's just Clara, Rodney, and Everett. We're going to see *Tarzan* downtown."

Clara had talked Mabel into a double date after Rodney asked her to the movies.

"That sounds fun." Mama touched Mabel's arm. "Seems to me that Mrs. King is trying to push Rodney on her daughter. What does Clara think of that?"

Mabel was a little surprised that her mother was so frank. Although, now that Mabel had graduated from high school, her mother was more forthcoming about so-called grown-up topics.

"It seems that way because she is," Mabel said. "She was right there when Rodney brought up going to the movies. Poor Clara couldn't say no, what with her mother standing there grinning from ear to ear. So she decided to drag Everett and me into it. I guess we're her chaperones tonight." At her mother's startled expression, Mabel hastily added, "I'm just joking, Mama."

"I wonder if it has something to do with—" Mama bit off the rest of her sentence.

"With what?" Mabel pressed.

Her mother hesitated then blurted, "I heard that they're in financial trouble. The Kings, I mean. Rodney is quite well-heeled, plus he's a favorite with the railroad, I heard. Sure to rise in the ranks."

"That's awful, Mama. Do you really think so?" Mabel had already been thinking along those lines, and it was disconcerting to have her mother confirm her fears.

Mama shrugged. "I'm just saying I've heard things. You said Clara's not happy about this date." Her expression grew fierce. "You're her friend. Don't let her get railroaded into marriage."

"Railroaded?" Mabel couldn't hold back a snort of laughter, and, after a moment, her mother laughed too.

"You know what I mean," Mama said.

Unfortunately, Mabel did. She glanced out the window at the car idling out front. "I'd better go." As she spoke, she spied Everett's lanky form stepping up onto the porch. A moment later, he rang the bell.

Seeds of Suspicion

Her mother hastily withdrew into the parlor, leaving Mabel to answer the door. "Hello, Everett." She stepped out onto the porch. "I'm ready to go."

Everett's gaze swept over her attire, her second-best blue dress and her white peep-toe pumps. "You look lovely tonight, Mabel." He extended his arm. "May I escort you to the automobile?"

Mabel laughed. She enjoyed the way he combined sincerity with good humor. "I'd be delighted, sir."

They descended the steps to the drive, where Everett opened the rear door for Mabel to get in. Then he slid in beside her.

Clara twisted around in the front seat. "Hello, Mabel. Don't you look nice."

"So do you," Mabel said, although she noticed that Clara wore the dreaded pink ruffled dress again. "Hello, Rodney."

He greeted Mabel politely, and they set off. Mabel sat back in the seat, enjoying the smell of new leather and the smoothness of the ride. Such a contrast to her father's Model T.

Downtown was busy. The stores were open late this evening, and people were window-shopping or going inside the restaurants to eat.

"Can we get an ice cream soda after the movie?" she asked. The drugstore soda fountain was a popular gathering place for Blackberry Valley's young folks.

"Your wish is my command," Everett said, smiling.

"I'll have to keep that in mind," Mabel replied pertly, tapping her chin as if dreaming up tasks for her date.

Rodney slid the roadster into a parking space along the street. "Close as I can get. We'll have to walk from here."

They were a couple of blocks from the theater with its brightly lit marquee. After the men helped Clara and Mabel out of the car, the two couples strolled along the street. Rodney extended his arm to Clara, but she pretended not to notice. Instead, she pointed out a pretty frock in a window to Mabel, who walked behind.

In contrast, Mabel didn't mind taking Everett's arm. He kept up a steady stream of humorous banter as they strolled along. She hadn't laughed so much in ages.

Now and then Mabel saw men loitering, crouched in an alley or standing in a doorway, watching the cars and pedestrians passing.

Mabel's heart clenched with compassion. These were men out of work, on the road, trying to find a good place to land. Her parents hired them now and then, giving them meals and a roof over their heads for a few nights. A few coins to keep them until their next stop.

They were almost to the theater when a man lurched to his feet and approached. "Rodney," he called.

"Who is that?" Clara asked, her voice full of concern.

Mabel's steps faltered. The man was tall and muscled, his skin ruddy from long hours in the sun, and there was something aggressive in his tone. Despite the ragged clothing indicating his poverty, he didn't have the hangdog demeanor of other men. Also, he called Rodney by his first name instead of Mr. Combs, as if they were on familiar terms.

Rodney threw the man a glance and kept walking, only to have the stranger call out again and begin to follow them down the sidewalk.

The station agent halted. "Why don't you three go on ahead? I need to have a quick word with someone." Despite his smile, uneasiness shone in his eyes.

Mabel realized he knew the man. Her father or Clara's would have brushed off the man's ill-mannered approach with a word, especially with women present. What was Rodney worried the man would say or do if he didn't stop to talk?

"We'll meet you in the lobby." Everett guided Mabel and Clara along the sidewalk.

When Mabel glanced back over her shoulder, she saw Rodney and the man standing close, talking in low voices. By their stance and gestures, she could tell that, although it wasn't a pleasant conversation, they seemed to have a lot to discuss.

Chapter Twelve

The television crew and Marshall were already at the King Farm when Hannah arrived the next morning to film the segment. This early in the day, there was still a hint of freshness in the air, although haze built in the distance, promising another scorcher.

Everyone was in the kitchen, including Blake. They sat around the island, drinking coffee and eating blackberry streusel muffins. A chorus of good mornings met Hannah, followed by Elaine's compliment. "Love the hat."

"Thanks." Hannah pulled off the straw sun hat and finger-combed her hair into place. "It's already getting hot. Don't want a sunburn on my scalp." They would probably make her take it off for the actual interview so they could see her face. Other than that, she was wearing it today.

Jada glanced at the clock and drank the rest of her coffee. "We'd better get out there before the sun is too high in the sky."

"How far is the patch?" Tiffany asked Elaine as they all rose.

"You'll want to drive down to the barn. From there, it's not far. We have a handcart if you want to use it."

Realizing that people were going out, Banjo began to circle and whine. "He doesn't want to be left out," Marshall said with a laugh. He patted the dog's head. "You're so cute." Banjo licked his hand.

"We need to leave him inside," Elaine said. "Blake, can you make sure that happens? The last thing we need is him running through the shot."

Jada tilted her head. "I don't know. That might be a nice touch."

"Except he'll bark," Elaine replied. "You don't want that."

"Probably not." Jada slung a handbag strap over her shoulder. "Ready, Tiffany?"

Hannah gazed longingly at the coffee.

Elaine saw her and laughed. "I'll make you a travel cup. Grab a muffin."

"They're really good." Blake snagged another, and his mother pretended to swat at his hand. "What? I need to fuel up for the day."

Coffee thermos in one hand and a muffin in the other, Hannah rode down to the barn with Elaine. A glance back at the house revealed Banjo sadly watching from a window.

"This is so exciting," Elaine said. "I asked them to take a shot of the sign by the road. Tiffany said they already did when they first arrived."

"You'll get some great PR out of the segment for sure." Hannah took a big bite of her muffin, enjoying the contrast of tart berries and sweet brown sugar topping.

They pulled up in front of the barn beside the broadcast van. Blake went into the barn for the cart. At Tiffany's instructions, he and Marshall loaded the equipment into it. Then Marshall wheeled the cart toward the patch, the women following. Blake stayed at the barn to do chores.

The sun beamed down, and insects sang. The heat slowed their footsteps. Today, Jada was dressed more casually in a blouse, linen trousers, and sneakers. Tiffany, who would stay behind the camera, wore shorts, as did Marshall. Hannah and Elaine were dressed in capris and crisp sleeveless blouses, much cooler than pants and neater than T-shirts.

Once they reached the blackberry bushes, Jada took them through the plan while Tiffany set up, checking the light and adjusting the camera and sound equipment.

"Elaine, I'd like you to talk about the kind of blackberries you grow and why." Jada peered more closely at the bushes. "They don't have thorns?"

"A thornless variety that blooms later than most," Elaine said. "I'll explain more during my speech."

Jada nodded. "Perfect. I've already filmed the local chamber head talking about the origins of the festival. Hannah, I want you to talk about why you like these berries from a culinary point of view."

For a moment, Hannah's mind went completely blank. Then she thought about her recipe for the cook-off. She wouldn't reveal it yet, but she could certainly talk about the qualities of Elaine's berries and why she liked to use fruit in her dishes, especially in surprising ways. *Take that, Corrie.*

"Remember, we'll do some editing," Jada said. "We'll make sure you look and sound great."

"Phew." Hannah swiped a hand across her brow in jest. "So glad to hear that."

Everyone laughed, Tiffany filmed a few establishing shots of the farm, and then Jada got to work. "We're at King Farm today in beautiful Blackberry Valley. I'm with Elaine Wilby, the farm's owner, and chef Hannah Prentiss, owner of the Hot Spot, a local farm-to-table restaurant."

Standing out of range, Marshall pumped his arms in a hurray gesture that made Hannah smile.

"Elaine, how long has your family been farming this land?" Jada asked.

"Over a hundred years." Elaine gave a brief history of the first King settlers. Then the conversation moved smoothly to the blackberries.

Sooner than Hannah could believe, Jada was saying, "Cut. And that's a wrap. Great job, ladies." She plucked a blackberry off the cane and popped it into her mouth. "I've been dying to do that the whole time."

Tiffany took one as well. "Yum. So good."

"I'll give you some to take with you," Elaine said. "Plus, I have homemade jam if you want a jar."

Jada laughed. "This is the best part of the job."

"Why do you think I became a critic?" Marshall asked with a grin.

Elaine had brought a couple of baskets with her as props, and now she and Hannah filled them for the television crew.

"You've been so helpful," Jada told Marshall. "Not to mention you have great taste. We need to talk. Soon."

Marshall beamed. "Anytime."

Hannah was glad that her friend was finding success in his chosen field.

Then a shout came from the direction of the buildings. "Banjo! Come back here."

Elaine rolled her eyes. "So much for keeping him inside. That dog is an escape artist."

The rest of the time they picked berries, Hannah expected Banjo to show up, tongue hanging out and tail wagging. When he didn't, she then thought he might intercept them on the way back to the barn. But there was no sign of him.

With Marshall's help, Tiffany loaded the equipment into the van. "You're spoiling me," she told him. "I usually do it all myself."

"Just being a gentleman," Marshall said as he shut the van door. "Hannah, Elaine, are you coming to the parade at noon?"

"Wouldn't miss it," Hannah said. "The Hot Spot has a float, thanks to Dylan."

"Awesome." Marshall moved around to the passenger side. "See you there."

Hannah and Elaine waved as Tiffany backed the van and then headed up the driveway.

"I wonder where Banjo went," Hannah said. "I thought he'd come find us."

"Me too." Elaine walked toward the open barn door. "Blake? Are you in there?"

Her son appeared in the doorway. "What's up?"

"I heard Banjo barking. Is he with you?"

Blake shook his head. "He took off into the field. I figured he was going to go find you."

Elaine rested her hands on her hips. "I thought I told you not to let him out."

"I didn't mean to," he protested. "He pushed past me when I went inside for a drink. You know how he is."

Elaine exhaled. "Well, we need to find him. I'm worried he'll get lost. He's too new here to wander without supervision."

"He went that way," Blake said, pointing to the farm's acreage. "Not down the drive."

"That's a relief." Elaine surveyed the property. "We'll each take a direction. Text if you find him."

Hannah was assigned the field past the hoop houses. Bottle of water in one hand, hat firmly on her head to block the sun, she ambled along the rows of growing vegetables. Once in a while she called the dog's name, hoping she'd hear a bark or the jingle of his tags.

Nothing. The grass was up to her knees past the gardens, a hay crop that would soon be mowed. Grasshoppers jumped, and butterflies flitted among the wildflowers. If she wasn't searching for a dog, she'd really enjoy this summer-morning stroll.

Ahead, she could see the property line between the King and Combs farms. At the end of the hayfield, acres of cultivation began, plots lined with growing rows of plants. The house and outbuildings were farther on, several acres in the distance.

Hannah saw two men fifty or sixty yards away working near a small, parked tractor with a trailer attached. They were picking something, placing the crop in bushel baskets in the trailer.

"Hello," she called. "Have you seen a black-and-white dog?"

One man cupped his hand to his ear, shaking his head.

Hannah walked closer to them, careful to walk between the rows of plants. She recognized Seth Bagsby, who had worked on the Hot Spot float. He also worked at the animal shelter, Hannah remembered.

The other man had been bent over, and when he straightened, Hannah's jaw dropped. "Phoenix," she said after a beat. "You're working here?" Hearing the note of astonishment in her own voice, Hannah winced. Just because he'd been fired by Elaine didn't mean someone else wouldn't hire him.

Phoenix adjusted his cap, frowning. "Yeah. Just started."

Seth looked back and forth between them, his brow furrowed. Rather than question the interaction, he said, "You said something about a dog? That's all I could hear."

"Yes." Hannah hooked a thumb over her shoulder. "Banjo. He got loose, and we're looking for him. He's medium size." She demonstrated his height. "Black and white, with a black spot over his eye. Really cute."

Seth nodded. "I remember that dog. He was at the shelter. Elaine adopted him? I knew she was thinking about it."

"She did." Hannah looked at Phoenix. "You know Banjo. Have you seen him today? He might have come over here to say hi to you. Or Seth."

This theory made sense. Dogs had excellent noses, and he would recognize both of them.

The young men looked at each other and shook their heads. "He hasn't come over here," Seth said. "If we see him, we'll let Elaine know."

"I'll give you her number," Hannah said, pulling out her phone. She supposed Phoenix might still have it, but didn't want to assume. "If you find him, try to keep him with you, okay? We'd hate for him to get lost."

"Lot of hazards on farms," Phoenix said. "Old barbed wire. Abandoned wells. Rusty metal."

Thanks for that. Hannah didn't need to imagine the trouble Banjo might have found during his wanderings. She recited Elaine's number to Seth, who entered it into his phone.

"Thanks," Hannah said. "I'll let you get back to work." As she walked past the trailer, she noticed the crop they were harvesting. Big, beautiful red onions.

Chapter Thirteen

Once Hannah was back on King land, she called Elaine. "Did you find him?" her friend asked before Hannah could say a word.

"Not yet." Hannah didn't know which piece of news to reveal first. Phoenix, she decided. "I went all the way to the Combs farm and spoke to Seth and Phoenix—"

"Phoenix? What's he doing there?"

"Working. It surprised me too. Anyway, they were harvesting red onions."

Elaine was silent for a moment. Then she said, "You know, there are a lot of red onion varieties in the world."

"You're right. I guess I have red onions on the brain." What if Cooper had already found the seeds? But it couldn't have happened recently. The onions the men were picking had been planted months before. But what if his claim to the Blackberry Red was based on past subterfuge? In other words, he could have been growing the variety for years without specifically naming it. Maybe his threat to get the seeds patented was to retroactively cover his tracks.

Hannah rolled her eyes. She was really reaching now. Putting the topic aside, she asked, "What about Blake? Has he had any luck?"

"I haven't heard—hold on. He's texted me."

She kept moving while waiting for Elaine to return, steadily crossing the field.

Elaine's voice came back on the line. "He found him at the old house. Hang on, I'm coming to get you."

Elaine disconnected before Hannah could ask for details. If Blake had found the dog, why didn't they all just meet at the barn? And what old house? Was it the one Timothy Buttonwood had mentioned seeing earlier in the week?

What if Blake or the dog was hurt? Hannah broke into a run.

A buzzing sound caught her attention. Elaine was at the helm of a four-wheeler with a cargo crate strapped onto the back rack. She raced right to Hannah and braked, the engine rumbling. "Hop on."

Hannah climbed on behind Elaine, and they took off.

Elaine circled a copse of trees and pulled up close to the edge. Hannah realized that, sure enough, there was an old house with trees and brush growing up all around it. Moss coated the roof, and a pane was missing in an upstairs window.

The quiet was deafening when Elaine shut off the engine. She started toward the house, pulling a pair of pliers out of her back pocket. "Banjo got tangled in some wire."

"Oh no." Hannah hurried after her friend.

Blake and Banjo were in a small clearing on the other side of the ramshackle building. Blake was sitting on the ground beside the pup, who whined and yipped when he saw Elaine. "It's okay, buddy. We're going to help you."

A strand of wire was wrapped around one of Banjo's legs. No wonder he hadn't come when called.

"Hold him still, okay?" Elaine knelt beside the dog and grasped the wire between her fingers. One snip, and Banjo was free. He flung himself at Blake, barking with joy.

"It's okay, buddy," Blake said, patting him as he ducked his slobbery kisses. "Think he needs to go to the vet?"

Elaine examined the leg. "Probably should. The skin is broken, and that wire is pretty rusty."

"I'll take him," Blake volunteered. "It was my fault he got out."

Elaine handed him the keys. "Clip him in the crate on the four-wheeler. Hannah and I will walk back." She pulled out her phone. "I'll give them a heads-up you're coming."

Blake carried the dog through the trees while Elaine called the vet. Hannah wandered around the clearing, careful to avoid the wire snaking through the grass.

When Elaine got off the phone, Hannah asked, "When was the last time someone lived in this house?"

"It's been empty ever since I can remember," Elaine said. "My dad told me it was built for farmhands to stay in."

Farmhands had lived here at one time. Had that included Wilson Barnes, Clara's beau?

Hannah stepped through long grass, careful to watch her footing, and peered through one of the dirty windows. She saw a big room, empty except for an old potbellied stove, table, and chairs.

"Want to go in?" Elaine asked. "It's in okay shape."

"Sure." Hannah liked exploring old buildings as long as she didn't fall through the floor.

She followed Elaine around the house to the front door, sheltered by a small porch. The door was unlocked.

Warm, dusty air with a hint of soot smell greeted them. "This isn't bad," Hannah said. "Quite cozy, in fact."

"Blake wants to fix it up for himself," Elaine said. "I told him he can if he pays for it. There's no electric or running water, so he'd be roughing it."

"Solar power would be a good option," Hannah suggested.

"That'll be up to him." Elaine started for the staircase. "Want to go up?"

Again, Hannah trusted Elaine. Even though the house had been unoccupied for decades, it looked fairly well taken care of. At least they hadn't allowed the roof to leak and eventually cave in. As her dad always said, "Once you lose the roof, it's over."

Upstairs were two rooms tucked under the eaves, both empty.

"You didn't see the seeds in this house, did you?" Hannah asked. "When you were a kid?"

Elaine thought for a moment. "I don't think so. We didn't come in here much when we were younger. My parents were deathly afraid we'd get hurt." She paused. "In fact, they used to keep the door locked. I'm not sure when it got unlocked. Maybe Blake found the key."

Hannah hoped seed thieves hadn't already come and gone with their stolen treasure. "Why do you suppose Banjo came over here?" She went to the dormer window and peered out. From there, she could see the Combs farm. Seth and Phoenix were still working in the field. "Maybe someone was messing around, and he came to say hello."

Elaine joined her at the window. "Phoenix is working over there, you said. Is that him?"

"Yes, and Seth Bagsby. I understand Seth works at the shelter sometimes."

Seeds of Suspicion

"Seth. Yes, he was working the day we went in to meet Banjo. I'd seen the photo online, and I couldn't resist. Fell in love with him right then. I'm so glad he was still available when we went back."

"I'm glad too. He's adorable." Hannah took a deep breath. "The thing is, Elaine—Banjo knows Seth and Phoenix. Do you think one of them has been here recently? And that Banjo followed one of their scents to this house?"

A horrified expression flashed across Elaine's face. "You think one of them locked Blake in the storage room? Maybe it was Phoenix, sneaking back for some reason. Maybe he lied about the hat we found in the barn." Her brows drew together. "Though why would he? He had permission to be there at the time. And what reason would Seth have to snoop around?"

Hannah could only make one connection. "They're both working for Cooper Combs."

Elaine nodded. "They are. You think Cooper would stoop that low?"

"I hope not," Hannah said. "But he was pretty worked up about the seeds and his claim that his family owned them." She thought of what she'd overheard. "He asked Timothy Buttonwood about patenting seeds when they were eating at the Hot Spot."

Elaine shook her head. "He's really determined to get ownership of them, isn't he?"

"If he can find them." Or maybe he already had, and the crop in the field was the elusive Blackberry Red variety. But that theory was probably a huge stretch.

Hannah's gaze fell on a set of drawers built into the wall. Maybe by some miracle, the seeds were inside one of them. "Mind if I look?"

"Feel free." Elaine stood with her arms folded, obviously a lot on her mind.

Hannah pulled open the top drawer. Nothing inside except a piece of wallpaper used as a liner. From the design—pink with blue ribbon stripes adorned with small flower bouquets—Hannah guessed it was from the 1920s or '30s.

She opened the other three drawers. Each was lined with the same paper.

In the bottom drawer, she found something else, tucked under the paper, which had shifted out of place. It seemed to be a page from a letter.

Hannah was tempted to read it. Instead, she called Elaine over. "Look what I found." She showed her the page with loopy, feminine handwriting in black ink.

Elaine took the page. "Huh. I can't believe no one ever found this. Want me to read it out loud?"

"Please," Hannah said. "I'm dying of curiosity."

"'Dear Wilson, I can't wait for us to be together,'" Elaine read. "Wow. A love letter."

"So there was something between Wilson and Clara," Hannah blurted. "Well, I'm assuming that's from Clara. Mabel said as much in her diary, that she thought Clara was sweet on Wilson. I was just wondering if Wilson might have stayed in this house, since he was a farmhand. I guess this answers that question."

Elaine flipped the page over. "Nothing on the back, and no closing, unfortunately."

"Keep reading," Hannah urged. She'd seen there was a lot more than one sentence.

"'Since our talk last night, I've been daydreaming about us living here on the farm, with our own little family. We'll name our first boy after you and the first girl after my mother—'" She flipped the page over again. "That's where it ends. The rest must be missing."

"Sounds pretty serious to me," Hannah said. "If she was talking about having children, they must have been planning to get married."

"Maybe they eloped," Elaine said. "I hope wherever Clara ended up, if it was with Wilson, that she was happy."

"Me too. Want to hear what I've found out so far?" Hannah was eager to share what she'd read in the diary as well as what she'd learned about Rodney Combs.

"Love to. I need a change of subject from mysterious intruders and my injured dog." Carrying the letter, Elaine started toward the stairs. "Tell me on the way back. We better get going if we're going to make the parade. Oh, and I'd better put a new lock on the front door. I don't want people inside this house unless I know about it."

Before they left the clearing, Hannah took another look at the old house. What other secrets were hidden there? Would they be able to learn the truth about Clara King and the man she'd loved?

Blackberry Valley
August 12, 1932

"Someone's got a beau." Everett watched Rodney escort Clara to the front door of her house after the movie.

Mabel couldn't hold back a scoff. "That's what he thinks." Rodney had fawned over Clara all night, solicitous and attentive to the point of being sickening. Her friend had gone along with it, but now, when Rodney tried to give her a kiss, Clara pushed him away and shook her head.

"Uh-oh," Everett said. "Trouble in paradise."

Mabel tapped Everett's shoulder. "Cut it out. Clara likes Wilson."

Everett turned to face her. "Wilson Barnes?"

"Yes. He's a great guy. And a gentleman, unlike Rodney." Mabel scowled. "Rodney is too oily. I don't trust him." It felt good to get that off her chest.

To her surprise, Everett nodded. "I see what you mean. He's a bigwig, sure. Throwing his weight around. I'd never take him fishing."

Mabel understood perfectly. Fishing trips were reserved for real friends. "Did you find it strange when he stopped to talk to that man on the street? It seemed like they knew each other."

Everett rubbed his chin. "Yeah. I was wondering about that. I mean, I'm sure Rodney knows lots of folks from all walks. Goes with his position."

"I thought that man was awfully bold. And I got the impression they were arguing."

Everett's brows rose, and humor danced in his eyes. "Were you spying on them?"

"You know it," Mabel declared. "I'm looking out for Clara, what with her folks pushing Rodney on her. As if she needs to grab a husband quick."

"She doesn't have to worry about that." He smiled at Mabel. "Neither do you. Is there any room in your book for another date with me?"

Mabel grinned. "Maybe. What do you have in mind?"

Instead of answering as she expected, Everett touched her arm. Mabel followed his gaze to the front porch, where a third person had joined the couple.

Wilson Barnes.

"What's going on?" Mabel leaned closer to the open car window, wishing she could hear what they were saying. "Maybe you should go over there, Everett. What if they start fighting?"

"I don't know, Mabel. I don't want to make things worse."

Suddenly, Rodney took a swing at Wilson.

Everett pulled on the door handle. "So much for that idea."

Mabel climbed out of the car as well, moving to stand within earshot. She could hardly believe her eyes. Were they really going to fight right there on Clara's front porch?

But instead of returning the blow, Wilson stepped back, holding up both hands and shaking his head.

Clara tugged at Rodney's arm, her voice rising in alarm. "What do you think you're doing? Cut it out."

Everett strode up the sidewalk, his stance loose yet confident. "Gentlemen, why don't we call it a night? You're going to wake up Mr. and Mrs. King. And that won't be pretty." He laughed.

Rodney, who had been glaring at Wilson, slowly relaxed. "I'm ready." He straightened his shoulders and pulled down his cuffs. "Good night, Clara." He descended the porch steps, joining Everett on the pavement.

Everett tried to put a hand on Rodney's shoulder, but Rodney shook him off as he marched toward the car. The two men and Mabel climbed back in, and they set off.

The silence was tense, and although Mabel was dying to ask for details of the argument, she didn't dare. One thing she knew for certain. The rivalry between Rodney and Wilson was out in the open now.

Her heart clenched. Would Rodney complain to the Kings about Wilson, even though he'd thrown the first punch?

Mabel was afraid that in a contest between the two men, Wilson would be the loser. He didn't have the social standing or the money Rodney had. What if he got fired and had to leave Blackberry Valley?

Clara would be heartbroken. How could Mabel help her friend? The Kings wouldn't listen to her.

Maybe they'd listen to her mother. Earlier tonight, Mama had expressed concern about Clara being forced into marriage with the stationmaster. Clara didn't like him either. Mabel thought his choice of companions, meaning the man on the street earlier, was strange.

Where there was smoke, there was fire, right? Mabel had an idea. When she got home, she would write to her cousin in Ellisville. If there was anything concerning in Rodney's background or behavior there, her cousin would know. The Kings would have to listen then.

One way or another, Mabel would help her best friend.

Timothy Buttonwood was coming down the drive when Hannah and Elaine reached the barn. "Is he still doing soil samples?" Hannah asked, uncomfortably aware that she'd forgotten to tell Elaine about Timothy's departure from the university.

"Apparently so." Elaine waved as Timothy climbed out of his truck, a quaint older-model Ford. "Morning."

"Good morning to you, ladies." Timothy inclined his head. "I have a few more samples to dig, if that's all right. I've sent the first batch off to the lab, with a rush order. A friend there owes me a favor. We should hear back shortly." He went to the rear of the truck to take his tools out of the bed.

"A rush order? Thanks." Elaine seemed pleased. "Now I just need to find the seeds."

Timothy's shoulders stiffened. "No luck?"

"I haven't had a chance to look," Elaine said. "We've been so busy, especially with the festival. A television crew was here this morning."

"Filming?" He turned abruptly, metal soil sampler in hand. "About the onions?"

"No, blackberries. Hannah's in the cook-off tonight, and they wanted to capture her in action, picking berries."

Timothy's gaze skipped over to Hannah. "Congratulations. Your restaurant is fabulous, and a television feature will help get the word out, as you deserve."

"Thank you," Hannah said, smiling. Now that he'd been so complimentary about the Hot Spot, she felt uncomfortable criticizing him to Elaine. Maybe he was embarrassed, even humiliated, about the loss of prestige after leaving the university. The article had said he'd resigned, perhaps under pressure. Double-dipping wasn't a light charge and called his integrity into question.

Which was why she needed to tell Elaine about it. Even if Timothy loved the Hot Spot.

Elaine's phone rang. "Excuse me. It's my son. He's at the vet with our dog."

"Banjo?" Timothy frowned. "I hope he's okay."

Elaine was already talking to Blake, so Hannah said, "Banjo cut his leg on some wire near an old house. Not too badly, fortunately, but they wanted to make sure it didn't get infected."

"Oh no. I hope he heals quickly." Timothy turned back to the pickup bed. "You have to be careful on these old farms. Lots of ways to get hurt."

"That's for sure," Hannah said.

Elaine hung up. "Banjo will be fine. He's been bandaged and gotten antibiotics. They'll be here soon."

"That's wonderful." Hannah started toward her car. "I'd better head out."

"See you later," Elaine said. "Oh, Professor? If you see anyone on the property, will you let me know? We've had people trespassing lately."

"I sure will." Timothy pulled a backpack out of the truck and slid the straps over his shoulders. "And now I'll be on my way."

As Hannah got into her car, she hoped he meant it when he said he'd keep a lookout. If he was in league with Cooper Combs, he might turn a blind eye to someone snooping around.

Or maybe he was looking for the seeds as well.

Instead of starting the car, she waited until he was well away from the barn on his way to the field. The opposite direction of the old house, she noticed.

Then she climbed back out, phone in hand, and went into the barn.

Elaine sorted through tomatoes at one of the tables. "I thought you left."

"I have something else to tell you." Hannah found the link Marshall had sent her and opened it. "About Timothy Buttonwood. Marshall found this, and I've been meaning to show it to you."

Forehead creased, Elaine read the article. "But he gave us cards. I had the impression—"

"I know. Me too. It's not okay that he misled us." Hannah gnawed at her bottom lip then decided to go for it. "What if he's trying to find the seeds too?"

"Oh no. That's possible, isn't it? He saw the article and came to Blackberry Valley, pretending he was interested in helping me. He wants the onions for his own use, I bet."

Hannah had to admit that sounded awfully plausible. "Or he's helping Cooper."

"Forget about the soil samples. I'll do it myself." Elaine marched toward the barn door. "I'm going to tell him to get off my property."

"Elaine, wait!" Hannah didn't think that was such a good idea. They didn't have any proof, only speculation.

Her friend didn't listen as she barreled through the open door. And ran right into Timothy Buttonwood himself.

Chapter Fourteen

Elaine stopped dead, her face flushing. Now that the professor was right there in front of her, her outrage and courage seemed to drain away. "I suppose you heard that," she muttered.

Timothy tilted his head, an uneasy smile on his face. "You want me to leave? Not a problem, Elaine. I certainly don't want to push in where I'm not wanted." He turned to go. "You should have said something earlier."

"I didn't *know* earlier," Elaine said. "Hannah just told me that you were fired from the university."

Timothy pivoted, his chin lifting proudly. "Resigned. I resigned. There's a difference."

Hannah was curious about the allegations of misconduct, wondering if he would deny them. That wasn't really her business though. The business cards were. "What's bothering me—us—is that you pretended to still be teaching at the university. Thinking it would give you more credibility, I suppose."

He ducked his head. "Yeah. I shouldn't have done that." His lips twisted wryly. "I could tell you it was out of habit, but I'd be lying. I'm used to the respect and open doors being a professor there gave me."

The trio stood in silence for a long moment. "I can understand that," Elaine finally said. "But maybe I should just take my own soil samples."

He shrugged. "It's your call. I was hoping you would find the seeds and raise a successful test bed. I've been involved with projects where very old seeds germinated."

The women must have looked doubtful, because he slid his phone out of his pocket. "I'll send you the links. Finding heirloom varieties and bringing them back is the core of my new venture. Not only am I creating a directory, but I also want to help farmers raise those crops. I'll be a consultant and a grower myself."

Hannah had to admit he sounded convincing. His cause was interesting, even noble. As a chef, she would love to incorporate rare and unusual heirloom vegetables into her menu. Marketing ideas and images flashed into her mind. What a great way to promote the restaurant while supporting the region's heritage.

"Hannah, you understand, don't you?" Timothy asked. "I can see it on your face. To think there was a time when supermarket varieties were all I knew about. There's a whole world of delicious, interesting, nutritious vegetables out there."

Hannah couldn't argue with that.

He tapped at his phone a few more times. "There. Elaine has the links. I'll get out of here for now, and if you want me to continue to take soil samples, Elaine, feel free to let me know later."

Hannah heard Elaine's phone beep with a notification. "Thanks. We'll check out the links."

Timothy turned away, still looking at his phone. He was halfway to the door when he stopped. "I have some news from the lab."

For some reason, his announcement made Hannah nervous.

"What did they say?" Elaine asked. She sounded as if she expected bad news about a loved one.

"It's not good. Your soil is deficient. Depletion is common after many decades of farming. You need to—"

Elaine waved a hand. "Send me the results, okay? And the bill. I don't have time to think about that right now. We don't have the seeds anyway." She picked up a ripe tomato and weighed it in her hand. "Guess the farm isn't that bad. Look at this beauty."

Timothy didn't respond as he left the barn. A moment later, Hannah heard his truck start up and roar away.

With a big sigh, Elaine set the tomato in a bin. "That went well," she said.

Hannah hastened to reassure her. "He's the one who was deceptive. Maybe now he'll get his business cards updated."

Elaine's forehead creased with concern. "Do you really think my soil is poor?" She moved to the fridge. "I've got your blackberries for the cook-off."

"It's hard to know without the test results," Hannah said tactfully. "Obviously, it's working for the crops you already grow. Besides, you're not even doing onions yet."

Her friend brightened. "That's true. If and when I find the seeds, there'll be time enough to improve the soil for the new bed. I'll find someone else to advise me."

"I'm sure you can," Hannah said. She glanced at her phone to check the time. "We'd better scoot if we're going to make it to the parade. They'll be closing off Main Street soon."

Elaine pulled the tray of blackberries out of the fridge. As they walked out to Hannah's car, she suggested, "Why don't I ride with you? Blake can meet me downtown and bring me home."

"Sure. He probably wants to see the parade, right?" Hannah clicked the button to lift the tailgate.

"Definitely. Kylie and the other contestants will be in it." Elaine set the tray gently on the carpet. "Stop at the house, and I'll change my shoes."

The pair stopped by the farmhouse where Elaine changed into sandals out of clogs and grabbed her bag. At the bottom of the driveway, she closed and locked the gate.

"Rather like locking the barn door after the horse is gone," she commented as she joined Hannah in the car. "The people snooping around aren't coming through the front."

Hannah thought the same, but she understood the desire to take any precaution. "It's hard to guard your entire property." The King Farm was bordered by either the road or other farmland, which meant access was almost impossible to monitor.

As they approached the entrance to the Combs farm, Hannah saw a truck with a wooden slatted back pull out. Whoever was driving had a lead foot and raced away.

"Cooper must be late for the parade," Hannah joked.

"Maybe," Elaine said. "The King Farm used to do floats. Maybe next year."

Hannah smiled at the thought that the Hot Spot actually had one. "It was so sweet of Dylan to build us a float. Frankly, I didn't even think about it."

"You have a lot on your mind," Elaine said. "The restaurant is really taking off. It's exciting to work there and see its success."

Hannah was touched. "Thank you for saying that. I want my employees to feel invested rather than thinking of it as just a job."

"We are invested," Elaine assured her. "Everyone is happy."

That was good to hear. "If you run into any issues or have any suggestions for improvement, please feel free to come to me."

"You've always made it clear that your door is open." Elaine took out her phone. "I'm telling Blake to meet me at the park."

Traffic was heavy in downtown Blackberry Valley, bumper-to-bumper and moving at a crawl. Although Hannah was happy to see so many extra people in town for the festival, it was annoying, frustrating, and hot.

They finally reached the restaurant. "I need to take the blackberries inside first," Hannah said. "Then we'll walk over to watch the parade."

Once the berries were safely in the walk-in, Hannah and Elaine strolled along the sidewalk, waving to people they knew. Traffic was shut down, and pedestrians milled around on both sides of the street and in the road. Children skipped along, holding balloons and pinwheels. Mothers and fathers pushed strollers holding adorable babies. Friends stopped to chat in clusters. Everyone seemed happy and in high spirits.

Hannah looked around, feeling a sense of nostalgia. She'd missed living in a small town, the good cheer and fellowship found at local gatherings. The sense of tradition and history carried on from generation to generation.

Someone called their names from across the street. Hannah glanced over to see Lacy standing on the sidewalk with her mother, Christine Johnston, and other women from the church group.

Hannah and Elaine joined them and were greeted with hugs.

"Isn't this great?" Lacy asked. "I think this is the best festival turnout we've had. Neil was supposed to join me, but he's swamped at the store." Lacy's husband owned a bookstore called Legend & Key.

"That's wonderful," Hannah said. "I'm glad business is good for him." She spotted her father and uncle across the street, standing with friends. They waved at each other. Zeus, her father's border terrier, tried to dart into the street to get to Hannah, but Dad had a tight hold on his leash. Hannah hoped she'd be able to catch up with them later.

"How's it going? Are you ready for tonight?"

There was far too much to tell her friend. Plus, this wasn't the best venue, in public on a crowded sidewalk.

"Want to have lunch?" Hannah suggested. "We can catch up then."

"Sure, if you have time. I'm staying in town for the day."

"I'll make us something at my place." That would give them privacy, and she'd be on-site to prep for the cook-off later that evening.

Drumbeats and the blare of trumpets sounded in the distance. The parade was coming. The crowd scattered off the road, finding places on the sidewalk.

A familiar figure wound through the bodies. Blake, carrying Banjo. When he reached them, he set the leashed dog on the sidewalk.

"Aw, what happened?" Lacy bent down to pat the dog, crooning over his new bandage.

"He cut his leg on some old wire," Blake explained. "He was a real trouper at the vet."

Elaine looked relieved to see her son and her pet. "Thanks for going, honey. I'm glad he's okay."

The music was louder now, and the high school marching band came into view, playing their hearts out. Majorettes stepped high and twirled batons. The audience clapped and cheered.

Next came a few people on horseback and in carriages, dressed in period clothing as early Blackberry Valley settlers. Then floats for local businesses, farms, and civic groups. Some riders threw candy toward the sidewalk, and the children darted to pick it up.

Then a farm truck approached, one with a wood-slat back, and Hannah noticed a banner draped across the hood. COMBS FARM, FEEDING BLACKBERRY VALLEY FOR 100 YEARS.

Cooper was at the wheel—and Timothy Buttonwood was in the passenger seat, waving and smiling at the onlookers. He must have gone straight to the Combs Farm when he left Elaine's. They'd seen this truck pull out earlier.

Elaine drew in a breath. "Oh, my. He *is* working with Cooper."

"Sure looks that way," Hannah said. "Though we already knew they were acquainted." She waved and smiled along with everyone else.

Seth and Phoenix were in the back of the truck, both wearing straw hats and overalls like old-fashioned farmers. They held up produce—ears of corn, tomatoes, and red onions—as if displaying them to the crowd. One joker called out, "Throw us an onion." Phoenix gestured as if to toss it to him, and people laughed.

With an excited bark, Banjo yanked his leash from Blake's hand and bolted into the street—directly into the path of the truck.

Chapter Fifteen

Fortunately, Elaine barely had time to cry out before Cooper braked to a halt.

Blake ran into the road with an apologetic wave to the driver. He scooped the dog up and returned safely to the sidewalk. He secured the leash around his wrist before setting the dog back down. "Don't do that, Banjo."

Banjo sat with a whine, ears drooping.

Hannah leaned toward Elaine. "I think that answers one of our questions. Banjo considers Seth or Phoenix or both to be friends."

"Sure seems that way," Elaine agreed. "He was really happy to see them."

"Hurray!" Lacy exclaimed from beside Hannah. "The Hot Spot float looks great."

"It's awesome," Elaine agreed. "I love the barn and the chickens."

"Yeah, the chickens are great," Lacy said with a laugh.

Other than Dylan and Raquel, Hannah didn't recognize the other young people in the bed of the truck, waving and smiling. She'd have to get their names and give them gift certificates to thank them for volunteering on her float.

The contestants in the Blackberry Queen contest were on horseback, dressed in Western garb of jeans, fringed jackets, and cowboy hats.

The young women stopped, each one allowing her horse to prance in a circle before going back into formation, to the applause of the onlookers.

When Kylie spotted Hannah and her friends, she gave them a huge smile and an extra-enthusiastic wave. Once again, Banjo tried to dart forward, but Blake had better control of him this time. "Not so fast, you."

"I think we'll leave him home during the next parade," Elaine said wryly. "We're lucky he didn't spook the horses."

The sheriff's department cruisers and fire trucks brought up the rear of the parade, flashing lights and siren blasts a big hit with the onlookers. Liam rode in the ladder truck, and he gave Hannah a wave and a thumbs-up as he went by.

"He's such a great guy," Lacy said. "We're lucky he decided to stay here. He's had offers from all over the state, you know. A lot of cities want him as their chief."

Hannah hadn't known that, and as she returned his friendly greeting, she felt really glad that he was still in Blackberry Valley. And that she had moved back home.

Elaine's tomatoes had inspired Hannah to make a classic summer sandwich: ripe tomato slices with mayonnaise, salt, and pepper. It was usually served on soft white bread, but Hannah liked to lightly toast hers to add some support and make the sandwich less messy.

After grace, Lacy took a bite. "So good," she said, rolling her eyes. "Remember how we used to take these on picnics?"

"Sure do. It was about the only thing we could make." Hannah had spent many lazy summer days with Lacy, riding bicycles, swimming, climbing trees, and just hanging out.

"And now you're a world-class chef." Lacy bit into a potato chip with a crunch. "What's new?"

"I hardly know where to begin," Hannah said. "Oh, guess what? The television crew filmed me and Elaine at her farm this morning. They've decided to feature me and the Hot Spot on their show. Isn't that exciting?"

Lacy grinned. "I'm not surprised at all. That's fantastic."

After Hannah told her about the filming, she moved on to a less agreeable topic. "Then, after the crew left, Elaine had a run-in with a professor who's been taking soil samples on her land. We think he might be working with Cooper Combs to try to grow the Blackberry Red onions. If they find the seeds before we do."

"Whoa," Lacy said, waving both hands. "Back up. I have no idea what you're talking about."

Reflecting over the past few days, Hannah realized she hadn't been keeping Lacy updated. "I'm sorry. We've both been so busy. Let me start at the beginning."

Between bites of her sandwich, Hannah took her through the sequence of events.

As always, Lacy was a great audience, listening closely and inserting comments here and there. The attack on Blake shocked her. "Oh, man. Elaine must have been beside herself. I'm so glad he's okay."

"Me too." Hannah felt upset at the mere mention of it. "I don't think whoever it was meant to hurt him. I think they tried to hide their identity. He fell inside the storage room, and that's where he bumped his head."

"It could have been a lot worse."

"You're right, it could have," Hannah said grimly, giving a silent prayer of gratitude that Blake had recovered fully. She checked their glasses. "More tea?" She got up to retrieve the pitcher from the fridge.

"So we have Cooper Combs, Professor Buttonwood, Seth, and Phoenix all on the farm property at one time or another," Lacy mused. "Or nearby. You haven't actually seen Seth at King Farm, right?"

Hannah filled their glasses. "I haven't. Though he's working next door, maybe even staying there, and Banjo knows him from the shelter. Banjo didn't warn Blake about a prowler in the barn, which is telling. And he ran off to the old house, possibly to greet someone. He definitely knows Phoenix from when he worked at Elaine's."

"The dog that didn't bark?" Lacy said with a smile. She took a drink of her tea, the ice cubes clinking. "If only Elaine could find those seeds. She could patent them herself and put an end to this."

Hannah returned the pitcher to the fridge and grabbed a container holding homemade chocolate chip cookies. She placed the cookies within reach and sat back down. "I'm worried Cooper found them already. At least a year ago, I mean. Did you see the red onions he's growing?"

Lacy's mouth fell open. "I did notice them, on his float. His behavior would make sense then. He might be trying to sow doubt regarding ownership then patent the variety and tell Elaine they belonged to his family all along."

Hannah smacked herself in the forehead. "I keep forgetting to ask Elaine if she has old farm ledgers. Blackberry Red should be mentioned in the entries in the early 1930s and even earlier. We already found an ad calling them proprietary and another saying 'only at the King farm,' but more proof wouldn't hurt." She picked up her phone. "While I'm thinking about it."

Hannah sent Elaine a text inquiring about the farm records. Before putting the device aside, she saw she had a new text.

Her heart thumped when she noticed a response from Micki about her request for Corrie Rice's new phone number. She left it unread for later.

Forcing thoughts of Corrie aside, Hannah said, "I have something to show you." She went to her bedroom to retrieve Mabel's diary. "This was written by my great-great-aunt, who was Clara King's best friend." She handed the book to Lacy.

"The missing Onion Queen?"

Hannah nodded. "Evangeline gave me special permission to take it out of the local-history collection. It's really interesting so far. And while I was at the library, I also looked through back issues of the *Blackberry Chronicle* from 1932. That's where I found the old Blackberry Red ad."

"What else have you found out?" Her friend also enjoyed digging into mysteries from the past as well as the present. She leafed through a few pages of the diary, glancing at the handwritten pages.

Hannah gave her a summary, including the letter she and Elaine had found in the old house that morning. "According to Elaine, the older generation hinted at a scandal as the reason Clara left town. The train station robbery is the only incident I've found so far that fits. Wilson was working on a float at the station when the robbery happened."

"So he got blamed?" Lacy guessed. "Maybe he and Clara ran away and got married."

"I don't know yet," Hannah said. "I need to see if there are follow-up articles in the newspaper. Oh, and the sheriff is going to look for the file."

"It pays to have friends in high places," Lacy said with a grin.

"I also discovered that Rodney Combs was engaged to another woman the year before he moved to Blackberry Valley. Obviously, that wedding never happened." Hannah had taken a screenshot of the announcement, and she brought it up for Lacy.

"An Ellis from Ellisville," Lacy commented. "I'm guessing her family was prominent."

"I thought so too. I wonder who broke it off." Hannah tapped her fingers, thinking. "If Rodney left town, maybe Mr. Ellis wasn't happy with him. I'm not sure Blackberry Valley was a promotion over Ellisville, regarding stationmaster positions. The towns are similar in size."

"How did you find the announcement?" Lacy asked. When Hannah told her, Lacy put the diary aside and began tapping on her own phone. She muttered to herself as she searched. "Aha. In April 1931, there was a theft at the Ellisville train station."

"Another one under Rodney's watch?" Hannah exclaimed. "What does it say?"

"According to the article, a wealthy woman discovered that a small travel case of valuables was missing after a stop in Ellisville. They blamed it on a vagrant. A man riding the rails who had been hanging around the Ellisville railyard."

"I suppose he could have done it," Hannah admitted. "But in both cases, the crime was blamed on someone who happened to be around. Were they fall guys?"

"Could be." Lacy frowned. "You do realize we're assuming that Rodney was guilty?"

"Yeah, we are. I have to admit I don't like him, going by what Mabel said in her diary. I'll try to keep an open mind though. The truth is what we want, right?"

Even if it meant the Combs family did develop the Blackberry Red variety first. Even if Rodney was innocent and the vagrant and Wilson were guilty.

Family stories passed down through the years could change with each telling, with each person's interpretation of events. Keeping an open mind was essential in solving mysteries.

The conversation turned next to the upcoming pageant. Lacy sent Hannah the agenda. "Hot off the press," she said with a laugh.

Hannah studied the sequence of events. Each contestant would present her talent, then each would give a short speech, and finally they would all sing a group number together. After conferring about scores away from the stage, the judges would announce the results.

"It's going to be a tough call," she said, thinking about the young women competing.

"Always is," Lacy said. "We have some runner-up prizes too. Everyone who enters will be recognized in some way."

Hannah remembered something from an earlier judge email. "Dress code for us is semiformal, right?"

Lacy nodded. "Usually the men wear suits and ties and the women wear dresses or skirts."

Suddenly Hannah was concerned that she didn't have anything appropriate. Should she go shopping? If so, when would she have time?

"What's up?" Lacy asked. As Hannah's oldest friend, she could read Hannah like a book.

"I don't think I have anything to wear," Hannah admitted. "I haven't dressed up much in years. Beyond a skirt and blouse for church." Or nice dinners out when she went on a date. Which was also ages ago.

Lacy pushed her chair back. "Let's take a look."

"Please." Hannah led the way to her bedroom closet.

Lacy flipped through the hangers. "If you don't have a dress, we can put together a skirt and blouse."

Hannah smiled, remembering similar occasions in high school, when they were getting ready for a dance or a double date. She and Lacy had always picked out clothes together, hunting for the elusive outfit that would make them feel confident and attractive. Lacy was a master at creating the perfect combinations.

"Here we go," Lacy said. She emerged holding a gold chiffon skirt with numerous layers. "This is pretty."

Hannah took the skirt, still on its hanger. "I forgot I had that."

Lacy was already back among the hangers. She found a breathable black blouse with elbow-length sleeves and beaded embroidery on the front. She handed it to Hannah and then dove for shoes, finally resurfacing with a pair of black slingbacks.

The last item was a paisley shawl with black and gold in the design. Lacy hung the outfit on the closet door, the shoes underneath. "What do you think?"

Hannah gave her a hug. "That you're a genius. Now I don't have to go shopping."

"The horror," Lacy joked. "Actually, we'll have to take a jaunt to Louisville sometime soon. I know all the best places to go."

"I'm sure," Hannah said. "Thank you. I'd be lost without you."

Lacy's gaze fell on Hannah's bedside clock. "Is that the time? I'd better run."

"And I'd better get to work." Hannah walked her out. "It was great catching up with you."

"Same." At the door, Lacy gave Hannah a hug. "Good luck tonight. Neil and I will be there to cheer you on."

"Awesome. Thank you." Hannah opened the door. "See you then."

"Keep me posted," Lacy said as she started down the stairs. "If you come across any more clues or information about our mysteries."

"Will do." Noting the use of *our*, Hannah smiled. As always, she appreciated Lacy's sharp eyes and wits. Her friend had already found another crime that had occurred under Rodney's watch. Whether or not the stationmaster had also been a thief was still up in the air.

They might never actually get answers, Hannah reminded herself. Not after ninety years. Still, she'd learned to start with what she had to work with and go from there.

As Hannah closed the door and walked back into the apartment, she remembered the text that had come in during lunch. She opened her messages to read it.

Here's Corrie's new number. A phone number followed. Don't tell her I shared the link about the show, okay? I don't want to be put in the middle.

I won't. Thanks for the number.

After updating Corrie's contact information, Hannah stared at her phone for a minute. She was officially out of excuses. A check of the clock told her that it was late morning in California. Not too early to call.

Taking a seat, Hannah thought about what to say. She would stay calm and not make accusations. It was possible—although not likely—that Corrie had forgotten exactly who had created the pizza. Pressure to be seen as an innovative chef might have convinced her to gloss over the details.

Whispering a prayer, Hannah pushed the call button.

Chapter Sixteen

Corrie's number rang and rang. Was she ignoring Hannah? Or was she busy?

Hannah almost hung up. Then she composed herself. She would leave a message, and hopefully Corrie would return her call. Otherwise, she would have to go through all this uncertainty again.

"Hello, Corrie? This is Hannah Prentiss. I hope you're doing well." She was careful to sound friendly. "I have something I'd like to talk to you about. Can you please call me back?" Hannah gave her number, although the caller identification would as well.

There. That chore was done and, better yet, she'd managed to keep her cool. Hannah put her phone aside. She needed to wash up and go downstairs to start prep work for the cook-off.

Jacob was already in the kitchen, slicing peppers and onions. "I have bad news."

Hannah stopped short. "About the staff?" She was immediately worried that one of her employees was ill or hurt.

A rueful expression slipped across his face. "Sorry. No. It's the cheese delivery. They're running late."

"What?" Hannah's head felt like it was going to come off. "I need the burrata cheese for tonight." She hurried toward the walk-in, hoping they already had some on hand. She was only making a couple of pizzas for the contest.

She scanned the shelves, seeing milk, cream, sour cream, ricotta, yogurt, and many other dairy products. No burrata.

Hannah ducked back into the kitchen, closing the door with a *clunk*. Her mind whirled. What could she do at this late hour, if the delivery didn't come in time?

The local grocery. Hannah pulled out her phone and brought up the website. They had the cheese in stock, but she wasn't familiar with the brand, so it might taste or behave differently in her dish. Standing in place, she closed her eyes, trying to think.

"Hannah, what are you doing?" Jacob sounded concerned.

Eyes still closed, she made a waving motion to let him know she was all right. What did the burrata bring to the pizza?

Her eyes popped open. "What do you think of ricotta as a substitute? That would go on before cooking." Ricotta wouldn't have the dazzle of the fresh burrata though.

Jacob tilted his head, considering. "That might work. But I wouldn't panic yet. Call the dairy and see where they're at. Maybe one of us can go meet them."

"Great idea. I'll go. I don't want to mess up your routine." Jacob was very methodical in how he worked his way through prep each day.

Hannah placed a call to the cheese vendor and explained her dilemma. The manager who answered the phone was pretty sure they'd make it to Blackberry Valley by four. But Hannah didn't want to take the chance, and soon a mutually agreed spot to meet was arranged.

"I'll let the driver know," the manager said.

"We're on," Hannah told Jacob. She grabbed a small insulated container and a bottle of water. "I'll be back."

"Good luck," Jacob called.

Hannah's knowledge of local roads would come in handy. Before she even got the car started, she had a mental route already mapped out. By cutting across the countryside, she'd approach her destination much faster while encountering less traffic. With the festival in full swing, Blackberry Valley was jammed with visitors.

After a brief period of gridlock downtown, Hannah reached the open road. She sailed along, her mind filled with her to-do list. As soon as she got back to the Hot Spot, she'd make the pizza dough. It only took half an hour to rise. While it did, she would load up the blackberries, grated fresh mozzarella and parmesan, olive oil, and basil for transport to the cook-off site. She was also taking a portable pizza oven to the event along with a pizza peel and other tools.

While the judges and attendees watched, she would assemble the pizzas and bake them. The other chefs would also be preparing their blackberry-themed dishes. Normally the judges circulated, interviewing the chefs while they worked. Today, the television crew would be part of that process. Which meant she needed a few minutes to check her hair and makeup before going over to the park. Another item for her list.

Oh, how she wanted that trophy, a metal spoon and whisk on a stand. She'd display it so proudly in the Hot Spot. If she didn't win, well, she'd congratulate the winner and check out their restaurant at some point. She could always learn something new. In fact, she loved discovering new tastes and techniques, ingredients and combinations.

Food was both basic and a blank slate for creativity. If not for God's marvelous creation, people's diets might be like the cows in the pastures she passed, content with grass, hay, and grain. Instead, there were almost endless possibilities. Each culture offered its own spin on seasonings and preparation methods.

Signs of civilization appeared as Hannah left the countryside behind. Houses lining the road, a sign welcoming her to town, a gas station, and soon, a grocery store. There was the cheese truck, parked at the loading dock. Perfect timing. Hannah drove through the lot and stopped next to it.

After a couple of minutes, a man came out of the open bay, pushing an empty dolly. Hannah got out and went over to intercept him. "Hey," she called. "I'm Hannah, from the Hot Spot. Did the office call you?"

He gave her a friendly nod. "Sure did. Are you taking your whole delivery?"

Hannah thought quickly. She only had the one cold box. "No, just the burrata cheese. The rest can be delivered whenever you get to Blackberry Valley."

"Fair enough. I'll get your burrata." He climbed into the truck. A couple minutes later, he brought out a small box. "Here you go. Six containers."

"Thank you so much." Hannah accepted the box, flipped it open to verify the order, and hurried back to her car. She would make it home even sooner than she'd hoped.

On her way, she came across a stranded motorist. An old truck was parked beside the road, hood up. There were no houses for at least a mile in either direction.

Hannah slowed to check on the driver. Although most people had cell phones and could call for assistance, she wanted to help if she could.

She pulled up beside the truck and, as she did so, a young man straightened in the front seat. Phoenix, the former farmhand at King Farm. His face brightened when he saw her.

"Do you need help?" she called through the open car window.

He scrambled out of the truck and came over to the passenger side. "Actually, I could use a ride to town, if you're going that way. The tow truck is coming, but he'll be taking my truck in the opposite direction."

"I'm going downtown," Hannah said. "Does that work?"

His nod was eager. "Sure does. I'm due at the park. Hold on. I'll grab my stuff."

While he rooted around in the truck cab, Hannah sent Jacob a text to let him know that she was on her way. She also mentioned helping Phoenix, a stranded motorist, laughing at herself as she included the information. She didn't sense any threat from Phoenix. He seemed like a harmless young man.

Phoenix shut the truck hood and then picked up his guitar case and a backpack. He put them in the back seat and then climbed into the car. "Thank you so much. I had no idea what I was going to do." He took out his phone and made a call. "This is Phoenix Barnes, owner of the 1990 Ford? Tell the driver that I left the key under the floor mat. I'm heading to Blackberry Valley now. Give me a call when you figure it out." A pause. "Thank you, ma'am."

Barnes. Hannah had heard that last name recently. Where?

"I think it's the alternator," Phoenix said when he hung up. "It's been acting up and finally quit on me." He laughed. "I'm lucky it didn't happen on my way east."

"Your way east," Hannah repeated. "Where did you come from?" This was the first time she'd been alone with the young farmhand, and she had to admit being curious. As she was about nearly everyone she met. She enjoyed hearing their stories.

"California," he said. "Outside Fresno." He rolled down the window and rested his elbow on the ledge.

Fresno County was an agricultural hub, Hannah knew from her work in California restaurants. A lush, productive area that grew much of the nation's produce. "What brought you to Kentucky?"

"I'm headed to the University of Kentucky in the fall. I saw the ad for a farmhand and decided to come early and work." He made a face. "With mixed results."

"Do you have experience working on a farm?" Hannah asked, thinking he might if he was from an agricultural area.

His grin was charming. "Not unless you count my mother's houseplants. Somewhere in family history, we owned a farm. Guess I didn't get that gene. Although I'm doing okay at Cooper's place," he added quickly. "My dad passed away a few years ago, and my mom is a music teacher. I'm planning to follow in her footsteps. UK has a great education program. Plus, we had family here a long time ago."

"You sounded great when I heard you play." Hannah winced when she remembered the rest of the scene. Elaine had berated Phoenix, believing he was responsible for pushing Blake into the storage room.

His expression sobered. "I didn't hurt Blake. He's my friend. Or was." Phoenix stared out the window. "I'm kind of embarrassed about how it all went down." After a moment he said, "Elaine was right to fire me. I wasn't focused on my job the way I should have been. I get that way sometimes when I'm writing songs. In my own little world."

Hannah thought of common ground. "I've been known to get lost in the clouds myself. When I'm dreaming up new recipes, I sometimes get a little obsessed."

Phoenix's face lightened. "And we enjoy the benefits. Elaine brought home takeout for us one night. It was amazing."

"Thank you. That's nice to hear. More than likely, Jacob actually made the food. He's the head chef." They had almost reached Blackberry Valley. "Where do you want me to drop you off?"

"The park, please," he said. "I'm part of a group doing a sing-along for kids."

Hannah slowed as a line of traffic appeared ahead. "That sounds fun." Relevant experience for his role as a music teacher too.

Once they reached the park, Phoenix climbed out and retrieved his guitar and backpack. "Thanks a lot, Hannah. Really appreciate you stopping."

"No problem." Phoenix disappeared into the park, and Hannah edged back into traffic, her thoughts already on the tasks ahead.

"That's a big batch of dough," Jacob commented an hour later as Hannah pulled the wrap off the bowl.

Hannah punched the dough down. "I made extra. Thought we could do mini pizzas as an appetizer." To be honest, Hannah had found herself automatically making the usual amount of dough she'd prepare for the restaurant. Much more than she needed for the cook-off.

"Yeah, we could. People love those."

"I can put them together," Hannah offered. "Then you just have to bake them." All she had left to do was load the carts when it was time. Dylan would help her transport the pizza oven, ingredients, and tools over to the park at four.

"Awesome. Thanks." Jacob stirred a stockpot on the gas range. He picked up a spoon and dipped it in. "Want to taste?"

"Definitely." Hannah hustled over to the stove and took the spoon, which held a red sauce. Flavors burst in her mouth—spicy sausage, basil, oregano, garlic. "Wow. This is incredible."

Jacob beamed. "It's for the Zowie Ziti." The popular pasta dish was baked in individual ramekins and served piping hot. "The sausage, spices, tomatoes, pasta, and cheeses are all local."

"Great job." Hannah was pleased at how much they could source from farms and locally owned food businesses. The pasta was an incredible find, handmade by an Italian American family that lived just outside the county.

Hannah bagged two portions of dough for the cook-off then rolled and lined the pans for the appetizers. Each pan represented an order of six. She added sauce, cheese, and toppings, and put the covered pans into the walk-in.

Dylan hurried through the back door. "How'd you like the float?"

"It was amazing," Hannah said. "Thanks so much."

"Really cool, man," Jacob added. "Loved the chickens."

"That's what everyone says." Dylan pulled out his phone. "We're getting tons of hits on social." He showed Hannah and Jacob the pictures a friend had posted, tagging the Hot Spot. There were a lot of positive comments.

"I never thought of a parade float in my marketing plan," Hannah commented. "Quite an oversight, I guess."

"We can use it again for the Thanksgiving parade," Dylan suggested. "We'll add some stuffed turkeys and wear Pilgrim hats."

Jacob patted his shoulder. "Always thinking ahead. Great job."

The young man glowed with pride. "Lots more ideas where that came from."

"Want to help me load the carts?" Hannah asked him. "The pizza oven is a little heavy."

Dylan flexed his biceps. "On it."

After Hannah changed and freshened up, they conveyed the carts over to the park. Dylan seemed to know everyone, and he frequently waved and shouted greetings. "Great menu at the Hot Spot tonight," he called out a few times. "Stop by."

"Wow. You're a one-man marketing machine," Hannah marveled.

"I want us to succeed," he said.

His loyalty—and the use of *us*—touched Hannah. Working in restaurants for decades, she'd seen the flip side far too often. She was grateful to have such loyalty from her staff.

A chamber volunteer directed Hannah to her spot under the big tent. She was placed in the middle of the seven chefs, a few that she had met previously. Others were from restaurants in nearby towns.

May the best chef win, she thought. "We can leave the oven on the cart," she told Dylan. "I'll take care of everything else."

"Are you sure?" he asked, hovering.

Hannah smiled at him. "I am, thank you."

Still, he lingered. "Will you need help getting everything back?"

"I'll call if I need one of you to come over," she assured him. "Maybe someone here can help me." Depending on who was around, she might be able to ask a friend.

Dylan took off, and Hannah got to work laying out her supplies for the pizzas. She spread a tablecloth and then placed the ingredients and tools in an attractive display. Next, she built a wood fire in the pizza oven.

"Are you properly permitted for that, ma'am?" a male voice inquired.

Hannah glanced up to see Liam grinning at her. "As a matter of fact, I am," she joked. "Perhaps you'd like to do an inspection?"

"Definitely." Hannah moved aside, and Liam bent to examine the oven.

"Nice little gadget," he said. "I could use one of these."

"They're handy," Hannah said. "I couldn't make my entry without it."

Liam moved back. "What is your entry?"

Hannah showed him the sign she'd made to put on the table: BLACKBERRY BURRATA PIZZA.

"Interesting," he said. Although he nodded, he looked uncertain.

"This is burrata," she said, taking a container out of the insulated cooler. She opened the lid to show him the cheese ball bobbing in liquid. "It's a casing made of mozzarella with cream and something called stracciatella inside. Stracciatella is basically shredded mozzarella. Burrata has recently gotten popular in all kinds of recipes." Hannah's chest tightened. Including her own, now soaring online thanks to Corrie.

"What's bothering you?" Concern flashed in Liam's eyes.

Apparently, he could read her as well as she could him. "Let me show you." Hannah brought up Corrie's video and showed him the title.

"You came up with the same idea?" He glanced from her phone back to her. "Does that happen a lot?"

"Sure. All the time." Hannah gave a helpless laugh. "But in this case, it's my recipe. Every single ingredient was my idea. She and I used to work at the same restaurant, and she was there when I came up with it."

He took the phone from her and studied the post. "Got a lot of engagement. Does she give you credit?"

"No." Hannah folded her arms. "And it's really bugging me. In fact, I called her earlier, but she didn't pick up."

Humor quirked Liam's mouth. "Were you going to chew her out for stealing?"

Hannah shook her head. "Not at all. I'm trying to approach this the Christian way. Confront in love." She swallowed. "But I'm having a hard time." Dread balled in her belly at the thought of speaking to Corrie. "I guess I don't like confrontation."

Liam sent her a sympathetic look. "Who does? Are you worried she'll be angry? Or defensive?"

Hannah considered. "Yes, I am. Corrie isn't the easiest person to get along with. She can be pretty prickly."

"Which means that she probably gets away with a lot, right? People don't want to deal with her attitude, so they just give up."

His insight was spot on. "You're right. She might be taking advantage of the fact that no one wants to cross her."

"I've been in your shoes before," Liam said. "Believe me. As fire chief, I've had to deal with all kinds of situations in the department. What I try to do is focus on what I need to say. I don't worry about their reaction. I can't control that."

The wisdom of Liam's words sank into Hannah's soul. It was a good reminder. How Corrie reacted to the situation with the recipe was beyond Hannah's ability to control. All she could do was speak the truth in love.

Chapter Seventeen

Hannah took a deep breath. The judges were at the next table along with the camera crew. In a couple of minutes, it would be her turn.

She surveyed the table again to be sure she had everything. Behind her, the pizza oven threw out heat, already up to temperature. Not the best idea on a summer evening, but the novelty of the wood-fired portable oven was already drawing attention from onlookers.

Finally, they approached her table. Hannah straightened, making sure she wore her biggest smile.

"Contestant number four is Hannah Prentiss, from the Hot Spot restaurant," the lead judge told the TV audience.

Behind him, Tiffany's camera light was steady and red, which meant she was filming.

"Good evening," Hannah said. "It's great to be here."

"What are you making for us, Hannah?" the judge asked.

Hannah oiled a pan then began to spread the pizza dough out with her fingers—practiced moves that took little thought. "My creation tonight is Blackberry Burrata Pizza." She gave a rundown of the ingredients.

"Interesting," the judge said, exchanging glances with the others, whose expressions expressed some doubt. "What was the inspiration for this recipe?"

"I invented it when I was working in California." She gave a summary of how she was inspired to use the cream-filled balls on the pizza in addition to the standard grated mozzarella.

Both pans were lined with dough now, so Hannah moved on to the next steps: oiling the dough and then crushing berries to make a sauce. She gave explanations, the camera continuing to record her actions.

Then they were gone, on to the next table where a chef was making a blackberry compote to be served over grass-fed filet mignon.

Hannah paused to drink some water then finished preparing the pizzas. She topped them with the blackberry sauce and shredded mozzarella. The fresh basil leaves and burrata would be added after baking.

She put the first pizza into the oven, timing it to be ready when the judges returned for the tasting. While it baked, she took a break, sitting in a folding chair someone had thoughtfully provided.

Colin meandered by on his sheriff's rounds, keeping an eye on the gathering. "Hey, Hannah," he said. "How's it going?" His gaze took in the oven. "I've got to get me one of those."

Hannah laughed. "That's what everyone says. They aren't that expensive, and they're a lot of fun to use." She explained a few of the features and told him where she'd gotten it.

Colin tapped a note into his phone and took a photo of the oven. "By the way, the evidence room wasn't able to locate the file you wanted, about that old theft. I'm sorry. It's just too long ago."

"I understand, and I appreciate you looking," Hannah said. She hoped her disappointment didn't come through in her voice.

He moved on, and Hannah returned to her post, checking the progress of the pizza in the oven. She pulled it out with the peel and then slid the second in to bake. Not an ideal situation, but the oven only held one pizza at a time. She was dealing with different conditions compared to a professional kitchen, and the judges understood that.

She hoped.

The judges watched with interest as Hannah pulled the second pizza out of the oven, placed a burrata ball in the middle of each, then sprinkled them with freshly torn basil.

"Why do you add the burrata after?" the head judge asked.

"Cooking would change the texture of it. You'll see how important that is when you try it." She picked up a large knife and deftly cut the first pizza with two swipes, making four slices. Then she did the same with the second pizza, the one hot out of the oven, and made sure that those were the pieces the judges took.

Tiffany and Jada each sampled a piece from the first pizza. "This is different," Jada said. "I love it." She took another big bite.

Her encouragement convinced one of the judges, who was dubious, to take a taste. After a tentative bite, he nodded in approval. "You could use this cheese with other pizza toppings, right? Like mushroom or sausage?"

"Definitely," Hannah said. "I made blackberry pizza today because of the festival."

"Of course, of course," he murmured. "Nice blend of flavors."

Although Hannah watched closely, the judges didn't reveal much. They made notations on clipboards and then moved to the next table. She picked up one of the two remaining pieces and sat in her chair to eat it. The performance was over, and she could relax.

Hannah analyzed as she chewed, seeing if there were any flavors or textures to tweak. The tart berries and creamy cheese were a nice blend, mouthwatering and rich.

The judges were taste-testing at the next table, the chef watching anxiously. He glanced over, and Hannah gave him a thumbs-up of encouragement. She suspected that the judges would have a hard time choosing a winner.

Just like she would at the Blackberry Queen competition. Now that she wasn't busy cooking, Hannah took in the crowd beyond the tent. The festival was hopping. Vendor booths seemed to be doing a brisk trade, and a crowd gathered in front of the bandstand to listen to the music. One young man juggled while another performed magic tricks.

She spotted Phoenix, guitar slung over his shoulder, talking to a young woman at a picnic table. When he shifted, she saw it was Kylie, enjoying a takeout meal. More cups and baskets on the table indicated that others had been seated with her.

Kylie's expression was attentive, even somber, as she listened to Phoenix. She shook her head and shrugged apologetically. He said something else and then walked off, leaving Kylie sitting alone. She watched him go then turned as several other young women joined her at the table, ice cream cones in hand. One handed Kylie a cone.

It wasn't any of Hannah's business, but she still wondered what Phoenix and Kylie were talking about. If she had to guess, she would say Kylie had questioned him about what happened to Blake. It was unfortunate that there was a rift between Elaine and the young man, although it would be justified if he was the one who had trespassed on the property and hurt Blake.

Lacy came up behind Hannah. "Look at this." She found another folding chair and pulled it close then displayed a video from the festival's social media.

"I came up with this one day while I was brainstorming new combinations," Hannah watched herself say on the video.

The camera panned across the table, taking in the array of ingredients waiting to be put together then showed Hannah holding the container of cheese. "My coworkers didn't know what to think at first," she said with a laugh. "But they all loved it."

Especially Corrie. Hannah's phone vibrated. She'd set it to silent during the contest. Thinking it might be one of the Hot Spot staff, she picked it up to look. And almost dropped it.

Corrie's name was on the screen.

"Are you going to take that?" Lacy asked when Hannah continued to stare at the screen.

Now was not the time and place. Not only was she in public, but she was also in the middle of a contest, so she had to stay put rather than find somewhere private to discuss the issue.

Hannah fumbled with the phone, choosing an automatic message to send. I'LL CALL YOU BACK.

Even though that ended the call, her heart still pounded. So much for being composed enough to talk to her former coworker. She had to move past the fear of confrontation somehow.

"What's the matter?" Lacy asked.

Hannah realized she hadn't told Lacy about Corrie's video. When they'd had lunch, there were so many other topics to discuss. "It's a long story, but a former coworker is claiming my entry tonight as her own recipe. I decided I needed to talk to her about that because she didn't give me credit." Hannah swallowed. "Maybe I should have left well enough alone."

Lacy tilted her head, her eyes warm with compassion. "Sometimes you have to confront people, unfortunately. Otherwise, they'll keep doing something wrong or hurtful. And in this case, you're now publicly saying you invented this pizza. What if people who see both videos start questioning you?"

Hannah put a hand to her face. She could imagine the comments, the possible outrage. It didn't matter that a pizza recipe was tiny in the grand scheme of things. In the online community, sometimes the smallest controversies became the biggest blowups. It was ridiculous, but it happened all the time.

"You're right, Lacy. I'll call her back when I have some privacy." She paused. "And after I pray. I really need God's wisdom and peace to do this."

"I hear you." Lacy's smile was knowing. "I'll pray for you, okay? That God will give you the right words to say. Words that will reach Corrie."

Her comment helped Hannah take a larger view. She had narrowed her relationship with Corrie to this one contentious point, this sense of injury and unfairness.

A voice came over the loudspeaker. "The judges will now take a brief recess to pick the winner. Let's give the chefs and judges a round of applause."

Everyone clapped then broke into chatter and laughter. Some of the chefs began packing up their stations, preparing to leave after the winner was announced.

"Want me to get you something to eat?" Lacy asked. "I can run to one of the food trucks."

Hannah realized how hollow her stomach felt now that the stressful part of the cook-off was over. That one piece of pizza hadn't been enough. "That'd be great." She found her handbag under the table and fished out some cash, which she handed to her friend. "Is the falafel truck here?" She'd seen it on the list of vendors. Hannah enjoyed authentic falafel, made with chickpeas and spices and served on pita bread.

"Uh-huh. Large or small?"

"Small." Even their small portions were generous. "Thanks so much."

Lacy headed off across the park, and Hannah began packing up her station. First, she put the pizza oven fire out. That would need a while to cool down before it could be transported.

A couple came up to the booth, looking around curiously. The man picked up the sign she'd made. "Blackberry pizza, huh? How does that taste?"

Hannah smiled. "Pretty good, I think. You should try it sometime. We'll be serving it at my restaurant tomorrow night." She pointed to the stack of printed cards promoting the Hot Spot. "You get a discount if you bring that."

The woman scooped one up, then a few more. "Mind if we take some for friends?"

"Feel free," Hannah said. It would be interesting to see how many resulted in visits to the restaurant. Elaine would keep them and make a tally.

Lacy came back with a paper bag. "I got one for me too. Let's eat."

Right after Hannah finished her falafel, the judges returned. The moment of truth was at hand. First, the chefs lined up for photos and compliments from the head judge, who declared this year the most difficult to choose the winner.

The second runner-up was a blackberry-glazed salmon cooked on a cedar shingle. Ribs barbecued with a blackberry chipotle sauce took the first-runner-up place.

Hannah held her breath. It was now or never.

"Our first-place restaurant is new to the area, although the chef is very experienced, with years under her belt at very prestigious eateries."

Her. There were two other female chefs remaining.

"Our winner's creativity and involvement in making our community a better place to live are off the charts. We're extremely proud to present this year's Top Chef award to Hannah Prentiss of the Hot Spot."

A thrill of disbelieving elation ran through Hannah. She'd won. Her little pizza had actually won. As the onlookers applauded, Hannah saw familiar smiling faces in the crowd, most notably Lacy and Liam, both beaming. And her father, who looked ready to burst with pride.

"Thank you so much," Hannah said to the judge as she accepted the trophy. Then she smiled for the cameras, and it wasn't hard at all.

A final word from the judge, and the event was over. People began to scatter.

Jada came up to Hannah as she resumed packing up her ingredients. "Congratulations. You deserved that win. Plus, it's going to be the perfect capper to our segment on you."

"Thank goodness, right? What if it had been a flop?" Hannah laughed. If she hadn't won, she would have enjoyed the experience anyway. She still had the privilege of cooking for people, which was her passion, and for that she was deeply grateful.

But the victory was certainly sweet. If only the impending conversation with Corrie wasn't a sour note in the back of her mind.

Chapter Eighteen

Trophy in hand, Hannah returned in triumph to the Hot Spot. Once again, Liam helped her transport the equipment and supplies, but this time he couldn't stay.

"I'd better get back to the park," he said when they reached the restaurant's back door. "Congratulations again, Hannah. You earned it."

"Thank you," Hannah replied. "I had very tough competition so, yes, it's a thrill."

He waved and set off.

Dylan poked his head out the door. Hannah had texted him that she was coming back. His gaze fell on the trophy. "You won?"

"I did," Hannah said. "I'm surprised the news didn't beat me here."

"We've been inundated," Dylan said. "If someone said something, I didn't hear it."

"Can you get the cart with the oven?" Hannah asked. "I'll take this one."

As soon as they entered the kitchen, Dylan called out, "Guess what?" Jacob, Raquel, and Elaine were all in the kitchen, an accident of timing. Dylan grinned at Hannah. "You tell them. After all, it's your news."

Hannah pulled out the trophy. "We won. The Hot Spot won." She gave shared credit because she wanted the win to be about the restaurant, to encourage her staff. After all, it was a team effort every single day.

They all erupted with cheers and applause.

Elaine grabbed Hannah's arm. "We should make an announcement out front."

Hannah followed the others into the dining room, and Elaine rang the bell at the hostess station. "Can I have your attention, please?"

Gradually the chatter and clatter of dishes stopped, and everyone turned to see what was going on.

"We have exciting news," Elaine announced. "The Hot Spot's owner, Hannah Prentiss, placed first in tonight's chef cook-off." She made a sweeping gesture. "Let's give Hannah a round of applause."

The customers reacted the same way her employees had. Raquel held up Hannah's arm, holding the trophy high for all to see.

Once the noise died down, Hannah announced, "Thank you so much. Dessert is on the house. Anyone who already had theirs, we'll take it off the bill." She put the trophy on display then returned to the back to wash up and put on a fresh apron. Time to pitch in.

Most nights, the Hot Spot was busy right up to closing, with people dining late. Tonight, the restaurant was empty by nine thirty. Due to the lack of customers, they began cleaning up early, keeping an eye out for late arrivals.

"I think they're all over at the park," Dylan said as he cleared a table. "Really good bands are playing tonight."

"That's what I heard too," Raquel said. "I don't mind. I already made a ton in tips."

"Me too." Dylan wiped down the table. "The customers were awesome tonight."

Hannah wondered if the news of her win had encouraged people to tip more than usual in response to the celebratory mood. She didn't mind an early night for a change. They'd all worked so hard this week.

And yet her mind still wouldn't rest.

She met Elaine at the hostess station. "I have a question for you. About the farm."

Elaine continued to tidy up. "Ask away."

"Do you still have any farm ledgers from the 1930s? I'm thinking there might be information in there about the Blackberry Red onion, like when your people started growing them, how many they planted, if they sold sets to other farmers in the area. I'm thinking we might find evidence that it originated with your farm."

Elaine put a hand to her chin. "I think so, yes. In the barn, there's a room that used to be sort of an office. We can check in there."

"When would be a good time to look? Tomorrow morning?"

Elaine grinned. "How about tonight? I'm pretty wired up, what with your win and all. It shouldn't take long. We can have dessert after."

Usually, Hannah was wiped out after a busy night at the restaurant, but not tonight. "I'd love to."

Hannah followed Elaine out to King Farm with blackberry jam cake in a container on the front seat.

They'd be busy tomorrow morning, making fresh desserts along with prepping for the Saturday night meal. Once again, Hannah would be gone part of the evening, this time to judge the Blackberry Queen contest. Elaine would be helping earlier with the logistics of the pageant, so she would be able to open the Hot Spot.

What a great team she had. Hannah mulled over ideas for special bonuses as she drove the familiar route to the farm. Maybe something extra in their paychecks. That was always welcome. And perhaps they could have a special meal out somewhere, at one of the high-end restaurants in the area. That would be a treat and an opportunity to check out the food and service. Knowing her gang, they'd enjoy the idea of being secret shoppers of sorts, evaluating every aspect of another operation.

Elaine stopped to open the main gate, and Hannah followed her through. Blake was still down at the park with his friends. Hannah didn't blame him. A glance at the festival as she passed had revealed a lively scene even at this hour. The food trucks were still serving, and a band played a number that had most of the audience on their feet.

In contrast, the farm was quiet in the moonlight, the towering trees shading the house. Elaine stopped there, so Hannah did as well, grabbing the container of dessert for later.

Banjo was ecstatic to see them, leaping and yipping. If his leg injury bothered him, he didn't show it.

"You'd think I'd been gone a week," Elaine said, patting him. "Just put the cake on the counter. I'm going to go change." She wore a skirt and low heels, not exactly the right attire for exploring a dusty barn.

"I'll take over dog duty." Hannah hunkered down and gave Banjo some love. "You're a good boy, aren't you?" She scratched his neck, making his tags jingle. He rewarded her with a lick on the cheek.

After the exchange of adoration, Hannah checked his water dish and added more. He cocked his head, but she didn't budge. "You need to ask your mom about treats. I don't want to get in trouble."

Elaine bustled into the room. "He wants a treat, doesn't he?" She grabbed one from a jar and tossed it. Banjo jumped and caught it in midair, which made them laugh. "Good boy, Banjo. Want to come with us?"

In response, he ran to the door and waited.

"Let's walk," Elaine suggested. "It's a nice night."

Hannah agreed, and they set off down the lane to the barn. The night air was refreshing, with a hint of coolness. When Hannah inhaled, she could smell green growing things, drying hay, and fragrance from Elaine's flower beds. At this hour, all was silent except for the whisper of the breeze in the treetops and the tall grass in the fields.

Banjo ran ahead, stopping to sniff then waiting for them to catch up.

"He really loves it here," Hannah commented. "I'm so glad you adopted him."

"He's a great dog," Elaine said. "Blake and I both fell in love with him the moment we saw him."

As they approached the barn, Elaine fished in her jeans pocket for a set of keys. "We keep it locked all the time now." She inserted the key into the padlock. "Never had a problem until this summer."

As they entered the barn, where Elaine switched on the lights, Hannah thought about the stray ball cap they'd found there. Had it belonged to Phoenix, despite his denials?

"You know how I had to go meet the cheese truck today?" Hannah asked. Jacob had told Elaine about Hannah's impromptu journey. "On the way back, I picked up Phoenix."

Elaine's footsteps faltered. "Why?" Then she kept going and opened a door off the main floor. She switched on a light in a side room.

"His truck broke down, so I gave him a ride." Hannah saw a small desk, the shelves behind it lined with books. Faded fair ribbons, ancient tack, and a few black-and-white photographs hung on the walls.

Elaine ran her finger over the desktop and grimaced. "As you can tell, I don't clean in here. We never use this room." She glanced back at Hannah. "How's he doing?"

"He seemed fine. He was on his way to perform at the festival. The reason I'm telling you is that he's a student at the University of Kentucky. I mean, he will be. He's starting this fall, he said."

Elaine whirled around, hands on hips. "Really? Was that his hat we found?"

Hannah shrugged. "Maybe? I don't know why he would lie about it though. He was working here when you found it, so it would have been reasonable for his hat to be in the barn."

"That kid drove me nuts." With a huff, Elaine turned back to the shelves. "Let's start with these." She pointed. "You take that end, and we'll meet in the middle. Look for any mention of Blackberry Red."

Hannah did as her friend suggested. For the next little while, they pulled down books, glanced inside, and then returned them to the shelf. Banjo made a thorough investigation of the barn then joined them in the office, where he sprawled on the floor, chin on his front paws.

As Hannah had hoped, the ledgers included information about each farm year—what was planted and where, farm expenses and income week by week, and crop tallies.

"Historians would have a field day in here," she said.

"True." Elaine studied a ledger, slowly turning the pages. "I could spend days reading these. You get a picture of the whole operation." She read a couple of entries aloud, mentioning a tally of hay bales produced and bushels of onions picked. "What a massive amount of work."

Considering the equipment used in the past, Hannah agreed. She selected another ledger from the row and opened it. "Here we go. 'Blackberry Red sets sold' in 1925. And apparently almost a thousand bushels were harvested here at the farm that year."

"Wow," Elaine said. "I can't even imagine that. Why don't you grab that ledger and the ones for a couple of years before? Maybe somewhere in those pages we can learn more about how Blackberry Red got started."

"How did farmers create new varieties before seed patenting and genetic science got involved?" Hannah asked.

Elaine added another ledger to the stack. "Through selection. It was a gradual process unless mutation intervened."

Suddenly Banjo leaped to his feet and dashed out of the room, barking loudly.

Startled, Hannah put her hand to her chest. "What's up with him?"

"It's probably Blake coming home." Elaine added one last ledger to the stack. "This should be enough to start with. Let's go have that cake."

Hannah could still hear the dog outside the barn. "I think Banjo's warning us about something. He's heading out to the fields."

"I suppose we should go check. I don't want him to run into a wild animal and get hurt."

Or an intruder. Hannah hurried through the barn, hoping that if someone was on the property, she would be able to spot them. Without getting attacked, of course.

Elaine was right behind her. "People ask how I stay in shape," she joked. "The answer is running after my dog."

"Plus running a farm," Hannah added. "And around the Hot Spot."

Once outside, they stopped to listen for Banjo. "He's over by the cabin." Elaine started in that direction.

Hannah did her best to keep up on the uneven ground. After a long day's work, her legs were tired. She'd sleep well tonight.

"Banjo," Elaine called. She pulled out her phone and switched on the flashlight function.

The dog stood outside the cabin.

"The door's open," Hannah pointed out.

Elaine continued toward the structure. "This is unbelievable."

"Wait," Hannah called after her. "What if someone is in there?"

Although Elaine didn't seem to hear her warning, she didn't enter the cabin. Instead, she stood a distance from the door and shouted, "I'm calling the police right now."

Hannah heard thudding footsteps—from behind the cabin. Banjo bayed and ran around the building.

Hannah stood rooted to the ground in shock. There *had* been someone inside.

Chapter Nineteen

"Banjo," Elaine called. "Banjo, come." She shook her head. "I hope I don't have to chase him."

Hannah squinted into the dark fields. Was that the dog? A slightly darker shadow seemed to be moving toward them. "Here he comes," she said, her statement confirmed by his jingling tags.

"Good boy," Elaine said. "Stay." She took tentative steps toward the cabin. "Think we should check it out?"

Although curious to see what the intruder had been up to, Hannah shook her head. "I think we should call the police. What if we mess up evidence?"

"Good point. I'll call them right now." She placed the call while Hannah continued to scan their surroundings. "They'll be right out," Elaine reported a couple of minutes later.

"Should we wait at the barn?" Hannah asked.

"Once we see them coming, we'll go meet them." Elaine started to walk around the small building. "Right now, I want to check the back."

Hannah hurried to catch up. "We should probably stick together."

The rear door of the cabin was wide open. Elaine used her light to peer inside. "I can't believe this."

Hannah moved closer so she could see inside as well. The entire kitchen area had been torn apart. Dishes, pots and pans, and upended canisters of flour and sugar were on the floor, along with packaged goods.

"I stocked the cabin before Phoenix moved in," Elaine explained.

About fifteen minutes later, Hannah spotted flashing lights moving along the road. "Here they come."

By the time the women reached the farmyard, the vehicle was easing down the lane to the barn. Elaine waved in greeting.

The sheriff's cruiser stopped, and Colin got out, joined by Deputy Jacky Holt. "Evening, Elaine," Colin said. "We got a report of an intruder?"

"Yes, someone broke into the cabin," Elaine said. "Banjo alerted us to their presence. When we went to check it out, they went out the back and ran away."

"Show us," the sheriff said.

After Jacky grabbed a duffel bag from the cruiser, they set off across the fields to the cabin. Banjo frolicked along beside them, excited by all the activity.

"Do you use this cabin for anything?" Colin asked as they approached, the powerful department-issued flashlights sweeping the area.

"Until recently, a farmhand stayed there," Elaine said. "He left a few days ago."

"Think he came back to grab something he left behind?" Colin asked.

"Possibly." Even in the dim light, Hannah saw Elaine frown. "But he could have just asked me. Or Blake."

That was what Hannah would have done, though she could understand the young man's reluctance to approach Elaine. Their last conversation hadn't been pleasant.

"How'd you leave things?" Colin asked.

Hannah had often noticed the sheriff's ability to put his finger on topics people avoided or would rather not address. It was part of his talent as a law enforcement officer.

Elaine didn't say anything for a moment. Then she admitted, "Not good. We'd had some incidents around here, including my son getting pushed into a storage room and hitting his head. Remember?"

"I do," Colin said. "You filed a report."

"Well, I may have accused Phoenix of doing that. Which was probably rash of me." Elaine bit her lip. "Not my finest moment."

"Understandable for a mom to be upset," Jacky murmured.

While Hannah found Colin's line of questioning to be reasonable, something made her doubt that he was on the right track. "Whoever it was ransacked the place. I doubt Phoenix would do that. He doesn't strike me as the vengeful type." In fact, when she'd given him a ride, she'd found him to be a polite and respectful young man.

"Ransacked?" Colin echoed.

"At least the kitchen was," Hannah said. "We could see it from the back door, which was open. We didn't go in."

"I wanted to," Elaine added. "But Hannah reminded me whoever it was might have left evidence."

They had almost reached the cabin. When Banjo bounded toward the open front door, Colin said, "Hang on to him, okay?"

Elaine caught the dog's collar. "Come on, Banjo, let's stay with Hannah."

The trio waited at a distance while the sheriff and deputy cautiously swept the cabin, making sure no one was inside. Then, while Jacky dusted the front door for fingerprints, Colin asked Elaine to come inside to see if anything was missing. Hannah kept Banjo out of the way.

Through the open doorway, the lights now on, she could see Colin and Elaine moving around the cabin, which was basically one large room.

"That's not mine," Elaine said, pointing to something on the floor. "Not anything Phoenix would own either."

"Okay, we'll take it as evidence." Colin pulled a plastic bag from his pocket.

When they emerged, Hannah called out, "What did you find?"

"A really nice silver pen," Elaine replied. "Nothing Phoenix would have owned, probably."

Hannah thought of another clue. "Plus, Banjo barked at whoever it was. Remember the other times, when he didn't, possibly because he knew the person?"

"That's interesting," Jacky said. "Should I try the back door, Sheriff? I'm not getting much here. Either a jumble of prints or nothing."

"Figures. The perp probably wore gloves." Colin tucked the pen into the duffel bag. "We'll try to get prints from this at the station."

Maybe they'd get lucky and get some evidence from the pen. But they'd still need people to match any fingerprints to...unless Elaine's intruder was already in the system.

"Besides your ex-farmhand, who else might have reason to break in?" Colin asked. "Any thoughts on what they might be after?"

"Seeds," Elaine said promptly. At the sheriff's puzzled look, she went on. "Ever since Marshall wrote that article about the missing Onion Queen and the famous Blackberry Red onions, people have been prowling around here."

Colin scratched the back of his neck. "Are the seeds really valuable or something?"

"I guess to some people," Elaine said. "My neighbor, Cooper Combs, insists they belong to him, and we have a fake professor sneaking around here too. They both want to grow those onions."

"To give you some context, Blackberry Red onions used to be one of the area's most popular varieties," Hannah said. "The King family developed them and grew the sets for other farmers and gardeners to grow. We've found old ads with that claim, and I can show them to you. But Cooper came over here and confronted Elaine about the onions, saying they originated with his family and accusing her family of stealing the seeds. I was with Elaine when he did that."

"Okay," Colin said, releasing a breath. "I'll take your word for it. Maybe I should have a little chat with your neighbor." His brows drew together. "What was that about a fake professor?"

"Timothy Buttonwood used to be employed at the University of Virginia at Charlottesville," Hannah explained. "He left the college but introduced himself to us as still working there. He was taking soil samples for Elaine in case she found the seeds and wanted to plant them. She told him to leave after finding out about his deception."

Deputy Jacky took notes. "Any idea how to reach this Buttonwood guy?"

Elaine took out her phone and shared his number.

Hannah hoped the sheriff's visits to Cooper and Timothy would be helpful. However, it was possible it would only make the men more determined.

"I suggest getting padlocks for the cabin doors," Colin told Elaine. "The kind that can't be snipped. Unless you have someone new moving in soon?"

Elaine shook her head. "Not right now. I should probably do the same on the abandoned house before that gets trashed."

"I'm sorry you're dealing with this," Colin said. "We'll do our best to find out who's behind it."

"Thank you, Sheriff," Elaine said. Her smile was wan. "Never a dull moment around here lately, it seems."

Hannah and Elaine set off for the barn, with Colin promising to swing by the house when they were finished at the cabin. Banjo accompanied them, loping along and sniffing at whatever took his fancy.

"I'm not sure how much more I can take," Elaine said, her distress evident in how fast she walked.

"I get it," Hannah said, her heart going out to her friend. "We need to find those seeds. That should stop them in their tracks."

Elaine huffed as she threw her hands in the air. "I haven't had time to look. If only I could remember where I saw them. It's as if I have a memory that keeps sliding away whenever I think too hard."

"I know what you mean," Hannah said. "Sometimes the answer comes to me in the middle of the night."

Seeds of Suspicion

Elaine barked a laugh. "That happens to me sometimes too. But then I can't remember it when I wake up." They had reached the barn, where light spilled out into the yard. "We'll grab the ledgers and take them up to the house."

They each carried several dusty old books. As they approached the house, another set of headlights came down the drive.

"That must be Blake," Elaine said.

By the time Hannah and Elaine reached the house, Blake and Kylie were climbing out of the car. "Hey, Mom, Hannah," he called. "Kylie and I are going to have a snack before I run her home."

"You can't eat my cake," Elaine joked. "Otherwise, have whatever you want."

As they walked toward the back door, Blake said, "I didn't know you were here, Hannah. If you need to leave before I take Kylie home, just let me know, and I'll unlock the gate for you."

"You'll have to do that right away," Elaine told him. "The sheriff is here."

Kylie gasped, and Blake asked, "What's going on, Mom?"

"We had another intruder." Elaine handed the ledgers to Kylie and then opened the back door and gestured everyone through. "Banjo must've caught the guy's scent, because he took off while he was with us in the barn. Someone was in the cabin."

"Phoenix was down at the park. We saw him right before we left. Didn't we, Kylie?"

She nodded. "He played with one of the bands. He's really good."

Elaine took the ledgers from Kylie and set them on the counter. "The prowler was in the cabin when we got there. He went out the back door. The place is a huge mess."

Blake began looking through cupboards. "Seriously? Who's doing this?" He pulled out a box of microwave popcorn packets.

"I'd like to know as well." Elaine moved briskly to the fridge. "Want a glass of milk with your cake, Hannah? I don't want a hot drink tonight."

"Sounds good." Hannah set her books down next to Elaine's pile.

"What are these?" Kylie asked. She began leafing through the one on top. "They look old."

"Ledgers from the farm," Hannah said. "We're going to go through them for information about Blackberry Red onions. Elaine has always understood that her family developed the onion. We hope we can find more proof than what we've seen in old King Farm ads."

Elaine brought two glasses of milk to the island.

Hannah opened the box of cake. "Wow, there's tons here, Elaine."

Her friend peered into the box. "You're right. Kids, you're welcome to some after all."

Kylie peeked at the cake. "I'd love a sliver, if that's okay."

"Sure thing." Elaine opened the freezer door. "With ice cream?"

"Yes, please."

When the microwave beeped, Blake emptied the bag of fresh popcorn into a big bowl and placed it on the island. Then he opened the fridge and pulled out a can of soda. "Want one, Kylie?"

"Please." Kylie accepted a dish of dessert from Elaine and dug in. "Yum," she said after a bite. "This is so good."

Hannah took her serving from Elaine. "It's an old recipe I found in the newspaper when I was researching the Onion Queen story." Using her fork, she cut a piece of cake and then scooped up some ice cream.

Seeds of Suspicion

"Can I help you look through the ledgers?" Kylie asked. "I love researching history."

Elaine capped the ice cream and put it back in the freezer. "I won't say no. Many eyes make light work."

Blake was seated on a stool, swiveling and eating popcorn. Now and then a kernel fell to the floor, where Banjo snapped it up.

Someone knocked on the door.

"That's the sheriff," Elaine said, hurrying to answer.

Blake slid off his stool. "I'll go unlock the gate. Be right back. Make sure Banjo doesn't steal all my popcorn."

Voices conferred at the door, and then Elaine returned. "They're going to keep me posted."

Hannah hoped something would break soon. For example, actually seeing a prowler's face. Or finding the seeds and announcing that to the world.

Kylie pointed at the ledgers. "Can we take a quick peek tonight? I know it's getting late, but I'm so curious."

"Me too," Hannah admitted.

Elaine made a scoffing sound. "You've already solved two mysteries since you got back to town," she said to Hannah.

Kylie's eyes were wide. "Really? That's awesome."

Hannah finished her cake while Elaine filled Kylie in on what had happened in the last two months.

Blake returned and immediately went to the fridge to forage. He began pulling out lunch meat, cheese, and sliced tomatoes.

Elaine rolled her eyes. "I'll never understand where you put all the food you eat."

"I'm always on the go, so it burns right off." He turned to Kylie. "Sandwich?"

"No thanks," she said with a laugh. She hopped down and collected the empty cake plates. "I'm going to wash these and then look at one of the ledgers."

"Thank you, Kylie," Elaine said.

Hannah and Elaine each chose a book and began to leaf through them. Hannah took out her phone, planning to snap pictures of anything interesting for future reference.

They hadn't gotten far when Kylie pulled a folded page out of hers and opened it. "It's a map of the farm." She bent closer. "It's showing where they planted crops in 1932."

Elaine and Hannah came around to peer over her shoulder, and Elaine began pointing out various areas of the farm. "Cattle corn in this field, which is the vegetable garden now. Oh, and in the west field, onions." Blake also came over, holding his sandwich.

The area marked ONIONS was sizable, at least a couple of acres, if Hannah had to guess. A large crop. She noticed that Elaine was frowning. "What's wrong?"

Elaine tapped her finger on the onion area. "That's right next to the land we sold to the Combses."

Hannah studied the map. "Where is the boundary now?"

"Right about there." Her friend traced a line on the page.

"Oh, Elaine," Hannah said. "That's where Cooper is growing onions now. I saw Seth and Phoenix harvesting them when I was out looking for Banjo."

Chapter Twenty

"But why does that matter?" Blake asked.

Hannah tried to organize her thoughts. "I'm wondering whether they've been growing Blackberry Red all along without anyone knowing it."

"Maybe they self-seeded," Elaine said as she returned to her stool. "Happens frequently with vegetables, including onions."

"It would explain why Cooper was so adamant about claiming ownership," Hannah said. "That way he can market the onions under their proper name. That could mean a lot of money for him, given the current interest in that variety."

Elaine rested her chin in her hand. "It makes sense. The thing is, I was always told that my family developed it. If that's what he's doing, he's being sneaky, and I don't like that."

Hannah didn't either. Since the Combs family had found the plants on their land, they were certainly within their rights to grow them. Too bad he hadn't approached Elaine with transparency and honesty—*if* that was what was happening.

"If he's already growing Blackberry Red, then we know why he wants to find those seeds," Elaine said. "He wants to stop me from growing them too."

"Would the seeds even germinate?" Kylie asked. "How old are they?"

"They might." Elaine pointed to the ledger in front of Kylie. "They were last grown here in 1932. The family stopped growing them after Clara King left. The last Onion Queen and the last crop of Blackberry Reds. Or so we thought."

"Wow," Kylie said, wonder in her voice. "Who knew onions could cause so much drama?"

Indeed, Hannah thought. "Elaine, do you mind if I take a couple of ledgers home with me? I'll take good care of them."

"Help yourself." Elaine started to say something else, and a huge yawn erupted instead.

The rest of them yawned in response, and she chuckled. "I think it's time to call it a night."

"Yep. Big day tomorrow." Hannah smiled at Kylie. "Especially you, young lady. I'd tell you to get your beauty sleep, but you don't need any."

Finally home, Hannah curled up in bed with Mabel's diary, hoping it would help her unwind. It had been another long and exciting day. On the one hand, she'd won the chef cook-off. What a thrill! But on the other, there had been another prowling incident at Elaine's farm.

Maybe she would find answers in the diary. Or in the farm ledgers now sitting on her coffee table.

She opened the book and began to read. She'd left off with the disastrous movie date Mabel had gone on with Clara, Rodney, and Everett Byrne. Rodney had tried to punch Wilson Barnes, bringing the rivalry for Clara's heart out into the open.

Blackberry Valley

August 15, 1932

Chatter and laughter filled the dining room at the King home. The Onion Queen contestants had gathered to make crepe-paper roses for their float. Mrs. King had declared that real flowers were impractical, as they were sure to wilt before the horse-drawn float had gone one block.

"I've made more coffee," Mrs. King announced, setting a carafe on a hot plate. "Help yourself. There's also coffee cake and fresh fruit."

"I'll take the fruit," Ada Young said, patting her slender waistline. "No cake for me until after the competition."

Mabel had no such qualms. "I'm having some. I get plenty of exercise." She deftly folded red crepe paper that would soon be another blossom.

Ada eyed Mabel's hands. "How do you get the grime out?"

Mabel frowned at her. "What do you mean?"

"From weeding." Ada held up her own slim, immaculate hands. "I've seen you out in the fields." A couple of girls giggled.

Heat burned in Mabel's cheeks. There wasn't any shame in honest work, as her mother always said. And with the farm being shorthanded, she'd been more than happy to pitch in.

Clara broke in, her voice cool. "Mabel is a Proverbs 31 woman. 'She plants a vineyard.' Better than idle hands."

Mabel hid a smile. Ada was known for her laziness, expecting others to wait on her hand and foot.

Ada's face darkened. Then she turned to one of the gigglers. "Will you get me a cup of coffee?" The young woman hurried to obey.

Mabel lost her battle with a smile. When she glanced up, Clara winked at her.

The phone rang in the front hall, and Mrs. King hurried to answer. A moment later, she appeared in the doorway. "Clara, dear, it's Rodney Combs for you."

Ada's glare was vicious, although she tried to hide it under her thick lashes.

Instead of getting up, Clara reached for another piece of crepe paper. "Can you tell him I'm busy, Mama? Thank you."

Mrs. King stared at her daughter for a moment as if trying to decide whether to argue. Then she turned, shoulders stiff, and returned to the hall.

"Playing hard to get?" Ada asked. "Aren't you the bold one."

Clara shrugged. "Not at all. I simply don't want to talk to him right now."

Ada chewed her bottom lip. Then she said, "He's the most eligible bachelor in Blackberry Valley." She sounded envious. "I'd snatch him up lickety-split."

"Maybe you should, Ada," Clara said.

Mabel still hadn't heard exactly what had transpired between Rodney and Wilson after the double date. She hadn't had a moment alone with Clara this morning. Maybe later, when they took the paper flowers and a section of lattice to the station, she could get the details from her friend. The floats were being built down there, in the lumberyard.

She and Clara had volunteered to tie the flowers to the lattice there so they wouldn't get damaged in transit. Bunting would also be draped on the float, and the contestants, dressed in flowing white dresses and flower crowns, would sit or stand to ride.

Mabel realized this was a covert way for Clara to spend time with Wilson, who was working on the floats. She certainly wasn't going to point that out to anyone.

After lunch, Clara and Mabel set off in the farm truck to the lumberyard.

"So," Mabel said as soon as the wheels were spinning down the drive, "what happened that night after the movie?"

Clara glanced over with a grin. "I could tell you've been bursting to ask me that since it happened."

"Can you blame me?" Mabel demanded. "I couldn't believe my eyes when Rodney threw that punch. Spill already."

Clara braked at the bottom of the drive, looking both ways before pulling out. Her lips curled in distaste. "Rodney tried to kiss me. I saw it coming and pushed him away."

Mabel rolled her eyes. "I saw. Ugh."

"You're telling me. Anyway, Wilson came along, and he apparently sized up the situation. He suggested to Rodney that it was time for him to go home." Clara lifted one shoulder. "Rodney didn't like that."

Mabel wrinkled her nose. "That was obvious. Good for Wilson, not hitting him back."

Clara shuddered. "I'm glad someone had some restraint. It would have been a real hullabaloo if they'd started tussling. Daddy would have had a fit."

"Rodney was pretty mad all the way home," Mabel told her. "Didn't say a word to me or Everett, even when we dropped him off at his cottage."

"Everett was a hero. He really helped calm things down." She glanced sideways at Mabel. "He's an awfully nice guy."

"He is," Mabel agreed, allowing herself a minute to think about Everett. The best part was that they'd been friends for years. She really liked him. And now—well, time would tell.

Clara, always able to guess what she was thinking about, sent her a smile.

Mabel changed the subject before Clara could decide to tease her. "Oh, guess what? I wrote to my cousin in Ellisville to ask about Rodney Combs and his time there. It occurred to me that we don't know much about him and maybe she'll have some information. Personally, I don't trust him."

"Why not?" Clara asked. "I mean, I have a definite aversion to the man. I tried to like him, since Mama's so intent on having him around. I can't stand him, but why wouldn't you like him?"

"You mean besides him being so fresh, trying to kiss you? Maybe you should tell your mother about that."

Clara rolled her eyes. "She'd probably tell me I should have let him."

Mabel burst out laughing, and so did Clara.

"There's another reason I don't trust Rodney," Mabel said. "Did you get a gander at the man he was talking to on the street? I thought that was really odd. The guy didn't look very reputable at all."

"He sure didn't. I know a lot of men are traveling now, and they can't help their appearance. But it wasn't that. He seemed pushy, almost demanding that Rodney talk to him."

"'Watch the company a man keeps,'" Mabel muttered. "That's what my mother always says. Speaking of Mama, she's worried that you're going to get railroaded into marriage with Rodney. She doesn't like him either, for what that's worth."

Clara raised a brow. "Railroaded? She used that word?"

Mabel shrugged. "She did. I guess she could see which way the wind was blowing after the dinner party at your house." She almost blurted the part about the Kings' financial troubles but managed to bite back the words. That would certainly be embarrassing for Clara.

"Yeah, it was pretty obvious, wasn't it?" Clara slowed the truck as they approached the lumberyard. "I'm going to have a little talk with my mother. After that awful date, I'm finished with Rodney Combs."

The railroad station was across the street from the lumberyard. Mabel could see several men, including Rodney, working on a switch beside the tracks. A freight train waited, smoke billowing from the stack.

"The floats are over there." Mabel pointed to an open area in the yard. Several wagons at various stages of decoration dotted the space. Mabel noticed Wilson moving around the first one in line. "There's Wilson."

The farmhand waved as Clara pulled up in the truck. He stuck out his thumb and said, "Going my way, miss?"

"If you're lucky," Clara joked back. She opened the heavy door and slid out to the ground, and Mabel did the same.

Wilson followed them to the rear of the truck. "What do you need me to do?"

Clara pointed. "That lattice needs to be fastened to the front of the wagon. We're going to tie these paper flowers to it." She showed him the one in her hand.

Wilson's eyes lit up. "So you'll be sticking around for a while? I've been by myself for the last couple of hours. Everyone left for lunch and didn't come back."

"We'll be here as long as it takes." Clara didn't seem unhappy about that.

Just then, a sheriff's car careened up the street, siren wailing.

"What's going on?" Mabel asked.

They watched as the cruiser screeched to a stop. Two deputies leaped out and ran inside the station.

"Let's go find out," Clara said.

"What if it's not safe?" Mabel objected. Maybe the deputies were after a dangerous criminal trying to get away on the train. There might even be a shootout.

"We'll stay outside." Clara trotted toward the road, leaving Mabel and Wilson little choice but to follow.

Others had started to gather as well—workers from the lumberyard, passengers arriving to take the next train, and curious passersby.

The sheriff emerged through the station doors. He stood on the porch, hands on hips, surveying the crowd. "Is Wilson Barnes here?"

Wilson stepped forward, his hand lifted. "I'm Wilson Barnes."

The sheriff gestured for him to come forward. "We need to speak with you."

Confusion flooded Wilson's face. "With all due respect, Sheriff, what's this about?"

People in the crowd began to mutter and whisper, nudging one another.

Clara put a hand on Wilson's arm. "Go on," she urged. "You can't refuse without looking as if you're hiding something."

Wilson squared his shoulders. "Guess you're right." He stepped forward, the crowd parting for him.

When he reached the sheriff, the officer put his hand on his shoulder and steered him inside the station.

After they disappeared inside, a deputy came out. "Station is closed right now, ladies and gentlemen."

An older man with spectacles dropped two bags with a thud. "What about my train?"

"Don't worry," the deputy said. "This won't take long. You won't miss your train."

Clara clenched her fists, dismay twisting her features. "What do they want with Wilson? He hasn't done anything."

"Maybe they just have some questions for him," Mabel said. Despite this reasonable theory, her insides twisted with fear. What had happened? Why was the sheriff here?

The answer wasn't long in coming. The news soon spread through the crowd. Someone had taken the money box from the stationmaster's office while he was otherwise occupied.

A terrible thought jolted Mabel. Wilson had been working across the street, alone for the last little while by his own admission. Did they think he was the thief?

Chapter Twenty-One

The next morning, Hannah mulled over Mabel's diary during her breakfast of cereal topped with fresh blackberries. *Wilson Barnes.* The same last name as Phoenix, the young farmhand from California. Could they be related? Surely that was farfetched though. Barnes wasn't exactly an uncommon name.

Hannah's phone rang, and she glanced at the screen. Ice trickled down her spine at the name showing.

Corrie Rice.

Did she have to call now, while Hannah was in the middle of breakfast? Plus, Hannah wasn't sure she was mentally ready for the conversation. However, if she didn't take the call, that meant more phone tag.

Hannah gritted her teeth. Better to get it over with. She connected the call. "Hello?"

"Hannah?" The clatter in the background made it hard for Hannah to hear Corrie.

"It's me. How are you?" Hannah scrambled to organize her thoughts. *Help me, Lord.*

The background quieted. Corrie must have changed locations. "I'm fine. You called?" Her abrupt tone and lack of return pleasantries immediately warned Hannah to tread lightly.

"I did." Hannah took a breath. "I came across one of your videos. Congrats on your success."

"Really?" Corrie sounded surprised.

"You have a lot of followers. That's awesome." Hannah girded herself. Now came the hard part. "There is one thing—"

"Isn't there always?"

Hannah swallowed. Of course it wasn't going to be easy. "I did see one video. The blackberry burrata pizza. Maybe you don't remember, but—"

She was interrupted by a bleep. Corrie had hung up on her.

Hannah stared at her phone in disbelief. *That went well. Now what?*

She picked up her spoon to continue eating. The breakfast she'd been enjoying was suddenly tasteless. Should she let the issue of the pizza recipe go? She'd certainly tried.

Then she remembered the cook-off. The television station would be broadcasting clips from the contest as well as the lead-up to the event. Those clips would probably also be posted on social media by the station, the chamber of commerce, and who knew who else. The Hot Spot should also post their own announcement of the win—and the winning dish.

Everyone was connected now, and Hannah was afraid that someone would see the posts and inform Corrie. Since Corrie's video had been posted first, it would look like Hannah had copied Corrie's recipe, rather than the other way around. That was the way the world worked.

She had to regroup and try again, before the situation blew up.

Hannah wished she'd never had that brainstorm now, even if it had led to a coveted award.

Hannah decided to get out of the apartment for a while. She'd go over to the park, where a farmers market was being held that morning.

But first, the coffee shop, where Zane was working behind the counter. "Congratulations," he called when he saw Hannah walk in. "Fantastic news."

Hannah ducked her head, heat rushing into her face as heads swiveled toward her. "Thanks, Zane. It's a real thrill."

Zane deftly unloaded a tray of clean cups. "Jacob's psyched, I can tell you that. He's already added 'award-winning restaurant' to his professional bio. What can I get you?"

Jacob should enter the next cook-off on behalf of the Hot Spot. He deserved recognition too. Hannah would be sure to mention it to him. "Um, a large coffee to go. I'm heading over to the festival."

"Don't blame you. It's a beautiful morning to walk around." Zane dispensed her coffee into a large to-go cup. "Farmers market today too."

"Yeah, I want to check that out." Hannah noticed a flyer on the counter, listing the farms that had booths at the market. King Farm was there and Cooper's farm as well. Though both farms sold most of their produce wholesale to stores, restaurants, and inns, they also sold directly to consumers.

An idea tickled the back of her mind.

Zane placed the coffee cup on the counter and rang her up. Hannah carried it to the condiment station, added cream, and went on her way.

People thronged the farmers market, strolling along the aisles and stopping to try samples and buy products. Besides produce, dairy products, and meat, there were prepared foods such as fresh-baked bread, various ethnic dishes, and sandwiches.

Hannah's mouth watered, even though there was no way she should be hungry yet. Still, she'd grab a meatball and mushroom sandwich on the way back through. She always had room for Italian food, especially when prepared with local porcinis.

Cooper's booth was at the end. Seth and Phoenix were on duty, replenishing bins and waiting on customers. As Hannah had hoped, there were red onions available. She wanted to buy a couple and try them. Blackberry Red had been distinctively sweet, and she wondered how theirs tasted.

Blake manned the King Farm booth. "Hey, Hannah."

She stopped to say hello and chose a couple of ripe red tomatoes. "Did you guys get any rest last night?" she asked when he suppressed a yawn.

"Some, but not nearly enough." Blake set her picks on the scale. "I kept waking up with every little noise, thinking someone was outside. We're going to put new locks on the cabin later today."

"Good to hear." Hannah paid for the tomatoes. "Is your mom here?" She could tell Elaine about the coincidence of Wilson's and Phoenix's last names.

Blake pointed toward the stage area. "She's helping get the pageant set up for tonight."

"Kylie must be excited." Hannah tucked the tomatoes into the cloth bag she'd brought.

"She is. She's really counting on the scholarship money." Blake smiled. "Can I get you anything else?"

Other customers approached the booth, so Hannah decided to move along. "I'm all set, thanks. See you later."

She walked on, checking out the wares at a candlemaker's booth and then buying some goat cheese, which would be delicious with the tomatoes.

Seth was waiting on a customer, but Phoenix leaned against the table, sipping from a to-go cup. He nodded to Hannah.

"Get your truck fixed?" she asked.

"All set," he said, straightening up. "Thanks again for the ride."

Hannah began to examine the vegetables in the bins. They were picture perfect. "Great produce."

Phoenix beamed. "Thanks. The soil is great, and Cooper knows what he's doing."

Hannah picked up an onion, which filled her whole palm. "I noticed you were picking these the day I was searching for Banjo."

"Yeah, they're really popular," Phoenix said. "People like to put them on hamburgers. They make nice big rings, so you get a good flavor in every bite."

"I like red onions in salsa," Hannah said. She put the onion on the scale and then added a second.

While Phoenix weighed the onions and calculated the cost, Hannah wondered how to frame her question. Finally, she went for it. "You said you had ancestors from Kentucky. Any idea where?" Besides his casual mention of ancestors, she'd seen him at the library, in the historical documents room.

His brows drew together. "Why do you ask?"

Hannah shifted her stance. Her question had been rather nosy. "I'm researching Blackberry Valley's history. One of the people I'm reading about is a Wilson Barnes. I recognized the name and wondered if he's related to you."

His expression thoughtful, Phoenix loaded the onions into a bag. Hannah had the sense he was weighing out what to tell her. Finally, he said, "I do have an ancestor named Wilson Barnes. He used to live in Blackberry Valley." His features darkened. "Until he was forced to leave town."

Blackberry Valley
August 15, 1932

The deputy shooed people away from the station entrance, except for the passengers leaving on the next train. He had them wait on the platform.

"Let's go work on the float," Mabel suggested. She could tell Clara was upset, and hoped the repetitive task would help soothe her. "We'll be able to see Wilson when he comes out."

Clara didn't argue, so they crossed the street again. Between the two of them, they got the piece of lattice up onto the wagon bed. Wilson would have to nail it in place later. Then they began to fasten the paper blossoms to the lattice with floral wire. Once done, it would look like a climbing rose.

Mabel couldn't help peering toward the station every few seconds. The deputy still occupied the doorway, poised as if to repel any intruders.

Then a movement caught her eye near the parked train cars. A man walked along the tracks, carrying a burlap sack over his shoulder. Not an unusual sight, except he seemed furtive, glancing around now and then as if wanting to know if anyone had noticed him.

Mabel nudged her friend. "Clara, look. What is that man doing?"

Clara lifted her head. "I don't know. Maybe he's planning to hop the train." Riders without money for tickets often did that, hiding in boxcars or scrambling onto a flatcar once the train was underway.

Although Mabel thought Clara was probably right, she couldn't stop staring at the man. Finally, the reason dawned on her. He was the man who had accosted Rodney in the street. She watched as he continued along the tracks, walking past the caboose and away from the station.

"The sheriff should be questioning him," she said.

"Who?" Clara's movements were listless as she placed another paper flower on the lattice and twisted the wire.

"That man. Remember the night we went to the movies?" Mabel could hear the excitement in her voice.

"The man who spoke to Rodney, the one we were so uncomfortable with. He was at the station, and now he's getting away."

Clara's arms hung limply at her sides. "Mabel, they've decided Wilson did it. I just know it." She blinked furiously, but not before Mabel spotted the sparkle of tears in her eyes. "It's so unfair."

Mabel handed Clara her handkerchief. "That's silly. Why would they suspect Wilson? He's a resident of Blackberry Valley, employed at one of the biggest farms. That man is a stranger, and a suspicious one. He'll take the money and run." This theory made sense to Mabel, although she had no evidence. "He was carrying a sack, Clara. The money is probably in there."

Clara didn't answer. She just kept twisting wires around the lattice.

Before she could talk herself out of it, Mabel climbed down from the float. "Be right back." She dashed to the train station.

The deputy, who was lounging against the doorjamb, straightened as she approached. "Miss, you can't come in here. Orders of the sheriff."

Mabel halted at the bottom of the steps. "I know that. It's you I want to talk to."

"Me?" The deputy's fingers went to his hat brim for an adjustment. "What about?"

She pointed along the tracks, where the man's figure continued to recede. "You need to go after that man. He walked away from here carrying a burlap sack. He might be the thief."

The deputy squinted into the distance. "What makes you think that? He's probably just a hobo, following the line."

"Seems to me like they should be talking to everyone who was around," Mabel pointed out.

His gaze returned to Mabel, cold and stern. "Maybe the sheriff already did. You think of that?"

Mabel shook her head. "No, I didn't. I'm sorry." She fled back to the float, her face flaming with embarrassment. She'd been put firmly in her place.

"Well, that was a mistake," she said as she climbed onto the wagon. She scowled. "He scolded me for interfering. Can you believe that? You'd think they'd appreciate an active public."

Clara had given up all pretense of decorating. She stared at the train station entrance, her expression somber. "What is going on in there?" She sounded desperate.

Mabel put an arm around her friend. "It'll be all right." It had to be. Wilson was one of the best men she knew.

"Can I tell you a secret?" Clara said, her voice barely above a whisper.

"Of course." Mabel inclined her head so she could hear better.

"Wilson asked me to marry him." A tremulous smile broke across her face. "He loves me, Mabel."

Mabel's heart soared with joy and excitement for her friend. "What did you say?"

"I—the station door is opening." Clara's spine went rigid, and Mabel's arm dropped away.

The deputy stepped aside, revealing Wilson coming through the door. He descended the station steps and strode across the street, head held high.

Clara scrambled down from the float and went to meet him, throwing her arms around him. Wilson put his arm around her, gazing into her face as if she were all that existed in the world. Thus entwined, the couple made their way toward the float.

If their love for each other was a secret before, it sure isn't now, Mabel thought ruefully.

"You're doing a beautiful job," Mama said, examining the beaded bodice Mabel was stitching onto her gown. She planned to wear the lavender chiffon dream of a dress in the Onion Queen competition.

"Thanks, Mama." Mabel had surprised herself with the neatness of her stitches and the evenness of the bead placement. Her mind had been occupied with thoughts of Clara and Wilson, Rodney Combs, and the train station theft.

Mama sat in the armchair across from Mabel, sighing as she lifted her legs onto an ottoman. "What a shock today. The train station robbed in broad daylight."

Mabel stopped stitching. "It really was. Especially when they questioned Wilson Barnes." Although she'd already told her mother about the incident, apparently, they were going to discuss it all again. Well, except for Wilson and Clara's affection and Clara's admission that he wanted to marry her. Mabel kept that to herself. It wasn't her news to share.

The doorbell rang, and Mama started to swing her feet off the ottoman. Mabel put aside her sewing. "You stay there. I'll get it."

Mabel hurried to the front door as the bell sounded again. They weren't expecting company, so she had no idea who it could be. Maybe one of her mother's friends, come to chew over the latest news while drinking sweet tea.

To Mabel's surprise, Clara stood on the steps. "Sorry to barge in like this, but I have to talk to you." She burst into tears.

Mabel stood back. "Don't apologize. Come on in." As she waited for Clara to enter, Mabel noticed a car creeping along the street.

As the roadster passed, she recognized Rodney Combs at the wheel. What was he doing? Following Clara around? Mabel sent the vehicle a fierce scowl before slamming the door, pretending she was shutting it in his face.

Clara jumped at the noise.

"Sorry," Mabel said. She was about to suggest they go upstairs when Mama bustled into the hall.

Seeing that Clara was upset, Mama put her arms around her. "There, there, my dear," she crooned. "What's the matter?"

Clara's answer was to sob into her shoulder. Mama had always treated her like a second daughter, and right now Clara seemed to need that.

Mama settled their visitor into a chair, fussing over her, then brought in sweet tea and cookies. "You take your time collecting yourself and then tell us all about it, dear."

Mabel nibbled on a cookie impatiently. She was dying to know why Clara had come over all upset like this. She was worried that Wilson had been arrested, but was afraid to ask, as if that would make it true.

After half a glass of tea, Clara said, "Thank you, Mrs. Prentiss. You've been so kind."

"Of course," Mama said. "You're always welcome here." By the anxious expression in her mother's eyes, Mabel guessed she was equally curious about Clara's situation.

"My parents told me something very upsetting tonight," Clara said, her face twisting in distress again. She took a couple of deep breaths before saying, "The farm is struggling. We're going to have to sell some land."

Mama gasped. "Oh no. I'm so sorry to hear that."

Although selling off parcels wasn't terribly unusual, especially in these times, acres of land represented so much more: a family legacy, the opportunity to create wealth, and even social standing in the community. Once sold, the land was rarely regained. Even in her short lifetime, Mabel had seen once-proud farms diminish in size, like patches being torn from a quilt.

"They didn't really say it," Clara said, "but I think that's why they've been hoping I would allow Rodney to court me. He's well-off, with a secure position. He has good prospects for the future. While the farm is supposed to go to my brother, it's possible Rodney and I could remain involved, as a married couple."

In this situation, Clara's parents would never approve of her marrying Wilson. Although he was a decent man, he couldn't offer anything except a strong back and willing hands. And they already had those from him. Unfortunately, they were thinking of their daughter's marriage as a possible benefit to them, not happiness for her.

"That makes sense," Mama said. "But only if you're willing. And I have the distinct feeling that you

Seeds of Suspicion

aren't." Her eyes were shrewd. "I think your affections are engaged elsewhere."

Clara's pink cheeks deepened in color. "How did you guess?"

Mama pursed her lips then said, "I know young women. Have you told your parents that you aren't free to marry Rodney?"

Clara shook her head. "I haven't dared. I was about to, but then Daddy told me the news. Now I don't know what to do."

"You need to be true to yourself," Mabel blurted. "If you marry the wrong man, a lifetime can be pretty long. Can you imagine fifty years with Rodney, or any other man you disliked?" She shuddered at the idea.

Mama nodded. "Mabel is right. You don't owe your family an advantageous marriage, unless you're willing. Maybe your brother should take on that burden."

"Good idea." Clara's mouth turned down. "Except he's still too young. My parents need solutions now."

Out in the hallway, the phone rang. Mabel hopped up. "I'll get that." She hoped it wasn't Clara's parents looking for her. She thought maybe Clara should spend the night. She needed time to unwind with her best friend and the comfort of Mabel's mother, not further hounding.

Mabel picked up the receiver. "Hello?"

When the operator gave the number calling, Mabel's heart skipped a beat. It was Evelyn, her cousin in Ellisville.

"I got your letter," Evelyn said without preamble. "I can't talk about this on the telephone, so can you come see me tomorrow? There's someone you need to meet."

Chapter Twenty-Two

Hannah was stunned by Phoenix's revelation. Was his ancestor the same Wilson Barnes who had left Blackberry Valley over ninety years ago? "What was his wife's name?" she asked hastily. "Do you know?"

"Clara," he said. "We have their marriage certificate at home."

They had to be the right couple. "Can someone send us a photograph of it?"

Phoenix looked taken aback. "Why do you want it?"

"Because Elaine had an ancestor named Clara King who was in love with a Wilson Barnes."

"Seriously? I had no idea." Phoenix took out his phone. "I can't remember her maiden name. I'll have Mom send us a picture. What's your number?"

Hannah's pulse thrummed with excitement as she shared her contact information. This might be a major breakthrough. Phoenix and Elaine could be related, even if distantly. A little awkward under the circumstances of Elaine firing him, but they'd probably get past that.

Hannah tucked the onions into her bag. She wouldn't say anything to Elaine yet, not until she had the picture of the wedding certificate.

After she left the market, Hannah went to the stage area to check on the progress for the evening's competition.

Elaine was directing the placement of banners, each displaying a photograph of a contestant. "A little more to the left," she called to a workman on a ladder. "That's it. Perfect."

Hannah took in the stage accoutrements: a backdrop, temporary curtains, a dais, and a podium. "Looking good," she said as Elaine turned to greet her with a smile.

"Thanks. We've been here since early this morning." Elaine watched as the workman moved the stepladder to place another banner. "Want to come to the farm for lunch? I think I might know where the seeds are."

"What?" Hannah yelped. "Are you kidding?"

Elaine shook her head. "You know how right before you go to sleep, your mind drifts? I had a memory of when I came across the seeds. I think. It was in the attic, while I was playing dress-up as a little girl."

"Oh, I'm so glad you remembered," Hannah said. "You didn't go right up and look? I probably would have."

"Well, it really was right before I fell asleep. And I didn't have time this morning. I had to get ready for the farmers market and then come over here. I'm finally going to look when I go home for lunch."

"I'll want to be with you for sure," Hannah said. "Text me with a time, and I'll see you there." She thought of the onions in her bag. "I'll bring salad."

Elaine's gaze was already fixed on the workman attaching the banner to a wire. "Sounds good. I've been craving quiche."

Hannah's steps were quick and light as she set off across the park. They were closing in on the truth about Clara and Wilson.

They might find the seeds today. And with any luck, they'd figure out who was prowling around the King Farm.

She couldn't wait to solve all these mysteries.

Blackberry Valley
August 16, 1932

Clara put a gloved hand on Mabel's arm as they entered the Blackberry Valley train station. "Oh, good. The assistant stationmaster is working. I didn't want to see Rodney today."

Neither did Mabel, especially since they were going to the town where he used to live, to find out his secrets.

When she said, "Two round-trip tickets to Ellisville, please," there was no reaction from the man behind the window, as there likely would have been from Rodney. The assistant dispensed the tickets, took her money, and handed her a train schedule as well.

Mabel thanked him, and they went out to the platform to wait, along with other passengers. The morning was fresh and cool, so they sat on a bench in the sun.

"How long is the ride?" Clara asked.

Mabel studied the schedule. "Not too long. Ellisville is about thirty miles from here, and there are a couple of stops."

"Do you see your cousin often?" Clara asked.

"Mostly at holidays and once or twice during the summer. She's great fun. I wish I could see her more." Mabel recalled the childhood mischief and pranks she'd gotten up to with Evelyn, who was her age. "Her father works in a bank and they live in town, so she loves visiting our farm."

A whistle in the distance announced their train, followed by the chugging of the engine. The passengers on the platform grew alert, gathering their things and moving closer to where they would board. Mabel and Clara joined them.

As Mabel watched the train slide into the station, the brakes hissing, she wondered if they would find answers today in Ellisville.

Evelyn waited for them on the platform, anxiously scanning the train windows to find Mabel. Short and curvy with a round, pretty face framed by dark bangs, Evelyn was always in motion. Tapping her toes, pacing around, turning to take everything in.

Mabel and Clara were the first to get off their car. "Evelyn," Mabel called, lifting her hand in a wave.

Evelyn raced toward them. "It's so good to see you." She threw her arms around Mabel for an enthusiastic hug before offering her hand to Clara. "Hello. I'm Evelyn Prentiss."

Clara shook Evelyn's hand. "Clara King. Nice to meet you."

Introductions taken care of, Evelyn took both their arms, guiding them along the platform instead of into the station.

"Where are you taking us, Evelyn?" Mabel asked.

"This is the scene of the crime," Evelyn replied in a hoarse whisper, her eyes wide.

Mabel exchanged an amused glance with Clara. They were here on serious business, but Evelyn's antics might lighten the mood. "What crime is that?"

But Evelyn's next words made it clear she wasn't joking. "Last year a passenger was robbed while the train was stopped." Releasing them, she pointed. "Mrs. Virginia Hardcastle left the train to get some refreshments in the station, assured by the porter that her baggage was secure. When she returned, she discovered that her jewel case was gone."

"Who was the stationmaster?" Mabel asked.

"Our mutual friend, Mr. Rodney Combs." Evelyn tossed her head, making her curls dance. "They blamed it on a vagrant, but don't they always?"

"Not always," Clara said sadly.

Evelyn's eyes narrowed. "Sounds like a story there."

"We have a story for you, Cousin," Mabel said. "And it sounds like you have one for us. Where can we talk without someone listening in?"

They walked to a nearby diner, where they took a booth at the very back. "We can stay here as long as we want," Evelyn said. "I'm friends with the owners."

They ordered bacon, lettuce, and tomato sandwiches with milkshakes, along with a big side of french fries. "The calories don't count if you share," Evelyn said as she grabbed a fresh, steaming fry.

Clara hadn't read Mabel's letter to Evelyn, so Mabel opened the conversation. "I wrote to Evelyn and asked her what she knew about Rodney Combs," she told Clara. "I sent it after Rodney tried to hit Wilson, but before the train station was robbed."

Evelyn's mouth dropped open. "*Your* station was robbed? And who is Wilson?"

"Wilson Barnes works at my family farm," Clara explained, her eyes shining. "He's a wonderful man who wants to marry me." She paused to swallow. "My parents think Rodney is a better match."

"He's not," Evelyn said bluntly. "But first, tell me about the robbery."

Mabel outlined the events for her cousin. "Rodney was outside the station working on a train switch when it happened."

Evelyn set her lips in a firm line. "Is that according to him? You cannot trust a word that man says."

"I've gotten the same impression, but I saw him myself, as did some men who were with him," Mabel replied. "Anyway, Wilson was working across the street, at the lumberyard. He was building our float for the Onion Queen contest. He told us he'd been alone there for a couple of hours because other men had left for lunch. Next thing we know, there's a report about a theft at the train station, and the sheriff wants to talk to Wilson. He wasn't arrested, but they grilled him pretty thoroughly."

"They badgered him is more like it, trying to make him confess to something he didn't do," Clara said angrily. "I have a feeling Rodney played him up as the prime suspect. I'm sure he's not the type to forgive and forget. Rodney tried to kiss me a few days before, but Wilson stopped him, and Rodney didn't take kindly to the intrusion."

"Wilson is a real hero, huh?" Evelyn asked in an admiring voice.

"I think so," Clara said. "He's always been reliable and upright and kind."

"Any suspects in the robbery?" Evelyn asked. "My theory is that Rodney gets someone else to do the actual dirty work."

Mabel thought back. "There was a vagrant who left the station with a large sack over his shoulder. I know it's quite a jump to say he did it. However, that same man accosted Rodney on the street when we were walking to the movie theater, and we didn't get the impression that he was a particularly respectable person."

Evelyn took a bite of her sandwich and chewed thoughtfully. "That's interesting," she said after swallowing. "Here, they had no problem blaming the theft on a vagrant. The thing is, they never found him."

Had it been the same man? If so, it was a link, however tenuous.

"Why did Rodney leave Ellisville?" Clara asked. "Did it have anything to do with the robbery?"

Evelyn considered this, her fingers tapping the tabletop. "There's not really an official story about that, but we all have our theories, especially since the burglary here wasn't solved. They never recovered Mrs. Hardcastle's belongings."

"What a shame," Mabel said. "You said you had someone for us to meet. Is it Mrs. Hardcastle?"

Her cousin shook her head, her gaze sharp. "Rodney's former fiancée, Ann Ellis."

Chapter Twenty-Three

Back at the apartment, Hannah tidied up a bit then made sure her outfit was all set for the Blackberry Queen competition later that night. Next, she ran down to the restaurant to make a quick check of inventory. All was in order, and the menu for the night's meals looked good. She left Jacob a note, telling him she'd be back around three.

Next up was the salad she would take to Elaine's for lunch. Hannah peeled one of the red onions then sliced it in half. What a beautiful red-violet vegetable, a nice shape and size.

She inhaled the aroma of a good onion while she sliced it into rings. She picked up a piece and bit into it with a crunch. The sharp flavor burst over her tongue, but it was sweeter than she'd expected.

As Hannah pulled the slice into separate rings to top the salad, she wondered whether this was the famous Blackberry Red. Had the Combs family been growing them for decades without anyone realizing it? The onions hadn't been labeled with a specific variety in Cooper's booth.

Another question was brewing as well. If Rodney Combs was involved in the thefts that occurred under his watch as stationmaster, had he been caught? If so, how had he then gone on to marry Ada Young with no repercussions? Did he change his ways? What about restitution for the thefts?

Hannah could see how easily a story could appear to lead in one direction. The danger was rushing to judgment and trying to make pieces fit instead of keeping an open mind.

She packed the salad into a container then whipped up a spicy Italian dressing and transferred it to a glass jar. Both went into a tote, and she was ready.

On my way, she texted Elaine.

Banjo's happy bark greeted Hannah when she arrived at Elaine's. He came bolting toward the screen door when she reached the house, skidding to a stop on the kitchen tiles.

"Hi, Banjo," Hannah said, laughing as he wagged his tail so hard his whole body wiggled with joy.

Elaine appeared behind him, wiping her hands on her apron. "Come on in."

Hannah opened the door, careful not to let Banjo escape, and slipped inside. Banjo leaped and danced around her legs as she made her way into the kitchen. "Good to see you too," she said with a laugh. "He really makes you feel loved, doesn't he?"

Elaine beamed at the dog. "I can't imagine life without him." A timer dinged, and Elaine opened the oven door with a mittened hand and pulled out a pie plate. "Perfect timing. The quiche is ready."

Hannah placed the salad and dressing on the island and removed the lids from each. "Do you have tongs and a small pitcher?"

Elaine provided both then proceeded to slice the quiche, which was flecked with mushrooms, onions, and bacon. She placed two slices on plates and set them on the table.

"That crust is a masterpiece," Hannah said with admiration. The edges were perfectly fluted and golden brown.

"My grandmother's recipe," Elaine said. "A mix of butter and lard and a little vinegar."

"The old recipes are often the best," Hannah commented. She regarded them as culinary treasures, with part of the enjoyment being the hunt for them.

They each served themselves salad, and then Elaine said grace.

Elaine took a bite of salad, nodding as she chewed. "Now that I'm a grower, I really appreciate good produce. Where did you get this?"

Hannah grinned. "The tomatoes are yours. I bought them from Blake." She named the farms that had provided the lettuce and cucumber.

"What about the onion?" Elaine speared a ring and studied it before putting it into her mouth. She ate it slowly. "It's fabulous. Not bitter at all."

"That struck me too," Hannah said cautiously. "This might be totally out there, but hear me out. That onion came from the Combs farm, from the land your family sold to them."

Elaine's mouth dropped open.

"I think that onion might be a Blackberry Red, descended from a self-seeded one many decades ago."

Elaine's mouth clamped shut, her brow furrowing. "I get what you're saying, Hannah," she said slowly. "Do you suppose they knew it was our onion?"

Hannah nodded. "Probably. Like we discussed before, that would explain why Cooper wants to patent the onion so badly. To cover up what his family has been doing for years. With a patent, he can claim it belonged to them all along. His onions probably sell well as they are, but if he could market them under the name Blackberry Red, sales would really take off."

Elaine led the way to the attic, reached by a set of pull-down stairs in the second-floor hall. A gust of hot, stale air greeted them as they climbed.

"I almost never come up here." Elaine stood with her hands on her hips, surveying the long room with its slanted ceilings. "Every time I do, I'm reminded I need to sort through everything."

Hannah took in the array of belongings that almost filled the space. An old wardrobe. Stacks of boxes and trunks. Furniture in various states of disrepair. A sewing machine on a table.

"It's hard to let go of family treasures," she said, thinking of the donations her own family had made to the library.

Elaine laughed as she edged past stacked dining chairs. "'Treasure' might be a stretch, but I get your point. I do feel sentimental about some of it." She picked up a large rag doll that had been sitting on a rocking horse. "Like Miss Molly here. She belonged to my grandmother."

Hannah touched the doll's faded purple gingham dress. Below a ruffled cap, the doll's yarn features smiled. "I think you should display Miss Molly in your sales room."

"Really?" Elaine held the doll up and studied her. "You're right. I'll have to air her out first. Not sure if I dare wash her. You're coming with me, Miss Molly."

They continued through the attic to a large trunk placed under a dormer window. From there, Hannah could see the barn and the fields beyond. She could also see Banjo sniffing around the backyard. "Banjo is out."

"Oh yeah. I meant to call him in." The dog had gone outside after lunch. With a grunt, she opened the window. "Banjo," she called. "Stay." Then she waved. "Hey, Kylie."

Hannah moved closer so she could see. Kylie had arrived on horseback. Banjo greeted the horse, who lowered his big head to the dog. Hannah was glad that the horse hadn't startled at Banjo's exuberant welcome.

"Hey, Mrs. Wilby," Kylie answered. "Okay if I ride through the fields?"

"Anytime, Kylie. You know that," Elaine said. "Excited about the competition?"

Kylie laughed. "Nervous is more like it. Riding always helps me calm down."

"Ride on then," Elaine said. "Banjo, stay." The dog was starting to follow Kylie.

"He can come with me," Kylie said. "He seems to have some excess energy."

"He always has excess energy." Elaine chuckled. "If he's not too much trouble, I'd appreciate you running him around. See you soon."

Horse and rider set off, hooves crunching over the gravel. Banjo trotted in front, as if leading the way.

Elaine left the window open. "The attic could use some fresh air. The exhaust fan in that window there turns on automatically."

Hannah was glad for that. It was quite stuffy.

Elaine lifted the trunk's lid to reveal a jumble of clothing. "You can tell I was here. When I was a kid, I really didn't understand the value of antique clothing." She held up a pink dress with torn ruffles at the hem and neckline.

"That looks like it's from the thirties," Hannah said, evaluating the skirt length and cut of the dress. "Maybe it belonged to Clara."

"That's possible." Elaine removed several other pieces of clothing from the trunk: soft white blouses, a floral print dress with pockets, and a simple blue skirt. She handed each to Hannah, who folded them and stacked them on a nearby end table she'd dusted off.

Elaine made a sound of surprise. "I don't remember these." She held up a bundle of letters tied with a ribbon. Then she sat back to examine them more closely. "The return address is C. Barnes in California." She tugged at the bow.

A rush of excitement made Hannah's nerves tingle. "Clara went to California." A further realization set in. "Her parents must have known where she was. What a relief." Having a child disappear was a nightmare for any loving parent.

Elaine started to slide the top letter out of its envelope. Then she stopped. "I should finish looking through the trunk first. Here." She handed the letters to Hannah, who set them on the table, even as her fingers itched to open them.

Elaine started searching again. "Here we are," she cried, holding a manila envelope aloft.

She opened the metal tabs and showed Hannah the contents—tiny round black seeds. "These are definitely onion seeds." She peered at the outside of the envelope. "Blackberry Red, according to the writing on here. I can barely read it, it's so faded."

Hannah stared at the seeds, joy flooding her heart. "You found them. This is incredible. I wonder if they'll grow."

"Me too," Elaine said with a laugh. Her phone began to ring, and she had to sit back to pull it out of her pocket. "Uh-oh. Kylie. Hope there isn't a problem." She swiped to answer the call. "Hi, Kylie."

From where she sat, Hannah couldn't make out Kylie's words, but she heard her urgent tone.

As Elaine listened, her features twisted.

"What's going on?" Hannah whispered, alarmed.

Elaine put the phone on speaker. "Kylie, I know your reception isn't great out there, but can you repeat that?" she asked.

Kylie's voice cut in and out, but Hannah heard enough. "He fell into the well…the old house…"

Elaine met Hannah's gaze. "That's what I thought you said. We'll be right there."

Chapter Twenty-Four

Elaine and Hannah raced across the fields on Elaine's four-wheeler to the old house. As she bounced along, wind streaming through her hair, Hannah prayed that Banjo wasn't injured. And that they'd be able to get him out of the dry well. Otherwise, they'd have to call for help. Maybe Liam, as fire chief, would know what to do.

This was the second time Banjo had run off to the old house once occupied by Wilson Barnes. What kept drawing him there?

As she had on the previous trip to the spot, Elaine pulled up as close as possible. They would have to push through the undergrowth to reach the clearing where the house stood.

Elaine slung the coil of rope she'd retrieved from the barn over her shoulder. "Here," she said to Hannah, handing her a sling and carabiners. They began making their way through the bushes.

Hannah was right behind Elaine, so when Elaine stopped short, Hannah bumped into her.

She looked past her friend to see what had startled her.

Cooper Combs stood in the clearing, talking to Kylie, whose horse grazed nearby.

Elaine lurched into movement again. She gave Cooper a scowl as she dropped the rope and other items on the ground. "Where's Banjo?"

Kylie guided Elaine to a hole in the ground. "He crashed through this old well cover. I'm so sorry, Elaine." Tears trickled down the young woman's face. "He ran over here, and he wouldn't come when I called."

Elaine patted Kylie's shoulder. "It's not your fault. I'm glad you were here to let me know he was in trouble. He doesn't always listen." She scowled at Cooper again. "Like some people I know who like to trespass." Elaine lowered herself to the ground so she could peer into the well.

Hannah joined her friend. Banjo was about fifteen feet down.

Banjo barked in joy when he saw his owner. "He's okay," Hannah cried. "Oh, thank goodness, he's all right." She threw her arms around Elaine, who blinked back relieved tears.

"We'll get you out of there," Elaine promised the dog. She studied the coil of rope. "I've got about twenty feet here." She glanced at the closest tree. "Not quite enough."

"I'll go get more," Cooper said eagerly. "My barn is closer."

Elaine studied him for a tense moment. "Take my four-wheeler. And hurry." She turned to Kylie as Cooper trotted out of the clearing. "When did he show up?"

Kylie gnawed at her bottom lip then said, "He was in the house. He came out when I screamed." She took a breath. "I was riding in the field when Banjo took off this way. I called, but he wouldn't come. So I followed him." Her features twisted with distress. "I heard him yelp when he fell in. I almost fainted with relief when I saw that he was okay."

"I'm glad you were here," Elaine repeated. She frowned. "So Cooper was in the house?" When Kylie nodded in confirmation, Elaine huffed. "I've been meaning to put on a new lock."

"It doesn't matter now," Hannah reminded her friend. "You found the seeds."

Kylie clasped her hands together. "The Blackberry Red onion seeds?"

"Yes," Elaine said. "Don't mention it to anyone yet, okay?"

"I won't. Promise." Kylie crossed her heart. "Blake will be thrilled."

"I sure am," Elaine said. "I'm going to see if any will germinate as soon as I can."

Hannah heard the sound of the four-wheeler's approach and was glad for the warning. "What will you say to Cooper?"

Elaine set her jaw. "I'm not sure yet. Still thinking about it."

Cooper pushed through the bushes, carrying a coil of rope and other gear. "While I was gone, I figured out how to get him out. Who wants to venture into the well? It will be perfectly safe."

Kylie volunteered, so Cooper strapped her into a climbing harness, explaining that rock climbing was one of his hobbies. He also donned a harness and set up the ropes, one looping around a strong tree, so he could lower her into the well. To get out, she would climb the stacked stones with Cooper tightening the rope against a fall.

"You doing okay?" Cooper called as Kylie slowly descended into the well. His muscles tensed as he fed the rope through the belay device.

"I'm fine," Kylie called. "Hey, Banjo." Joyful barking greeted her.

Hannah and Elaine crowded close to observe the scene inside the well.

Kylie crouched to pat Banjo, gently feeling his legs and torso. "He seems fine. He isn't flinching away from me or anything, the way he probably would if he was in pain."

Elaine blew out a breath. "That's amazing. He must have landed just right."

Seeds of Suspicion

Kylie stomped on the dirt, releasing a puff of dust. "The soil is pretty soft down here."

Cooper fed a second rope into the well. "Kylie, slide Banjo into the sling at the end of this. He's small enough that I can pull him straight up."

"We're getting you out of here, boy," Kylie said as she slipped the sling around Banjo's body. She tugged on the rope. "He's ready."

Holding her breath, Hannah watched as Cooper slowly pulled the little dog up from the well floor. As if he sensed they were helping him, he remained perfectly still.

As soon as Elaine could reach the dog, she pulled him the rest of the way up and out. "Oh, Banjo." With fumbling, eager fingers, she removed the sling. He leaped into her arms and licked her face, making them all laugh.

"He's a real cutie," Cooper said, grinning. He kicked at the edge of the opening. "We should probably nail a cover over this right away so he doesn't fall in again."

Elaine threw him a sharp look, and Hannah could guess her thoughts. It was Cooper's fault that Banjo had been here in the first place. If he hadn't been trespassing, Banjo would never have come to the house to investigate.

With an annoyed shrug, Elaine turned back to the well. "Let's get Kylie out of there. She's going to be late for the pageant." The young women were meeting for preliminaries soon.

Hannah peered down the shaft again. Kylie wasn't in view. "Where is she? Kylie?"

Kylie emerged from the shadows near the well wall. "Right here." She held up a metal box. "Look what I found. Want me to bring it up?"

"Go ahead," Elaine said. "Can't imagine what could be in there."

Once Kylie was safely out of the well, Elaine took the box from her, handed it to Hannah, and then hugged the young woman. "Thank you for rescuing Banjo. Now you'd better scoot so you can get ready for tonight."

Kylie returned the hug. "Wish me luck." She crossed the clearing and mounted her horse. "Stay out of trouble, Banjo." She nodded goodbye to Hannah and Cooper then clucked to the mare. The pair made their way through the woods and were gone.

Cooper grinned as he coiled a rope. "All's well that ends well."

Elaine took a deep breath and blew it out slowly. Hannah could practically hear her friend counting to ten to keep her temper. Then Elaine said, "Listen, Cooper, I really appreciate your help today. You made the whole rescue effort a lot easier."

He lifted a brow. "I can hear a *but* coming, Elaine. What's up?"

Elaine folded her arms. "But you were in the house. This roaming around my property has to stop." A thin smile curved her lips. "I already found what you're looking for, so you might as well give it up."

Hannah sat on the grass, patting Banjo, the metal box on the grass beside them. She thought about leaving but decided it was best that Elaine have a witness to her conversation with Cooper. That way, Cooper couldn't falsely report it later, when it would be only Elaine's word against his. He'd been great with the rescue, but that didn't erase the less-wholesome things he'd done.

Cooper stopped looping rope. "What are you talking about?" The color had drained from his complexion, belying his feigned ignorance.

Elaine didn't fall for it. "You know full well what I'm talking about. The Blackberry Red onion. You've been growing it without telling me, haven't you?"

He glanced back and forth between Elaine and Hannah. "How... what...?"

Hannah chimed in. "I think you are. You're growing red onions on land that used to belong to Elaine's family. That's why you wanted the seeds, right? So you could patent them first, making it official after the fact."

Cooper's shoulders drooped, an admission of guilt in Hannah's eyes. He dropped the coil of rope onto the ground.

Elaine shook her head. "You know, I don't care that much about the onions. It's not like I want to make a fortune with them. It's the sneaking around I don't like. Going into my buildings. Hurting my son." She pulled out her phone. "I'm calling the sheriff."

The bushes behind the house rustled, and everyone froze. "Hey, boss," a voice called. "You find anything?" The undergrowth parted, and Seth stepped into the clearing. He threw up his hands, his eyes wide. "Whoa. I didn't know anyone else was here."

"Clearly," Elaine said. "So I take it you two are working together."

"And not just in the fields," Hannah added. She was disappointed in Seth. He'd been great about helping with the float and in general had seemed like a nice young man.

Cooper and Seth exchanged looks. In tandem, they took a step back.

"You can run, but you can't hide," Elaine said. "I can't let you get away with hurting Blake."

"I didn't mean to," Seth blurted. "Honest. I didn't want to hurt anyone."

"You did something to Blake?" Cooper's face reddened. "You shouldn't have gone that far. What were you thinking?"

"It was an accident," Seth said. "I left my hat in the barn, and I went to get it back."

"A blue UK ball cap?" Hannah guessed.

The young man nodded. "That's the one. Anyway, I thought Blake was either not home or out in the field. I didn't hear him, anyway. And then, there he was." He hung his head. "I panicked and threw a sack over his head and then pushed him into that old storage room. I was so worried he'd be able to identify me. I didn't realize he'd get hurt."

Cooper rested his hands on his hips. "I promise you, Elaine. That was not part of the plan. Seth was just supposed to look around for the seeds. Get in, get out."

"Which is still a crime," Elaine reminded him. "Trespassing with the intent to steal. I should probably press charges." She paused. "For ransacking the cabin too. Did you know about that, Cooper?"

Seth's expression was appalled. "I didn't ransack anything. Seriously, Elaine, I didn't even go in the cabin, except while Phoenix was living there."

Cooper folded his arms, his features settling into hard lines. Hannah guessed that the implications of getting caught were finally sinking in. He had a lot to lose. He faced possible jail time and fines as well as the loss of his reputation and standing in the community.

A terrible thought flashed through Hannah's mind. Were they safe out there alone with these two men?

Banjo, who had been sitting at Hannah's feet, must have sensed Hannah's fear, because he growled. A low, ominous sound, loud enough to remind people that he was here too, ready to defend his mistress and her friend.

"We're not going to hurt anyone, boy," Cooper assured him.

Elaine stepped a short distance away. She pulled her phone out of her pocket and tapped at the screen. "And I'm calling the sheriff right now."

While her friend placed the call, Hannah turned to Cooper. "By the way, we found an expensive pen in the staff cabin. Was it yours?" When he reluctantly nodded, she shook her head. It was all so unnecessary. "Elaine's one of the most reasonable people I know. Why didn't you just talk to her?"

Cooper shook his head. "I didn't think it would do any good. My family has always thought that her family resented selling us that property, so I thought she would just get mad. Frankly, I'm not sure how they came to sell us such a profitable piece of land to begin with, if that was where they grew those onions."

"We have a theory about that," Hannah replied. "We don't think that was where they grew the onions. It's more likely the Blackberry Red self-seeded on that property."

Understanding lit in his eyes. "Ah, that makes sense."

Elaine completed her call. "They're sending a deputy. Apparently, one is in the area, so it will only be a few minutes."

The men's expressions became even more despondent, but neither moved. They seemed resigned to their fate.

Hannah had one more burning question. "What about Timothy Buttonwood?" she asked. "Was he working with you too?"

"No, Timothy wasn't involved," Cooper said. "He was going to help me test the old seeds and compare them to what we're growing now to confirm they are Blackberry Reds. Then help me patent them and make my claim official."

"Why was he taking soil samples from my farm for an onion crop then?" Elaine was puzzled. "I don't get it."

Cooper sighed. "I was going to offer to buy more of your land if it was right for onions." He hesitated then said, "He actually did find a good piece near the land that used to belong to your family."

Elaine snorted. "That's not what he told me." She shook her head. "Unbelievable."

"I think he might have been embarrassed that we found out he wasn't teaching at the university anymore," Hannah said. "Still, it was petty of him to give you false information."

"It really was." Elaine gestured to the path. "So, are you two following us to my house? Or will you be waiting for the deputy to come find you?"

Cooper squared his shoulders. "I will take full responsibility for my actions. All of this was my fault." He slid a stern glance toward Seth. "Well, most of it."

Seth gulped before nodding. "I'm going too. I want to make things right."

Chapter Twenty-Five

"And they're gone," Elaine said when she returned to the kitchen after escorting Deputy Jacky Holt, Cooper, and Seth to the door. She leaned against the counter. "I'm so glad that's over."

The meeting with the deputy had gone as well as could be expected, considering the painful nature of the conversation. As promised, Cooper and Seth had freely confessed their crimes. Elaine had decided not to press charges but suggested the men do community service as a restitution of sorts. One task had been decided upon, at Jacky's suggestion. The Blackberry Valley Festival cleanup crew was short a couple of members. Cooper and Seth would be filling in.

"It's such a relief," Hannah said. "No more prowlers." She pointed to the island, where the metal box Kylie had found waited beside the envelope of seeds and the packet of letters. "Mind if I look inside?"

"Feel free," Elaine said, glancing at the clock. "We'd better keep an eye on the time, though."

"This won't take long." Hannah opened the lid. Only a few objects were inside.

Elaine, who had given in to curiosity, reached into the box and pulled out a narrow paper band. "This looks like what you put around money."

"And this box is the right size to be a cashbox." Hannah inhaled sharply. "Maybe this is the box that was stolen from the train station."

Elaine stared at her with wide eyes. "And we found it in the old well near the house where Wilson Barnes lived. Do you suppose—"

"That he was guilty after all?" Hannah finished for her. "I don't want to believe that."

Hannah picked up what looked like a metal pin and turned it over. It was embossed with *L&N Stationmaster*. She handed it to Elaine. "I wonder if this belonged to Rodney."

Elaine examined both sides of the badge. "I bet it did. Why would Wilson have it?"

"I have no idea." Hannah removed the last item from the box—a once-white envelope, now yellowed with age. "I wonder what's in here."

She glanced at Elaine, who nodded eagerly. Inside was a letter, signed by Rodney Combs.

Ellisville, Kentucky
August 16, 1932

Ann Ellis lived in a yellow stucco mansion with tall white columns and black shutters. Mabel and Clara stared at the place in amazement as Evelyn led them up the walk to the front door.

Evelyn gave them a reassuring smile as she pressed the bell. "Don't worry. Ann's one of the girls. She's as down to earth as they come."

Her assessment was immediately verified when a young woman with platinum-blond hair answered the door. "Evie," she said with a huge smile, "it's good to see you." She hugged Evelyn, who then made introductions. "It's so nice to meet you. Please come in."

Mabel instantly liked Ann Ellis. What a fool Rodney Combs had been to lose her. This impression was only reinforced as their hostess ushered them through the house, making them feel right at home. She settled them on a screened-in porch and then brought out a pitcher of sweet tea.

"I understand you've been graced with Rodney Combs's presence in Blackberry Valley," Ann said dryly. "How's that going?"

Mabel and Clara burst out laughing. "Well," Mabel said, her tone just as wry, "he's been trying to court Clara, and now it looks like he's trying to have her beau put in jail."

Ann's eyes widened with shock. "He's worse than ever then. I'm sorry."

"Not your fault," Evelyn said. "He's a bad one, plain and simple."

"He used to hide it well, at least," Ann said. "I can't believe I was taken in by him. At the time, I was bowled over by his good looks and smooth talk. It didn't help that Daddy thought the world of him."

Clara nodded. "Mine does too. Come to think of it, he's pretty smart to butter up the men of influence first. Then any objection we have seems silly. Once our parents like him, it makes no sense to them why we don't want to step out with him."

"Exactly." Ann lifted her glass. "A toast to those who can see through Rodney Combs."

The women clinked glasses.

"Tell us why your engagement ended," Clara said. "If you don't mind talking about it."

"Not in the least." Ann refilled their glasses before going on. "You know about the burglary, right?" They all nodded. Ann lowered her voice, even though they were alone in the room. "It wasn't the first one under Rodney's watch."

"There was another one here in Ellisville?" Mabel asked in shock.

Ann shook her head. "No, at his previous post in another small town. Someone stole a valuable shipment of tools destined for the coal mines. The culprit was never caught."

Each theft was different, Mabel mused. That would make it more difficult for officials to realize that the same man might be behind them all. "What made you suspect Rodney?"

Ann pursed her lips. Then she said, "The way he was always buying me gifts. And he bought a brand-new roadster right after Mrs. Hardcastle's jewelry went missing." She frowned. "I overheard him talking to a really dreadful man one day, down at the station. He didn't see me standing there, and something made me wait to approach him. The other man said something about Rodney owing him, and Rodney handed over a fistful of money."

"Was the man dressed like a traveler?" Mabel asked.

Ann shook her head. "No, he wore a suit. He wasn't a gentleman though. He used coarse language and mannerisms." She described him for them. Except for the attire, he sounded like the man Mabel had seen in Blackberry Valley.

"After that, Rodney started talking about moving on to a new position. I made it plain that I wasn't going anywhere." Ann folded her arms over her chest. "I broke the engagement and gave him back the ring. Within a couple of months, he took the position in Blackberry Valley."

Ann's story confirmed Mabel's doubts about Rodney Combs. To be fair, there was no evidence that Rodney was involved in the robberies. His relationship with the mysterious man was troubling though. Why would Rodney give him money? And why was the man following Rodney from town to town?

On the train back to Blackberry Valley, Mabel and Clara discussed the situation at length. "Even if I wasn't in love with Wilson, I wouldn't consider Rodney as a suitor," Clara confided. "He's too flashy and a social climber."

"Not to mention that strange man," Mabel said. "If he's a friend, why didn't Rodney introduce us to him?"

"A very good point," Clara said. "I'll bring it up when I talk to my parents."

Mabel didn't like the idea that Clara had to present arguments when it came to rejecting or accepting a suitor. "Are they going to pressure you anyway?"

Clara's shoulders curled inward. "I don't know. It's possible. Or I might be pressuring myself. Now that I know they're struggling. I don't want to be the reason we lose the farm."

Mabel shook her head. "You're not responsible for that, Clara. Almost everyone is having a hard time right now. It's up to your father and brother to make decisions. Not marry you off like a medieval maiden."

"Medieval maiden?" Clara cracked a smile. "Now there's an image. One thing's for sure—Rodney is *not* my knight in shining armor."

The girls laughed at the idea of Rodney in a suit of armor, riding a white steed to the King Farm to ask for Clara's hand in marriage.

Changing the subject, Clara said, "Your cousin is nice. It was wonderful to meet her."

"Yes, Evelyn is a lot of fun." Mabel reflected on the meeting. "I liked Ann too. I'm glad she didn't marry Rodney."

"Although if she had, and they'd moved to Blackberry Valley, she would be our friend. I'm sure of it."

"Me too. She's a peach. But I wouldn't condemn her to a life with Rodney for our benefit," Mabel said, wrinkling her nose.

The miles clicked by as the train rolled toward Blackberry Valley. Mabel's thoughts turned to what lay ahead. Would Clara's parents accept her love for Wilson? And what about the money that had disappeared from the train station? Who had stolen it? Was it the traveler they'd seen with a burlap sack?

"Come over for dinner," Clara said when they disembarked at Blackberry Valley. "We can try on our dresses for the pageant."

"I'm still working on mine," Mabel said. "I have beading to finish."

"We'll stop by your house and get it," Clara suggested. "And tell your mother that you're coming home with me."

"That sounds good."

They set off in Clara's family Ford, which they'd left at the train station. The Kings owned two vehicles—this sedan and the farm truck. Mabel's family only had one. Her father still used a horse to pull wagons and carts. At least they had a tractor now. Mabel still remembered when her father had used a horse to plow the fields before planting.

When they reached her house, Mabel ran in, grabbed her dress, and explained her plans to her mother.

"Did you learn anything new in Ellisville?" Mama asked.

"We did." Mabel pecked her mother on the cheek. "I'll tell you all about it when I come home. One thing I can tell you now though. Clara is definitely not going to marry Rodney."

Her mother nodded in satisfaction. "I'm so glad. She deserves better."

"She sure does." With that, Mabel flew out the door and jumped back into the Ford.

At the King Farm, they carried their handbags and Mabel's dress into the house. "Let's put your dress in my room, and then we'll go see Wilson." Clara's eyes sparkled, and there was a definite lilt in her voice when she said Wilson's name.

Clara's mother wasn't in the house, and Mabel was glad to avoid her a little longer. She expected that

Seeds of Suspicion

Mrs. King would grill them about their visit to Ellisville.

The young women walked down the lane in search of Wilson. He wasn't working on the tractor in the barn or bent over the vegetables in the fields. In the distance, they could see Mr. King and Clara's brother stacking hay bales on a horse-drawn wagon.

"Maybe he's at the farmhands' house," Clara said. "Want to go over there?"

"Sure." Mabel didn't mind stretching her legs after the train ride.

The air was intensely hot, the sun oppressive. Mabel was glad when they reached the woods, where the shade was marginally cooler.

As they approached the clearing where the house stood, a shout rang out.

Clara turned to Mabel, her eyes wide. "That's Wilson." She broke into a run.

In the clearing, Wilson grappled with another man. With a jolt of shock, Mabel recognized the traveler they'd seen before.

On the grass nearby lay a metal box. Mabel's blood ran cold. Was that the missing cashbox from the train station? If so, why was it here, where Wilson was staying?

"You won't get away with this," Wilson said. He had finally managed to wrestle the other man to the ground. He sat on his chest, pinning his wrists.

"Clara, can you get me the clothesline?" Wilson called. Someone had strung a line between the corner of the house and a tree.

Mabel hurried to help Clara pull down the line. Once they managed to untie it, Clara rushed it to Wilson.

Wilson tied the man's wrists and ankles with the line. "Just keeping you like this until we get help." His face when he looked up at Mabel and Clara was full of distress. "I found him here at the house. He was planting evidence, I figure."

"This?" Mabel went over to the box. She flipped it open. "There's nothing here. Only some money bands." She gestured to the man lying on the grass. "We saw him walking along the tracks with a burlap bag the day of the robbery."

"Hear that?" Wilson said to the man. "We have witnesses. You aren't going to pin this on me."

Clara sank down onto the grass. "They must have planned this together. Rodney wanted you to be blamed." She put a hand to her mouth. "I can't even imagine such a thing."

Mabel couldn't either. She was outraged. "You'd better tell the sheriff the truth," she told the man. "We don't like crooks in Blackberry Valley."

Rustling in the woods announced the arrival of someone else. Mabel, Wilson, and Clara froze, waiting to see who it was.

Rodney stepped out of the woods, his gaze fastening on Clara then Wilson. "I thought I might find you here," he said to Clara. He sneered. "Like attracts like."

Clara's chin went up. "I'm not even going to dignify that with a response." She moved aside, gesturing to the man on the ground. "Maybe you can tell us what your friend is doing here."

Rodney took a step back. "Erlon? Why are you here?" His gaze skittered around the clearing, landing on the box and then dancing away.

Wilson crossed his arms. "You mean you didn't send him?" He snorted. "Tell me another. You tried to frame me so you can have Clara all to yourself." He stepped forward until he was face-to-face with Rodney. "I'm not a violent man, but you're really testing that. You and your henchman here will soon be under arrest."

"I was trying to help you, Rodney," Erlon said from the ground. "You said you wanted to marry this dame. Now the jig's up."

"What is he to you, Rodney?" Clara asked. "How do you know someone like him? I don't understand."

Several expressions flashed across Rodney's face as he backed away from Wilson. "I know you won't believe me." He shrugged his shoulders to straighten his clothing. "Erlon is my stepbrother. I've been trying for years to get him on the straight and narrow."

Erlon laughed. "Good luck. I learned from the best. Dear old Dad."

Rodney moved to stand over his brother. "I suffered too. But I found a way out, and I'm trying to make something of myself. You could do the same."

Erlon turned his head away. "Nah. It's too late for me."

"It's never too late," Mabel burst out, her heart wrung by the sorrow of a man's soul forever lost. "Maybe you don't have to go to jail. Make restitution and earn a second chance."

Erlon's eyes lit with hope. "Is there a way to do that? I promised Mama I would keep trying."

"Maybe so," Wilson said. "But if we help you stay out of jail, part of the deal is that I'm cleared." He put an arm around Clara. "I want to start my marriage with a clean slate, as I deserve."

"Done." Rodney's nod was decisive, and he looked at Erlon, who also nodded. "What are you thinking?"

"It'll cost you, Combs," Wilson said. "Then it will be up to Erlon. Think you can get on the right path, fella?" he asked the prone man. "This is a second chance, and those don't come along that often in a lifetime."

Erlon nodded again. "Yes, please. I'll try for Mama, Rodney. Okay?"

"It's a start," Rodney said. He reached for Wilson's hand and shook it. "Thank you."

Chapter Twenty-Six

"This is incredible," Elaine said, folding Rodney's letter and sliding it back into the envelope. "He was trying to help his stepbrother. Only to have him get in trouble again and again."

"What a heartbreaking situation," Hannah said. "Rodney was using his own money to pay for what was stolen." She'd been impressed to read that in his confession letter. Regarding the jewelry theft, he'd tracked some pieces to a pawn shop and given the sheriff an anonymous tip. Those had been returned to Mrs. Hardcastle.

Elaine picked up one of Clara's letters from the attic. She and Hannah had given them a quick read-through, trying to glean details that filled out the story. Mabel's diary had provided quite a bit of background information, but she hadn't written down this part of the tale. Hannah didn't blame her. Rodney's family troubles were his own, not hers.

"Clara told her mother where the metal box was, in case it was needed. Wilson threw it in the dry well when they left. What did she say again?" She scanned the page. "Ah, here it is. 'Wilson wanted to put the past behind him. The fact that he was ever a burglary suspect still hurts, I suspect, although he says he's forgiven everyone. That being said, we had no choice but to leave. You know how small towns are, Mama. Once a man's reputation is tarnished, he can't often recover. And of course I had to go with him. I belong with him.'" Elaine paused, swallowing hard. "Sorry. This part chokes me up, even though this is the second time I'm reading it."

"It's okay," Hannah said, her eyes stinging. "It got to me too."

After a moment, Elaine went on. "'I've forgiven you, Mama, and Daddy too. I know that you were only trying to do your best by me, in your own way. Wilson is a wonderful husband, and we're doing very well for ourselves. He's a foreman on a large farm, where his skills are valued. We're saving up to buy a piece of land to start our own operation. Right now, Wilson is learning, studying all the options. Almost everything grows in California, so there are lots of choices.'"

Phoenix was descended from Clara and Wilson, so they had succeeded. As if summoned by her thought, her phone chimed with a message. A glance revealed that Phoenix had sent a copy of the marriage certificate. Hannah opened the image, using her fingers to enlarge it. "Elaine, you'll want to see this. It's Clara and Wilson's marriage certificate."

Elaine took the phone. "Where did you get it?"

"Phoenix." Hannah's voice rose with excitement. "Elaine, he's descended from Wilson and Clara." As Elaine continued to study the document, Hannah relayed the conversation she'd had with the young man.

"Wow." Elaine handed Hannah the phone. "Can you forward that to me? I guess I'd better reach out to Phoenix, since he's family and all." Her stunned expression gave way to concern. "Hopefully he'll forgive me for losing my temper."

"Hey, it happens." Hannah sent the image to Elaine's phone. "I think he'll be glad to have relatives here. He's far from home. By the way, Wilson and Clara did get their farm. Phoenix told me about it."

"I can't wait to hear more. And to connect with his parents. They're my cousins too." Elaine glanced at the clock. "I'd better go get ready. And you have judging duty tonight."

With so many questions answered at long last, Hannah was actually grateful for the reminder. Perhaps she would be able to focus on enjoying the Onion Queen contest now.

The stage area for the pageant buzzed with excitement. Hannah wove her way through the crowd, trying to reach the cluster of judges standing near their table.

Lacy spotted her and waved. "You made it." She gave Hannah a hug then pulled back to take in her appearance. "You look lovely."

"Thanks," Hannah said, returning the once-over. "So do you."

Lacy wore a forest-green wrap dress with a bolero jacket and matching shoes. She fluffed out her skirt. "Quite a change from muck boots and overalls, isn't it?"

"You clean up nice," Hannah joked. She glanced around the crowd, spotting people she knew. Including Timothy J. Buttonwood, former professor at the University of Virginia. *Uh-oh.* She'd caught his eye. And he was coming over.

"Hannah," he said with great enthusiasm. "Not helming your restaurant tonight?"

Lacy's eyes went wide, and she ducked away, leaving Hannah to speak to Timothy. Hannah gestured toward the stage. "I'm judging the Blackberry Queen contest, and then I'll be heading back to the Hot Spot."

Timothy leaned closer, looming over her. "I heard Elaine found the seeds. That's fabulous. If she needs help with the patent process, I'm here for her."

Hannah wasn't sure how to respond. Suggesting he approach Elaine to make his offer might not be welcomed by her friend. So she merely said, "That's great to know. It's a very interesting topic."

"It is." Timothy drew a deep breath, appearing about to launch into a lecture.

Before he could get out a single word, Hannah saw Blake coming across the grass, Banjo running ahead on his leash. "Excuse me," she told the professor. "I need to speak to someone."

When the duo reached Hannah, she bent to pat Banjo, who jumped and yipped with joy. "He seems good as new after his big adventure."

Blake tilted his head, studying the dog with a smile. "He's certainly lively. Pretty excited about being here with all these people." His face sobered. "Mom and Kylie filled me in. I'm so glad Kylie was there when he fell into the well. She blames herself, and I keep telling her it's not her fault. Banjo likes to roam. We're going to have to dog-proof the farm."

Hannah laughed at the idea, wondering if such a thing was possible. "He also likes to say hello to people," she said. "Your mom and I think he went to the house because Cooper was there."

"That guy." Blake shook his head. "Hopefully the prowling is at an end, now that Mom's found the famous Blackberry Red onion seeds. Who'd have thought they'd be such a hot commodity?"

Marshall Fredericks stood nearby with the television film crew for the pageant. He must have caught what Blake said about the seeds, because he approached them and said, "If I'd known all the problems my little article would cause, I never would have written it. I heard you had trouble at the farm?"

"We did, but it's over now," Blake said.

"Your article did a lot of good too," Hannah added. "I understand this is the best year the festival has had. Plus, you brought a lot of attention to Blackberry Valley in general. All the businesses here are getting a big boost, including my restaurant. I'm thrilled to be featured on the television show." She was excited to see the segments about the Hot Spot and the cook-off. As long as the recipe issue with Corrie was worked out by then. A sour taste filled her mouth. That might take a miracle.

"So is Mom," Blake said. "And we're getting calls every day asking about produce. We'll have to expand next year."

"Phew," Marshall said, putting a hand to his forehead. "I'm so glad it's all working out."

There was more to tell the reporter, namely that they'd solved the mystery of the last Onion Queen. But Hannah decided to keep that to herself for now. It was Elaine's story to tell, not hers, like Clara's story hadn't been Mabel's to share.

Lacy came forward and touched Hannah's arm. "Sorry to interrupt, but we're about to get started."

Hannah glanced toward the stage, where Kylie and the other contestants waited. She couldn't help but think of Mabel and Clara and the other young women of 1932. Blackberry Valley certainly had a tradition of turning out fine young citizens. In her eyes, every single contestant tonight was a winner.

After Kylie was crowned Blackberry Queen, Hannah was putting her belongings on her kitchen counter when her phone rang. Glancing at the screen, the name she saw there made her pulse lurch in surprise.

Corrie Rice. The last time they'd spoken, Corrie had hung up on her. It hadn't been a pleasant experience, and Hannah wasn't eager to talk to her former colleague again.

The phone continued to ring. With a silent prayer, Hannah accepted the call. "Hello?"

Silence met her greeting. Maybe Corrie hadn't meant to call her. Maybe she'd hit Hannah's number by accident.

Hannah was about to hang up when she heard a tentative voice. "Hannah? It's Corrie."

"Hi, Corrie." Hannah kept her tone brisk. "What's up?"

"I'm sorry."

Hannah was silent. Had she heard correctly? Had Corrie actually apologized?

"Don't hang up," Corrie said in a rush. "Hannah, I mean it. I'm sorry I hung up on you last time. And I'm sorry I used your recipe without giving you the credit."

Hannah was amazed at this turn of events. *Thank you,* she said silently. Her prayer had been answered. Corrie had apologized for presenting the recipe as her own. Not an easy admission for someone as proud as Corrie. For anyone, actually.

"I appreciate your apology," Hannah said graciously. "Are you going to change the information on your website?"

"Already done. Check out the video, and you'll see. I added it in the caption. If that's not enough, I'll take the whole thing down."

Now that Hannah had gotten an apology and acknowledgment, she was ready to say all right and let it go. Instead, she made herself pause. "Let me have a chance to look at it, and I can let you know."

"Please do. I'll send you the link right now."

Hannah's phone pinged, and she opened the link. *Blackberry Burrata Pizza, created by Hannah Prentiss, owner of the Hot Spot.*

Back on the call, she said, "You mentioned my restaurant? That's awesome. Thank you."

"Not a problem." Corrie's voice was gruff. "Maybe I'll see you there. I checked out your website, and it looks great. I might be taking a road trip around the country, checking out local food."

"Let me know, and we'll comp you a meal," Hannah offered. "I'm having a great time finding and using local ingredients. There's an amazing amount of variety and quality around Blackberry Valley."

"And you grew up there, right? It must be nice to be home."

Hannah felt a smile break across her face. "You know what, Corrie? It really is."

From the Author

Dear Reader,

Welcome to this installment of the Mysteries of Blackberry Valley! The month is August, and locally grown vegetables and fruit are abundant. One of my favorite summer activities is browsing farmers markets for locally grown produce. Ripe red tomatoes picked moments ago. Crisp heads of lettuce, kale, and cabbage. Cucumbers and green beans. Varieties that are fresh, tasty, delicious—and often part of our heritage.

In recent years, I've learned about heirloom vegetables and decided to feature one, the fictional Blackberry Red onion, in this book. Heirloom varieties have been passed down from generation to generation, some hundreds of years old. Over time, certain strains and hybrid vegetables came to dominate commercial agriculture. These popular varieties are more reliable, have a long shelf-life, and are disease-resistant.

However, heirlooms are delightfully varied in appearance and taste. Examples include rattlesnake pole beans, "white wonder" cucumbers, and Cherokee purple tomatoes. Seeds for many heirlooms are now available, and I've made a point to buy their seeds for my own garden in addition to seeking them out at farmers markets. Have you tried heirloom vegetables? If not, check them out.

Signed,
Elizabeth Penney

About the Author

Elizabeth Penney is the Mary Higgins Clark-nominated author of more than three dozen mysteries, women's fiction, and romantic suspense novels.

Raised in Maine, Elizabeth spent her early years in England and France. She now lives in the mountains of New Hampshire, where she enjoys walking in the woods, kayaking on quiet ponds, trying new recipes, and feeding family and friends. Oh, and trying to grow things in the frozen North.

The Hot Spotlight

The story of the Blackberry Red onion was inspired by a piece of real history, the Wethersfield red onion. Wethersfield, Connecticut, was an early English settlement on the Connecticut River, and soon became a commercial hub. From the 1700s through the early 1900s, the Wethersfield red onion was one of the town's most productive crops, with over five million pounds exported annually. Onions were even used in lieu of cash by some Wethersfield residents, and a local church paid its taxes in that currency as well.

Although Wethersfield onions are interesting due to their role in early trade, the myth of the Onion Maidens really cemented the town's reputation. In the somewhat inaccurate and opinionated *General History of Connecticut*, published in 1780, Samuel Peters wrote that the Onion Maidens worked the fields for silk dresses. He went on to say that the maidens were ridiculed by women from other towns. A 1968 children's book, *Onion Maidens*, by A. K. Roche, repackaged the myth for a new and young audience.

The actual onion boom is long over, but Wethersfield businesses and organizations still feature an onion theme, including on the town's welcome sign. Despite the inaccuracy of Peters's portrayal of the Onion Maidens, the story intrigues visitors to this day.

From the Hot Spot Kitchen

HANNAH'S BLACKBERRY BURRATA PIZZA

When Hannah brainstormed a recipe for the chef cook-off, she wanted something different yet delicious. Pizza topped with ripe blackberries and creamy burrata cheese proved to be a winning entry. You can either use premade pizza dough or make your own 12-inch crust.

Ingredients:

Quick pizza dough:

- 1 packet or 2¼ teaspoons yeast
- 1½ teaspoon sugar
- ¾ cup warm water, 110–115 degrees
- 2 tablespoons olive oil
- ¾ teaspoon salt
- 2¼ cups all-purpose flour

Pizza toppings:

- 2 cups fresh blackberries
- 1 cup shredded mozzarella cheese
- 1 cup parmesan cheese
- 1 burrata ball
- Fresh basil leaves for garnish

Directions:

Mix yeast and sugar with warm water in large bowl and allow to bloom for ten minutes. Add oil and salt. Add flour until dough comes away from bowl. Knead gently, adding more flour as needed until dough is elastic, still soft but doesn't stick to your fingers. Place in oiled bowl and set to rise for half an hour.

Preheat oven to 450 degrees.

Press dough in oiled 12-inch pizza pan until thin and uniform. Brush with olive oil. Mash ½ cup blackberries in bowl until completely broken. Brush mashed blackberries on crust, distributing evenly.

Sprinkle mozzarella and parmesan cheese on pizza, followed by remaining blackberries. Cook until bubbling and browned, about 10 to 15 minutes. Remove from oven, add torn basil leaves, and place burrata ball in center of pizza. Slice and serve.

Read on for a sneak peek of another exciting book in the *Mysteries of Blackberry Valley* series!

A Likely Story

BY ROSEANNA M. WHITE

Hannah Prentiss pushed through one of the swinging doors separating the kitchen from the restaurant floor, a tray of food in her hands for table twelve. The dinner rush was just getting started, and Raquel had called in sick, so Hannah had left her orders and spreadsheets and happily covered for her.

One of her favorite parts of running her restaurant was moments like this. Moments when she got to interact with the crowds of hungry neighbors. When she saw the expressions of appreciation as they took their first bites or watched them debate over the menu offerings, unable to decide which dish tempted them most today.

She slid the plates of burgers and hand-cut chips onto the table in front of Alice Tyler and her twentysomething granddaughter, Jules, with a smile. "Here you go, ladies. Can I get you anything else?"

Before the Tylers could answer, the door swung open. Ordinarily that wouldn't have stolen anyone's attention in the bustling restaurant, but Neil Minyard didn't just come in with the breeze. He charged inside like a force of nature, holding up a cardboard box as if it contained the secrets of the universe. "The books are here!"

Ordinarily, *that* wouldn't have caused much of a ruckus either. No one else in town was ever quite as excited about books as her best friend's husband. Neil regularly went incommunicado when he got lost in the pages of a book in his favorite chair in his bookstore, Legend & Key.

This time, however, he might as well have been decked out like Santa in a room full of preschoolers. Shouts of pleasure arose, and every local at her tables stood, following Neil as he paraded through the dining room to an empty table at the back. Hannah wondered if tonight's packed crowd had as much to do with Neil as with the Hot Spot's new autumn menu items. Had he told everyone to come there for their book deliveries rather than his own shop?

Alice patted Jules's hand. "Go get ours, will you, sweet pea?"

Hannah settled a hand on Jules's shoulder. "I'll bring it over. I have to get mine anyway. One or two?"

"Just the one," Alice said. "We'll share it. Sounds like this B.B. Smith fellow is already raking it in. He doesn't need that much of our help."

Hannah figured she was right about that. She had no idea how many sales *Blackberry Secrets* had yet—only that it was enjoying its second week sitting on several national bestseller lists in one of the top spots. She didn't know what that meant for the author, whoever he or she was.

She moved toward the line of locals who had swarmed Neil. Taking her spot at the back of the line put her near a table of unfamiliar faces. They must have found her restaurant from the highway or online, because they frowned in clear confusion.

"Are we missing something?" one of them asked her, the lovely gray-haired woman craning around Hannah to try to see what was going on.

Neil brandished a box cutter as if it were a legendary sword and attacked the packing tape.

Hannah chuckled at his antics. "There's a historical novel that released a couple weeks ago and has hit the bestseller lists—and it's set right here in Blackberry Valley, apparently. Neil, the bookstore owner acting like that tape is a monster putting up a fight, gave us all a discount if we put in a bulk order."

The woman's companion, a man who looked enough like her that he must be her brother, wore an expression of epiphany. "*Blackberry Secrets*? No kidding. I just downloaded the e-book. Haven't read it yet though. I knew it was set somewhere in the South, but didn't realize we'd stopped in the exact location. That's a fun coincidence."

"We're all pretty excited to read it." Hannah, her empty tray tucked under her arm, watched as Neil pulled the topmost copies out of the box. "Though I didn't realize he'd be hand-delivering them here." She supposed it made sense, though, for him to bring a box to the Hot Spot, where quite a few of their mutual patrons would be this time of day.

Two of her Wednesday regulars, Jim and John Comstock—identical twins in their fifties who styled themselves so differently that no one had any trouble telling them apart—were at the front of the line and took the first two copies from Neil's hands.

Hannah pressed her lips together, waiting for commentary. She didn't know what form it would take, but those two always had something to say about everything.

John shook his head, huffing out a breath. "This cover's atrocious. If that's an actual photo from anywhere in Blackberry Valley, then I'm a swimsuit model."

A ripple of laughter rang out at the idea.

Jim, of course, couldn't be seen agreeing in public with his brother. "Oh, don't be such a snob. Book covers don't have to be perfectly accurate. They take artistic license to create additional appeal. Personally, I like it. Nice colors, real dramatic. And I love this font. I think I have this one. It's called—"

"Nobody cares what the font is named," John interrupted. But he was grinning. "Only you try to identify every font you see on every cover or billboard or menu."

Jim shot a smile over the crowd between them, straight at Hannah. "Nice use of both serif and sans serif on your menus, by the way. Perfect pairing."

Hannah grinned. "Thanks. I hired this great local graphics designer to help me."

Jim winked—he'd pretty much begged her to let him do her menu design, claiming that if she hired it out to a bigger firm, he'd boycott the Hot Spot out of principle—and flipped the book over to read the back cover.

Neil had his tablet out and must have pulled up a list of purchasers, because he made a few taps and then looked to the next person in line and made another. The line moved quickly, though the neighbors lingered at the counter with their books rather than returning to their seats. Hannah didn't mind, even if it meant she had to nudge Liam Berthold out of the way as she reached the counter.

He shot her a warm smile and granted her only a couple inches. To be fair, it was all the space he could make without bowling over Pastor Bob. "Now, now," he teased. "No need to get pushy. There are enough books for everyone. Can I have your phone real quick?"

Knowing he was about to change his contact again, as he did frequently when he saw her, she handed it over.

He tapped quickly then handed it back.

"Ah, yes. 'The Obstacle.' Because you were in my way just now."

She had to grin.

"I try to keep it fresh and interesting."

Neil looked up, smiling when he saw her. "Hey, Hannah. Didn't figure you'd mind if I did some delivering here. Jim mentioned when I saw him earlier that they'd be here for dinner, so I seized the inspiration."

"Of course not." She hooked a thumb over her shoulder. "I told Alice I'd get hers too."

"Cool." He made a couple notes on his tablet and handed her two copies. "Lacy's coming in for dessert later. She said something about forgetting what you look like."

Hannah laughed and ran her fingers over the smooth matte finish of the cover, loving the way the glossy embossed title felt in contrast. "It hasn't been *that* long. I saw her at church a few days ago."

"According to her, that doesn't count." He peered into the box, presumably counting the books left, cross-checked his list, and nodded. "She's worried you're overworking yourself. And she says your goat nieces and nephews will forget you if you don't come out for another visit soon."

Hannah had to laugh. She'd been meaning to make it back out to her best friend's farm for a week...or two. Time simply hadn't allowed it. "She's one to talk. No one who gets up at four thirty in the morning gets to lecture anyone else about working too hard."

Neil grinned, hefting his box again. "She goes to bed early to make up for it though. Not your MO, from what I hear."

Given that the restaurant didn't close until ten, and then there was cleanup and closing, he had a point. Though rather than answer, she slid the tray onto the counter to be used again and waved the books as a farewell. "Thanks, Neil."

"Take the time to read it," he called after her as she wove her way back toward Alice. "It'll do you good."

She smiled. According to him, most problems could be solved with a good book and a few quiet hours. And it wasn't that Hannah disagreed, exactly. She loved a nice novel as much as the next person. It was just that she spent so much time staring at her computer when she wasn't on the restaurant floor schmoozing customers and smiling at neighbors, that the thought of opening a book made her eyes ache in protest some days. Not to mention that the busier the restaurant got, the less she could justify spending her free time on a book, as much as she loved them.

But she'd make an exception for *Blackberry Secrets*. She'd seen a few reviews in some of the social media groups she belonged to in the last week that made it sound like exactly the sort of escape she'd enjoy. A historical tale of a simpler time, full of mystery, suspense, and a touch of romance. And she was more than a little curious as to how the author portrayed their little town.

Probably inaccurately. That was the usual complaint, right? Unless the author had spent a lot of time here, they would get things wrong—and according to town gossip, nobody knew anyone whose name could be shortened to B.B. Smith. Hannah prepped herself to forgive any errors. But as she handed Alice her copy with a smile, the pinch of the woman's lips made her wonder if everyone else in town would choose a different tack.

"Thanks." Alice took the book, frowning as she looked it over. "All that money for this? It's not even a hardcover."

"Neil gave us a great discount, Nan," Jules said. "I couldn't find it online for less. That's just what new books cost these days. Paper's expensive."

Alice harrumphed.

Jules grinned. "Of course, if you'd let me get you an e-reader—"

"I don't need any more electronic doodads to figure out. I'd go back to my old flip phone if you'd let me. These smart ones just make me feel stupid."

"But you can adjust the size of the type on an e-reader. I think you'd like that, since you talk about how everyone prints their text too small these days."

"I like paper books." Alice set the book down and returned to her burger. She shot Hannah a glance that was surprisingly warm, given her complaints. "And I *am* looking forward to this one. I hope you enjoy it too, Hannah. I was thinking maybe we should have a book club on it in a couple weeks, after everyone's read it. What do you think? Maybe have it here, so we can have refreshments? We could do it before you open. Evangeline won't let us have so much as coffee in her new meeting rooms in the library."

"I'd love to have a book club here. If you end up organizing one, let me know the date and I'll reserve a few tables." Hannah smiled at each of the women, sending a wink toward Jules for her fruitless technology crusade, and then moved off.

Another order was up in the window, but it was Dylan's, so Hannah ducked into her office to put the book away. Though the moment she stepped inside, the relative quiet wrapped around her. Rather than rush back out, she paused long enough to take a deep breath.

She ran her fingertips over the cover again. And then she flipped through the pages. Not to read it yet, but to glance at the stylized chapter starts, see the pretty section dividers, and smile when familiar names jumped out at her.

Familiar roads. Familiar landmarks. Just a few seconds of flipping showed countless examples of those.

Then another familiar name caught her eye, and she halted the fan of her pages to see if her vision had deceived her.

Nope. Right there, on page 179. First line of the third paragraph.

Max knocked on the kitchen door of the Prentiss house, waiting for Hannah Jane to let him in. His eyes tracked to the cookie jar, full as always. He wondered how many cookies were in it today. Hannah Jane would know, down to the last crumb, and she looked at him as if he'd forgotten her warning about it from last time and might try to steal one.

They were probably dry and tasteless anyway.

Hannah blinked. It wasn't *her*—she knew that. Merely a fictional coincidence, no doubt. If the author had researched local names,

Prentiss would have come up. And Hannah was a relatively common first name. Not to mention that her own middle name was Marie, not Jane.

Even so, she couldn't help the irrational surge of defensiveness. "My cookies are delicious, thank you very much." Then she had to laugh at herself.

With a shake of her head, Hannah set *Blackberry Secrets* on her desk and headed back out to the dining area. Everyone else in town might be chattering about the book all evening, even before anyone had a chance to read it, but Hannah had work to do. People to feed, food to order, and a best friend to placate. She didn't have time to pore over more pages and figure out what role her name played in that story.

Even so, with her curiosity piqued, it promised to be a long, long night. And for once, she didn't intend to let a little thing like exhaustion keep her from reading before she went to bed.

Loved *Mysteries of Blackberry Valley?*
Check out some other Guideposts mystery series!

Whistle Stop Café Mysteries

Join best friends Debbie Albright and Janet Shaw as they step out in faith to open the Whistle Stop Café inside the historic train depot in Dennison, Ohio. During WWII, the depot's canteen workers offered doughnuts, sandwiches, and a heap of gratitude to thousands of soldiers on their way to war via troop-transport trains. Our sleuths soon find themselves on track to solve baffling mysteries—both past and present. Come along for the ride for stories of honor, duty to God and country, and of course fun, family, and friends!

Under the Apple Tree
As Time Goes By
We'll Meet Again
Till Then
I'll Be Seeing You
Fools Rush In
Let It Snow
Accentuate the Positive
For Sentimental Reasons

MYSTERIES OF BLACKBERRY VALLEY

That's My Baby
A String of Pearls
Somewhere Over the Rainbow
Down Forget-Me-Not Lane
Set the World on Fire
When You Wish Upon a Star
Rumors Are Flying
Here We Go Again
Stairway to the Stars
Winter Weather
Wait Till the Sun Shines
Now You're in My Arms
Sooner or Later
Apple Blossom Time
My Dreams Are Getting Better

Secrets from Grandma's Attic

Life is recorded not only in decades or years, but in events and memories that form the fabric of our being. Follow Tracy Doyle, Amy Allen, and Robin Davisson, the granddaughters of the recently deceased centenarian, Pearl Allen, as they explore the treasures found in the attic of Grandma Pearl's Victorian home, nestled near the banks of the Mississippi in Canton, Missouri. Not only do Pearl's descendants uncover a long-buried mystery at every attic exploration, they also discover their grandmother's legacy of deep, abiding faith, which has shaped and guided their family through the years. These uncovered Secrets from Grandma's Attic reveal stories of faith, redemption, and second chances that capture your heart long after you turn the last page.

History Lost and Found
The Art of Deception
Testament to a Patriot
Buttoned Up
Pearl of Great Price
Hidden Riches
Movers and Shakers
The Eye of the Cat
Refined by Fire

MYSTERIES OF BLACKBERRY VALLEY

The Prince and the Popper
Something Shady
Duel Threat
A Royal Tea
The Heart of a Hero
Fractured Beauty
A Shadowy Past
In Its Time
Nothing Gold Can Stay
The Cameo Clue
Veiled Intentions
Turn Back the Dial
A Marathon of Kindness
A Thief in the Night
Coming Home

Savannah Secrets

Welcome to Savannah, Georgia, a picture-perfect Southern city known for its manicured parks, moss-covered oaks, and antebellum architecture. Walk down one of the cobblestone streets, and you'll come upon Magnolia Investigations. It is here where two friends have joined forces to unravel some of Savannah's deepest secrets. Tag along as clues are exposed, red herrings discarded, and thrilling surprises revealed. Find inspiration in the special bond between Meredith Bellefontaine and Julia Foley. Cheer the friends on as they listen to their hearts and rely on their faith to solve each new case that comes their way.

The Hidden Gate
A Fallen Petal
Double Trouble
Whispering Bells
Where Time Stood Still
The Weight of Years
Willful Transgressions
Season's Meetings
Southern Fried Secrets
The Greatest of These
Patterns of Deception

MYSTERIES OF BLACKBERRY VALLEY

The Waving Girl
Beneath a Dragon Moon
Garden Variety Crimes
Meant for Good
A Bone to Pick
Honeybees & Legacies
True Grits
Sapphire Secret
Jingle Bell Heist
Buried Secrets
A Puzzle of Pearls
Facing the Facts
Resurrecting Trouble
Forever and a Day

Mysteries of Martha's Vineyard

Priscilla Latham Grant has inherited a lighthouse! So with not much more than a strong will and a sore heart, the recent widow says goodbye to her lifelong Kansas home and heads to the quaint and historic island of Martha's Vineyard, Massachusetts. There, she comes face-to-face with adventures, which include her trusty canine friend, Jake, three delightful cousins she didn't know she had, and Gerald O'Bannon, a handsome Coast Guard captain—plus head-scratching mysteries that crop up with surprising regularity.

A Light in the Darkness
Like a Fish Out of Water
Adrift
Maiden of the Mist
Making Waves
Don't Rock the Boat
A Port in the Storm
Thicker Than Water
Swept Away
Bridge Over Troubled Waters
Smoke on the Water
Shifting Sands
Shark Bait

MYSTERIES OF BLACKBERRY VALLEY

Seascape in Shadows
Storm Tide
Water Flows Uphill
Catch of the Day
Beyond the Sea
Wider Than an Ocean
Sheeps Passing in the Night
Sail Away Home
Waves of Doubt
Lifeline
Flotsam & Jetsam
Just Over the Horizon

A Note from the Editors

We hope you enjoyed another exciting volume in the Mysteries of Blackberry Valley series, published by Guideposts. For over seventy-five years, Guideposts, a nonprofit organization, has been driven by a vision of a world filled with hope. We aspire to be the voice of a trusted friend, a friend who makes you feel more hopeful and connected.

By making a purchase from Guideposts, you join our community in touching millions of lives, inspiring them to believe that all things are possible through faith, hope, and prayer. Your continued support allows us to provide uplifting resources to those in need. Whether through our communities, websites, apps, or publications, we inspire our audiences, bring them together, and comfort, uplift, entertain, and guide them. Visit us at guideposts.org to learn more.

We would love to hear from you. Write us at Guideposts, P.O. Box 5815, Harlan, Iowa 51593 or call us at (800) 932-2145. Did you love *Seeds of Suspicion*? Leave a review for this product on guideposts.org/shop. Your feedback helps others in our community find relevant products.

Find inspiration, find faith, find Guideposts.

Shop our best sellers and favorites at
guideposts.org/shop

Or scan the QR code to go directly to our Shop

More Great Mysteries Are Waiting For Readers Like *You*!

Whistle Stop Café Mysteries

"Memories of a lifetime...I loved reading this story. Could not put the book down...." —ROSE H.

Mystery and WWII historical fiction fans will love these intriguing novels where two close friends piece together clues to solve mysteries past and present. Set in the real town of Dennison, Ohio, at a historic train depot where many soldiers once set off for war, these stories are filled with faithful, relatable characters you'll love spending time with.

Mysteries & Wonders of the Bible

"I so enjoyed this book....What a great insight into the life of the women who wove the veil for the Temple." —SHIRLEYN J.

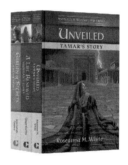

Have you ever wondered what it might have been like to live back in Bible times to experience miraculous Bible events firsthand? Then you'll LOVE the fascinating **Mysteries & Wonders of the Bible** novels! Each Scripture-inspired story whisks you back to the ancient Holy Land, where you'll accompany ordinary men and women in their search for the hidden truths behind some of the most pivotal moments in the Bible. Each volume includes insights from a respected biblical scholar to help you ponder the significance of each story to your own life.

Mysteries of Cobble Hill Farm

"Wonderful series. Great story. Spellbinding. Could not put it down once I started reading." —BONNIE C.

Escape to the charming English countryside with **Mysteries of Cobble Hill Farm**, a heartwarming series of faith-filled mysteries. Harriet Bailey relocates to Yorkshire, England, to take over her late grandfather's veterinary practice, hoping it's the fresh start she needs. As she builds a new life, Harriet uncovers modern mysteries and long-buried secrets in the village and among the rolling hills and castle ruins. Each book is an inspiring puzzle where God's gentlest messengers—the animals in her care—help Harriet save the day.

Learn More & Shop These Exciting Mysteries, Biblical Stories, & Other Uplifting Fiction at **guideposts.org/fiction**

Printed in the United States
by Baker & Taylor Publisher Services